FUM

FUM

ADAM RAPP

CANDLEWICK PRESS

Copyright © 2018 by Adam Rapp

First edition 2018

Library of Congress Catalog Card Number pending
ISBN 978-0-7636-6756-6

17 18 19 20 21 22 BVG 10 9 8 7 6 5 4 3 2 1

Printed in Berryville, VA, U.S.A.

This book was typeset in Baskerville.

Candlewick Press
99 Dover Street
Somerville, Massachusetts 02144

visit us at www.candlewick.com

For Hallie Bananas

―――――――――

"O God that madest this beautiful earth,
when will it be ready to accept Thy saints? How long,
O Lord, how long?"

—George Bernard Shaw, *Saint Joan*

―――――――――

PART 1

1

In the guidance counselor's office of Lugo Memorial High School—a ten-by-twelve-foot bunker situated in the basement of the stout three-story rectangular limestone building—sits Corinthia Bledsoe, elbows on thighs, her wood splitter's hands cradling her face, her mosquito-bitten knees trembling only as infinitesimally as knees this large can tremble.

As advised by the adult sitting across from her, Corinthia is inhaling and exhaling through her nose, the troubled breaths sluicing through the great caves of her nostrils, tainting the tenaciously humid late-August air of the sublevel public-school office.

"In and out, through the nose, just like that," she hears.

Corinthia was escorted here by the firm, resolute, not to mention hairy-in-a-storybook-ogre-way hands of Virgil Task, Lugo Memorial's varsity football coach. Coach Task, stalwart as a fire hydrant, with dark tufts swirling through the open collar of his knit cream-and-crimson athletic-department shirt, was aided by Gene

Hauser, the algebra II teacher and JV math team mentor. Mr. Hauser trailed behind them in a gymnastics-spotting fashion, ready to help should anyone collapse, blow out a knee, or sprain an ankle. Yes, that was indeed Gene Hauser, rarely seen beyond the confines of his classroom (which doubles as the math lab), whose personal scent Corinthia found to be suspiciously mulchy, as if he'd been spending all morning in a garden, digging up cabbages.

Guidance Counselor Denton Smock's office, which is painted the color of cougar eyes, boasts a phantasmagoric lavender-and-cotton-candy-colored aquarium; a kind of undulating liquid brain, which is home to, among an assortment of underwater wisteria and banana plants, a lone striped clown fish, whose almost staggeringly inactive floating state is the one thing Corinthia relates to at this moment.

"Is it alive?" Corinthia finally asks, referring to the fish.

Mr. Smock has been waiting for her to speak for twelve minutes. He knows that it's been precisely twelve minutes because he measures such things. There is a small digital clock on his desk that reports minutes and seconds in pulsing blue numerals. He keeps all of his "waiting" data logged in a little spiral notebook of lima-bean-green graph paper: minutes, followed by a colon, followed by seconds. Row upon row of "waiting" statistics with student initials beside each entry. If one were to find this notebook on, say, the pilling wool sofa in the Wallace Keebler Faculty Lounge, one might mistake Mr. Smock for the Lugo Memorial track and field coach. The meticulously gathered data could easily be misconstrued as recorded relay splits. He's especially interested in student silences and their accompanying behavior: how a body leans away from the steady, relentless thrum of the overhead fluorescent light; what the shoulders do during one of his unblinking, half-smiling stare-downs. Do a student's shoulders disappear into the back or seize up and crowd the neck? Does the left shoulder sit higher than the right, or vice versa? As far as Mr. Smock is concerned, he doesn't need language to make student assessments. The anxious body of the fourteen- to eighteen-year-old says it all.

"Rodney is very much alive," Mr. Smock replies about his clown fish, whose stripes alternate between blood-orange and white so perfectly, it's like a thing that's been painted with great care. A forgotten heirloom found at a garage sale. "After his lunch, he likes to float."

Speaking of fish, not quite an hour ago, at precisely 2:23 p.m., in Bob Sluba's life sciences class, in the middle of Lugo Memorial's oldest and most-beloved teacher's articulation of the marine-life relationship between bottom-feeding krill and phytoplankton, Corinthia Bledsoe, in an impassioned, heraldic one-part move, rocketed up from her custom-made desk and announced to Mr. Sluba and her seventeen fellow life sciences students that a family of tornadoes—three in total—was making a beeline toward Lugo, directly toward the small community's high school, in fact, and that everyone, students and teachers alike, should get to a safe place and assume the proper tornado position: hands clasped at the back of necks, knees on the floor, rumps kissing heels, chins tucked into chests. It's a vaguely religious-looking position, a supplication, even, as if a mass bowing of heads will somehow turn away God's angry weather beasts.

It is late August, after all, and the stubborn, insufferable humidity—that thick southern Illinois air that coats the skin like gelatin—often coincides with extreme weather alerts, especially in this part of the state, where tornadoes touch down as often as lightning along the fairways of certain Florida golf courses. Which is to say that tornado paranoia is not uncommon here. There were three warnings in July alone, although no funnels actually materialized in Lugo.

"Horn's gonna wail," Corinthia simply states, still catching her breath. Her deep voice is unusually high and reedy.

She's referring to the tornado horn, of course, whose earsplitting siren is so loud, it sounds as if it's being blown from some fabled, invisible Midwestern mountain. The actual horn, as unthreatening-looking as a chipmunk cleaning its paws atop a fence post, is attached to a one-hundred-foot aluminum rod at the outskirts of town and spins 360 degrees while blaring Federal Signal 2001-130, which warns that a tornado has been spotted at a dangerously close proximity and that one and all should seek immediate shelter, preferably underground.

"Why the need to personify a municipal warning system?" Mr. Smock says. "Children wail. Children and emotionally distraught widows in wagon train movies."

Corinthia is well aware that he is dismissing her prediction, which she is smart enough to know seems ludicrous — in her very large heart, she truly understands this — but to be scorned with such mockery, to drag wagon train movies into it! It makes her want to kick the front of his desk, but she resists the impulse and continues wiggling her knee.

"You'll see," she warns solemnly.

Mr. Smock nods and smiles. His job is to be sympathetic, after all. His lips sort of disappear as he thinks. For some reason this look makes Corinthia wonder whether or not he possesses nipples, or, rather, if under his clothes he is some other kind of being: a fish person with gills. Instead of a penis, does he possess a little hidden ventral fin? A spout? Mr. Sluba might be able to diagram such a thing on his life sciences whiteboard.

"And you claim these tornadoes were something you *saw,*" Mr. Smock says, still trying to make sense of the matter.

"Yes," Corinthia replies.

"Out the window?"

"In my head," she says.

"So you were asleep," he says. "I know how your medication can make you drowsy."

"I was about as drowsy as a wet dog caught on an electric fence."

The image seems to cause Mr. Smock's face to twitch, just at one corner of his mouth. It's barely perceptible, but it's certainly a twitch — indeed it is. At this moment, very little slips past Corinthia Bledsoe. Glimpsing those tornadoes has somehow tweaked her entire sensory system. According to Mr. Sluba, the normal human being possesses five senses: sight, hearing, taste, smell, and touch. But today Corinthia is keenly aware that something beyond this arrangement is at play. She can *feel* the ozone in the air, *hear* the humidity creeping through Mr. Smock's little moldy office, and practically *taste* the cheap, yeasty foot powder whose scent is wafting up from under his gunmetal desk.

"So then your eyes were open when you *beheld* this trio of tornadoes?"

"To behold something carries with it a connotation of beauty," Corinthia says.

Mr. Smock appears to be stumped. What little color lives in his face has gone away. That tan he worked so hard on this past summer while vacationing in the Michigan sand dunes has turned a pale, waxy blue.

"I suppose you're right," he finally admits.

"And *trio*?" Corinthia says, almost bitterly. "It's not a singing group."

He asks her what word she would use to qualify the three tornadoes. "A trinity?" he suggests before she can answer.

"A triumvirate," she replies in a beleaguered voice. "A trinity refers to a Christian godhead. Triumvirates are solely about power and destruction."

"Well," he says, "there's apparently nothing wrong with that vocabulary of yours."

Corinthia won the past two Lugo Memorial spelling bees. Last year, as a sophomore, she defeated senior valedictorian Sophia Bristol-Soffit, and as a freshman, in the final round, she wowed everyone by spelling *aerenchyma* without skipping a beat. For that bee, she defeated junior Junior Zobrist, who is rumored to be headed to MIT next year.

It's important to point out that Corinthia Bledsoe's desk is custom-made because when she stands at her full height, she is seven feet four and a quarter inches tall.

And she weighs 287 pounds.

Regular school desks just don't work for her. By all definitions, be they medical, standard, mythical, or otherwise, Corinthia Lee Bledsoe of Lugo, Illinois, born in the birthing ward of St. Joseph's Hospital up north in Joliet, just off Interstate 55, is a giant. She built the desk in shop class. Fashioned from pine and featuring a meticulously sanded, lacquered finish, whose sloped lid contains grooves for pens and pencils, it emits a faint, pleasant smell of resin and wood glue, collapses conveniently at its hinged, outermost edge, and folds in half for easy transport.

Although she is broad-shouldered, with enormous hands and equally enormous feet (size 22, men's), she has penetrating deep-brown eyes that not only balance her face, but also radiate a loving warmth and at times a generous, childlike vulnerability. These eyes belie her Paul Bunyanesque skull and monumental chin. And despite her teeth, which are as long, wide, and dimpled as dominoes, Corinthia possesses a full, attractive mouth. She has learned to maneuver her lips in such a manner as to reveal only a portion of this haunting, epic dentition.

At the onset of her puberty—at around age eleven and a half—a tumor attached itself to Corinthia Bledsoe's pituitary gland and caused her condition, gigantism, to manifest with nothing less than an undeserved, almost biblical tenacity. By her fourteenth birthday, she was a staggering six feet nine and a half inches tall, larger than most professional basketball players.

And she's grown almost seven inches since then.

Yes, she is a giant.

She is gigantic.

Because of those magnetic pupils and lovely mouth, her face defies the usual clichés ascribed to the monolithic storybook ogre, the grotesque monster with the cauliflower brow and sunken Beowulf eyes. Corinthia possesses a girlish, nicely positioned nose, unblemished skin, and cinnamon-colored hair, which she often pulls back into a classic ponytail.

But despite this beauty, by medical definition, Corinthia Lee Bledsoe, daughter of Brill and Marlene Bledsoe, sister to senior star wide receiver Channing "The Lugo Heat" Bledsoe (who is a mere six two, 185 pounds), is still a giant.

Thus, the very large heart and need for a special desk.

She and her shop teacher, Dolan Yorn-Pamutmut, whose hyphenated name is as mysterious as his missing left ear, chose pine because it's both a lightweight and extremely sturdy wood.

So, to say the least, the act of Corinthia Bledsoe reaching full verticality — exploding up from her custom-made portable desk — is nothing less than a thrilling event and a celebration of the genetic mysteries of the human race, certainly more thrilling than microscopic phytoplankton and nonexploding krill and Mr. Sluba's glabrous Benjamin Franklin face, especially when everyone else is sitting down at standard-size Illinois School District–issued desks, collectively fighting through post-lunch digestion comas (pizza pockets, lima beans, and fruit cups [which were mostly green grapes and little wedges of room-temperature melon]), everyone except for Mr. Sluba, who, at a modest five nine, often assumes a slightly bowlegged southwestern rancher's stance, perpetually within arm's reach of the science department's archaic manually operated overhead projector.

Some say he dates it like he would a woman.

As Corinthia sits across from Guidance Counselor Smock, whose thin, smooth face defies age and whose outward patience verges on ecclesiastical, her pine desk, which was collapsed and brought to the basement by Mr. Sluba himself, leans against the wall beside her.

"Do you think you're making the most of your junior year, Corinthia?" he asks. It's an oddly general question, considering the circumstances.

"Yes," she replies, although the past few days haven't been easy. Not because of any one incident or her health challenges. Not because Corinthia has grown more and more aware of the acute feeling of not caring. *Ineffectual* is the word she's heard before. Or the phrase *lack of affect*. Her schoolwork has been excellent. Based on her grade point average, she's currently ranked third in her class, and her attendance is impeccable. And yet this lingering blankness has been metastasizing somewhere deep inside her, like a small, cold stone slowly gaining mass, perhaps the phantom cousin of that tumor that attached itself to her pituitary gland some five and a half years ago.

"Have you thought more about where you might want to go to college?" Mr. Smock asks.

About a month ago, Corinthia was drawn to Northland, a small college in Wisconsin's remote upper hinterlands. The thing that grabbed her attention was the expanse of tall trees featured in their modest four-color brochure. Ancient black spruces, seemingly hundreds of feet high, an endless forest of them. Corinthia could see herself walking among these trees, drunk with the smell of pine, not a care in the world, no cumbersome door moldings or low classroom archways to negotiate, striding out in the open air, where hawks and eagles soar.

The campus of Northland College, home of the LumberJacks and LumberJills, is located in Ashland, Wisconsin. Its curriculum is geared toward the environment and sustainability. Corinthia likes the fact that their student population isn't mentioned in any of their marketing materials, which probably means that it's very small. The campus is located a mere ten-minute walk from the shores of Lake Superior.

Corinthia daydreams about shedding all her clothes and wading into this Great Lake, swimming out an impossible distance and just floating there on her back while staring up at the endless night sky, the stars wheeling above her as she waits for some prehistoric creature to emerge from the depths and lead her to the next phase of her life.

Floating in Lake Superior like Mr. Smock's little striped clown fish, Rodney.

"You continue to generate keen interest from Northwestern, Marquette, even the University of Chicago," Mr. Smock says, clearly attempting to keep the conversation focused on practical matters. "Those scores of yours are piquing real interest from the big boys."

The scores that he refers to are Corinthia's SATs, which she took at the end of her sophomore year, along with three other accelerated classmates. She found the test so stultifyingly easy that it actually bored her. And it was also just plain absurd. The idea of one's immediate future being dictated by the act of filling out endless arrangements of ovals with a number two pencil makes Corinthia want to pursue a vocation as a cashier at, say, the local gas station (Pewman's Gas and Go), just to spite all the career-crazed adults in her life. Wouldn't she be something to behold? After filling up the SUV, one would enter the little kiosk and—*KA-BLAM*—there she'd be, all seven feet four and a quarter inches of her, a veritable mountain of customer-service flesh, the crown of her head practically scraping the ceiling.

"I've spoken with your parents," Mr. Smock continues, "and I think they're coming around to the idea of Northwestern."

Her parents have mentioned no such conversation, and the fact that her guidance counselor is going behind her back to speak to them makes her want to snatch his notebook off his desk and tear it in half.

"Your mom seems quite taken with the North

Shore of Chicago," he continues. "Northwestern boasts a legacy of extraordinary alums."

"The Wildcats," Corinthia utters.

"The purple-and-white," Smock adds, citing the university's colors.

"What exactly is a wildcat anyway?" Corinthia asks.

"I believe a wildcat is any cat that is wild."

"Wild meaning feral?"

"Sure," he answers. "Feral."

"A state of savagery," she adds, "especially after escape from captivity or domestication."

Mr. Smock asks Corinthia if she's thinking of college as an escape.

She doesn't answer.

"Have you been feeling trapped?" he adds.

Corinthia is suddenly aware of the buzzing overhead fluorescent; the whirring, burbling aquarium; and another mysterious tremor that seems to be emanating from somewhere deep under the school building.

"Do you feel that?" Corinthia asks.

"Feel what?" Mr. Smock says.

Corinthia squints, trying to home in on the source of the tremor. Is she the only person who can feel this? Does the tremor have anything to do with the tornadoes? Is it coming from *inside* her?

"Look, it's hot," Mr. Smock offers, fanning himself with a pamphlet that reads SMARTPHONE DEPENDENCY: *Is a Device Ruling Your Life?*

Corinthia recently gave up her large-format smartphone. Despite its bigger dimensions, it was still too small. Whenever she'd arrange it against her face to speak, the mouthpiece barely cleared her cheekbone. Communicating with anyone effectively required her to toggle the device between her ear and chin, which made it look like she was using a man's electric razor. She tried a set of earbuds, but even the largest ones kept falling out. Now the phone, not much smaller than a standard-size digital tablet, lives in a shoe box on her dresser at home.

After a pause, Corinthia says, "You don't want to talk about the tornadoes."

"You've made it abundantly clear that there are three of them," Mr. Smock says. "A *triumvirate.*"

"They're gonna pull the roof off the field house."

"Corinthia . . ."

Lugo Memorial's guidance counselor is clearly tiring of this absurd subject, not to mention Corinthia Bledsoe's newfound maverick attitude.

"It's going to wind up in Brainard," she says, "in a half-harvested cornfield."

"Do you realize how silly you sound?"

"And in the field house, there will be a cow at half-court," Corinthia continues willfully. "Not a thing wrong with it. Like it's been there its whole life."

Everyone on the faculty is well aware of Corinthia Bledsoe's various medical issues. The hypothyroid condition and blood sugar problems. The terrible shoulder acne and sore gums and the perpetually sweaty palms. The excruciating joint pain suffered as a freshman when she couldn't get out of bed for two days and was prescribed an anti-inflammatory powerful enough to soothe an ailing racehorse. The various medications and their side effects: shortness of breath; wobbly balance ("Don't Operate Machinery . . ."); nausea; the seemingly irreversible dehydration.

Despite these challenges, Corinthia has always been known to be polite, courteous to her peers, and especially so to the faculty and staff of Lugo Memorial.

Mr. Smock passes her a paper cone of water, the second one he's given her, dispensed from his upside-down jug, which glugs like a creature with uneasy bowels. Corinthia downs the water and inadvertently crushes the paper cone into a piece of damp popcorn.

Entire faculty meetings have been called to discuss Lugo Memorial's physically unique student's special needs. At one such meeting, urged by the kindhearted choir director, Dolores Slenderschundt, it was decided that a special private bathroom should be built for Corinthia, approximately ten feet west of the normal girls' second-floor bathroom, the thinking being that placing Corinthia's bathroom there would split the difference of the three-story building, and in order to make use of it, she'd never have to negotiate more than a flight of stairs on those big ailing knees.

In terms of contractor specifications, her size would require more porcelain. The reason for a personal bathroom was that she'd already broken two toilets; the first episode occurred when Rinna Buss, the student council president and co-captain of the varsity cheerleading squad, was urinating discreetly, if not beautifully, when a tremendous crash occurred in the stall beside her. Rinna was the one who brought the delicate matter to Principal Margo Ticonderoga and her devoted vice principal, the soft-spoken, bowling pin–shaped Doogan Mejerus.

The broken toilet caused a flood in the girls' bathroom from which Corinthia emerged as though she'd survived an epic shipwreck, soaked from head to toe, her cinnamon hair pasted to her broad, stunned face.

After breaking her second toilet, which happened on the final Thursday of her sophomore year, Corinthia carried the porcelain remains down the hall to the principal's office as if it were an offering. To the few students loitering by their lockers, it looked like she was carrying an otherworldly candy dish.

At the final faculty meeting of the school year, thanks to Dolores Slenderschundt's impassioned appeal to civic kindness, the faculty unanimously approved the private bathroom after a quick vote, and a local contractor from nearby Benton arrived three weeks into the summer break to complete its installation. It took nearly five days to get the project going because the custom toilet had to be made from a special ceramic-and-graphite arrangement, with a thicker porcelain and reinforced stainless-steel buttresses to support Corinthia Bledsoe's considerable weight.

At one point, the facilities manager, Shoreland Splitz, had to interrupt Corinthia's summer break and ask her to come back to school and sit in a large vat of chalk dust and then sit again on a retired, repurposed chalkboard so they could have a proper measurement for the toilet seat.

"Sit in that," he said, clearly uncomfortable with the unusual request. "And then sit on that."

Shoreland "The Lamp" Splitz, a tall, bony man with hands like hawk talons, had to help Corinthia out of the vat of chalk dust, and the action aggravated a hernia he'd suffered some years back. For the rest of the summer and into the first few weeks of the new school year, he had to wear his old, ill-fitting double-spring truss with scrotal pads.

With regard to Corinthia's special toilet, the faculty took into account the sensitivity issue, God bless those benevolent adults, and decided to splurge for a soundless flushing mechanism, so that students passing by in the hallway wouldn't be able to easily identify when their prodigious peer was partaking of the customized services.

Despite fire code regulations, Corinthia was given a key and the bathroom was outfitted with a simple, easy-to-turn bolt-action lock. Again, the faculty was willing to bend on certain student handbook matters.

Corinthia's bathroom was never discussed with the Lugo Memorial student body, but when it (the bathroom) materialized, it was Facebooked, Instagrammed, Tweeted, Foursquared, WordPressed, Tumblred, Snapchatted, and so thoroughly digitally disseminated that it was as if pictures of Rinna Buss's breasts had been leaked. And they (the student body, not Rinna Buss's breasts) knew *why* and *for whom* the oversize latrine had been created, boy, oh boy, did they ever. How could they not? It came to be known as "The Rinth's Rectal Recliner," which Corinthia found to be discursively lazy, as neither her private toilet nor her personal rectum—a comparatively straight, terminal section of the intestine (as taught to her by Belinda Hnath, Lugo Memorial's willowy, allergy-prone anatomy teacher)—cantilevers in any direction.

One sophomore boy, Jordan Sheehey, even posted a smartphone movie of himself washing his dog, Demetrius, a 117-pound black Lab, in Corinthia's toilet. He'd planned with great care (miniature smartphone tripod and all), as he knew it would be all but impossible to sneak a dog of that size and unabashed enthusiasm into Lugo Memorial during normal hours. (As evidenced by the sudsy footage, Demetrius obviously loves getting baths.) How Jordan Sheehey got into the bathroom in the first place is anyone's guess. The only other key in existence lives in a metal strongbox down in Shoreland Splitz's office.

In any event, the first two years of high school haven't, to put it mildly, been easy for Corinthia. She never seems to fit anywhere, meaning literally, a cruel facilities fact she has accepted with self-effacing grace and at times a mock-woeful sense of humor. And this difficulty has extended beyond the entryways and corridors of Lugo Memorial. Once, after receiving the standard-issue P.E. clothes from the girls' phys. ed. instructor, Carla "The Human Birdbath" Snells, Corinthia—all seven feet four and a quarter inches of her—came bounding into the girls' locker room theatrically head-banging and rocking an air guitar.

Her extra-large shorts, which looked absurdly mini-ature on her frame, were riding so high they were practically thonglike. In order to span the width of her shoulders, her T-shirt was so stretched that the letters LUGO PHYS. ED were distorted into a blown-out Milky Way of unrecognizability. It was as if someone had forced an infant's onesie onto some prehistoric infant pterodactyl.

Yes, these moments have endeared Corinthia to her peers, but the continuous ducking under door-ways, the edging sideways through entrances, the twisting her neck to avoid lamps, projection screens, hanging 3-D mobiles of RNA/DNA helices, and the wooden dowels of anatomy charts, not to mention the five- to seven-part move of negotiating her legs under the cafeteria tables, has caused a scourge of knots to settle up and down her spine. She has walked into the third-floor clock three times. Once, its hard plastic fac-ing came crashing to the marble floor and went spin-ning down the locker-lined corridor like a runaway hubcap.

Mr. Smock utters something inane about the unbearable humidity and the tenacity of this year's mosquitoes and the upcoming standardized tests (Corinthia will again be taking the SATs). He, of all people, knows about Corinthia's medication, about the thyroid and blood sugar problems, about the crippling Osgood-Schlatters (oh, those awkward NFL knee braces she had to wear *outside* her pants during her entire freshman year!), inflamed arches, the awful bunion on the joint of her left toe, and the sudden waves of fatigue; how the faculty has had to be very forgiving of her occasional midclass nap. Despite his somewhat impenetrable demeanor, Lugo Memorial's guidance counselor has mostly been a steady voice of understanding.

One faculty member, girls' varsity basketball coach Wilbon Von Treese, has been less sensitive. When Corinthia wasn't interested in trying out for the basketball team, he called her parents immediately.

"There could be a HUGE future in this for her."

Corinthia could hear Coach Von Treese's voice wheedling through the phone's handset. Her father, Brill, listened politely, if not generously, rolling his eyes and smiling patiently at his daughter, who was lying on the kitchen floor with her knees tented and a phone book under her head (the "constructive rest" position intended to relieve lower back pain).

"Just *HUGE*," Coach Von Treese squawked repeatedly, insensitive to the angst this particular four-letter word might cause the Bledsoe family. *"HUGE, HUGE, HUGE!"*

Mr. Smock polices a few sesame cookie crumbs from the surface of his desk, brushes them into a cupped hand, and disposes of them into the trash can below. He rubs his palms together in a slow, priestlike manner and asks if everything is okay at home.

Corinthia replies, "Everything at home is dandy, Mr. Smock."

"Denton," he corrects her, reminding her of their first-name-basis "friendship," intended to transcend faculty-student formalities.

But the truth is that Lugo Memorial's only guidance counselor doesn't seem to exist beyond the four walls of his austere, eucalyptus-scented room. It's as if the office itself willed him into existence. He's rarely seen walking the halls. Oh, sure, he'll occasionally show up at a boys' basketball game or be clapping it up at the finish line of a cross-country meet, but these sightings are few and far between. Although he encourages the students to trust him — *"You can tell me anything. You really can!"* — few actually do.

One thing that can be said for Mr. Smock is that he exhibits admirable hygiene and style. He is so clean-shaven, his face appears to have been painted on with acrylics. He sports slightly-cooler-than-Clark-Kent-style-glasses, in that they're the tiniest bit cat-eyed, as well as skinny rockabilly pants. And basically the most stylish black leather shoes in southern Illinois. They have two-inch soles and big brass buckles.

His iPhone case boasts a zebra-print pattern.

He's as asexual as the stunted ceramic donkey featured in the annual Lugo Memorial holiday Nativity scene.

"Things at home are only 'dandy'?"

Corinthia brings the pads of her index fingers to her temples, which are suddenly throbbing again.

"*Dandy* can also mean lonely. Or sad. Or difficult," Mr. Smock adds, shoveling forth the clichés like clumps of steaming asphalt from the back of a truck.

He goes on to say something about how *understanding* everyone has been about Corinthia's various medical and physiological issues during these past two school years and reassures her that he knows—or at least he *thinks* he knows (as surely he can only *imagine* it)—how difficult it must be for her to face them on a daily basis. Again, the voice contains about as much music as a newly installed refrigerator. Corinthia gets the sense that he's ticking off some prescribed line of questioning he learned from a training manual.

"And now you're a junior," he adds. "One's junior year can be a time to turn the corner. . . ."

What specific figurative corner is he referring to? Corinthia wonders. *The social corner? The student-as-citizen corner? The corner of mentally sound behavior? The corner of college candidacy?*

For some reason, Corinthia sees herself manning the popcorn wagon in Lugo Memorial's Connie and

Dillard Deet Field House, dressed like a toy soldier, a red wool parade uniform complete with yellow piping and bright brass buttons, a black egg-shaped bearskin hat atop her head, little balloons of rouge enlivening her cheeks. The legendary field house packed to capacity for a boys' varsity basketball game, cheerleaders cartwheeling through the air like hairless cats flung by larger creatures.

The upside-down water jug gurgles.

The aquarium whispers and pulses with brain light.

Mr. Smock's eyes twitch behind the lenses of his designer glasses. He opens his mouth as if to impart more wisdom, then closes it, then opens it and leaves it open. *He has nothing left to say,* she thinks. *He's finally run out of clichés.* Corinthia notices a dull, chalky stripe down the center of his tongue and wonders if he sometimes keeps the clown fish in there as some perverse exercise in oral pleasure.

The air-conditioning system at Lugo Memorial — all those convoluted tin ducts and chutes — seems to be a thing that only makes noise, as there isn't anything remotely cool issuing from it. In her American literature class, Corinthia sits under the terminal vent of one such duct. Sometimes she imagines she is basking in the breath of a great African lion — just her and a hundred-year-old jungle king with a colossal, radiant mane, lying together in the long grass, breathing each other in.

And then, just like that, the sweltering heat seems to be a thing that is coming from *within* Corinthia, a cauldron that bakes not only her body but also the landmark limestone school building, the pond of recently refinished asphalt ringing the flagpole, the stunted neighborhood cottonwoods, and the sad tar paper–shingled roofs crowning the mostly one-story homes that make up the town of Lugo; roofs that, once the tornadoes hit, will fly off toward Arkansas and Missouri and Kentucky like the wings of weakened blackbirds.

The sky will turn brown, green, yellow.

Confused crows will skitter across the ground like lost rickety men.

Dogs will scamper in circles, their faces crazed.

Cats will slink backward down the trunks of ancient sycamores.

Trees will lean away from the sky.

The air will grow as thick as maple.

After Corinthia had urged her fellow life sciences juniors to get to a safe place, in an effort to alert the rest of the school, she exited as fast as she possibly could, bursting through Mr. Sluba's classroom door, literally rocking it off its hinges, and then went bounding from classroom to classroom like some wild-eyed

WWE wrestler, pleading with teachers and students alike — "We MUST, we absolutely *MUST* get to a safe place!" — the words hissing through her teeth.

These deranged visitations included Linda Lister's English class and Harden Mlsna's calc II class and Pru Tenderloin's European history class and Nola Heck-Burden's sophomore speech, drama, and journalism class at the precise moment when senior ingenue Skyler "Don't You Dare Call Me Sky!" Montreal was bringing the back of her perfect Virgin Mary hand to her finely concaved alabaster forehead while performing Desdemona's final speech in *Othello*.

Corinthia didn't have time to explain anything in detail; her objective was to use her enormous, masculine, often congested French horn of a voice to sound an alarm, to trigger nervous systems and make people *MOVE*.

She basically looked like a very large, crazy monster person.

It was a strangely uncomfortable scene when she had to be physically coerced by Coach Task, Mr. Hauser, and Doris Dabaduda, the head librarian with the thick varicose ankles and koala-bear eyes, who just so happened to be in the hallway. As they got Corinthia prostrate to the floor, Doris Dabaduda cried out like a creature caught in the jaws of a trap, having severely pulled her left hamstring.

The most disturbing moment, though, was when Coach Task had to deploy a full nelson and wound up riding Corinthia to the ground with his knee planted between her shoulder blades. He literally rode her like a bucking bronco or, say, a felled, mechanically failing alpaca fighting for its final breaths in the Andes.

Coach Task couldn't help imagining what an effective offensive lineman — or line*person* — Corinthia Bledsoe would make. Her great strength seemed most powerful when her hips were engaged. How incredible would it be if a *girl* started at left guard on the varsity football team! A *girl*! She would protect quarterback Drake Sirocco in a kind of mercenary *maternal* fashion, and Drake would have that much more time to survey his receivers and unleash a laser beam to Corinthia's older brother, speedster wide receiver Channing "The Lugo Heat" Bledsoe, who would be jetting down the right sideline, sprinting the way only God can make sprinters sprint, and the ball would be caught just shy of the thickly padded goalpost stanchions like a loaf of freshly baked bread — it would seem that miraculously soft — and the band would strike up the chorus of some eighties pop song, likely the title track to a classic Sylvester Stallone movie, the brass and strings and woodwinds dulcet and beautiful, the timpani drum rolling out end-zone thunder, causing the reinforced aluminum bleachers to shudder and spasm, the cream-and-crimson pom-poms airborne and plump with halos of halogen stadium lights, this particular Friday night in Lugo delivered like a southern Illinois sacrament to all 4,208 of its citizens.

Even those who weren't able to make it to the game — those less fortunate housebound few — would feel the tradition and beauty practically pollinating the air, and all would be gilded in the annals of Lugo Memorial gridiron legend.

Yearbook dedications would never be the same.

It wasn't easy getting Corinthia facedown on the marble floor, especially while students were spilling into the hallway and trying to digitally capture the incident.

"Smartphones down!" Becky Lujack cried, doing her absolute darnedest to corral her freshman boys and girls back into her American Government and the Founding Fathers classroom.

Coach Task, in the later stages of middle age, is still strong as a blue-blooded ox and, post–full nelson, was forced to deploy some incapacitating judo involving Corinthia's neck/shoulder relationship. Once he got her prostrate, he spoke to her in a direct but calming fashion, the same way a dog owner might admonish a misbehaving beloved German shepherd.

"Submit to Coach Task," he said, referring to himself in the third person as he has occasionally been known to do. "Submit now, Bledsoe."

After Corinthia's arms stopped swimming out and started sort of flapping around at her sides in a less intentional, more overpowered manner, between desperate breaths, in torn syllables, she promised Coach Task and Mr. Hauser that she was in control of herself.

"No retaliation now, Corinthia," Mr. Hauser warned.

"Mmmmnnnnmmmmnnnooooooo" is all Corinthia could muster.

"DO YOU SUBMIT?" Coach Task pleaded again, dark thistles pulsing through the rims of his nostrils.

After Corinthia pledged her self-control with "I *ssssbbbbmmmmmmmmmtttttt*!" they continued pinning her head to the base of the small trophy case that exhibits the few conference championships in football, baseball, and cross-country, her nose and mouth mashed into the joint where the wall meets the marble floor.

"Breathe it out now, Corinthia," Coach Task instructed her. "Breathe it all out."

Coach Task finally removed his knee from between her shoulder blades, and she remained on her stomach, inhaling the penitentiary smell of institutional disinfectant and dirty shoes.

A few minutes later, after Doris Dabaduda was carried off to the gymnasium to have her leg tended to by the athletic trainer, Coach Task and Mr. Hauser helped Corinthia off the floor, which was like trying to right some toppled medieval iron throne. They then escorted her to the infirmary—Coach Task gently but ever so firmly guiding her by her enormous elbow— where she was administered to with several conical paper cups containing an electrolyte solution and calmed by the school nurse, Oona Kleinschmidt, who offered Corinthia aloe-and-eucalyptus HandiWipes.

After Corinthia's heart rate returned to an acceptable level and it was determined that a hospital visit wasn't necessary, she was deposited at Guidance Counselor Smock's office, where he offered herbal tea and sesame cookies, which, per usual, Corinthia refused. She simply sat across from him, physically spent, unblinking, and tried to *not think* about those tornadoes for some twelve minutes.

Finally, Mr. Smock speaks again.

"So we were talking about your junior year," he says. "What lies ahead?"

But before she can answer him, it happens again—that dreaded family of tornadoes overtakes her. The image seizes her mind: a triumvirate of bulging, undulating funnels, spinning and contorting improbably toward Lugo.

Corinthia's chin collapses into her Adam's apple. A fault line emerges in her broad, smooth forehead. Her unblinking eyes are as wide as ostrich eggs.

"Corinthia . . . ?"

When she opens her mouth to speak, she bellows a kind of human dial tone. She closes her mouth, opens it, and tries to speak again, but only a dirgelike sound issues forth. Guidance Counselor Smock removes his black-framed glasses. His brows gather at the center.

This will be the last thing Corinthia recalls from her visit to the guidance counselor's office in the basement of Lugo Memorial High School: Mr. Smock's tense, gathering brows. It doesn't occur to her that she's walked away until she's halfway up the basement stairs.

"Corinthia!" Mr. Smock calls after her, in perhaps the most emphatic version of his voice she's ever heard. "Corinthia Bledsoe, you're not walking away from your guidance counselor's office! You are NOT doing that!"

But she is. And she doesn't even bother answering, because she's too busy taking the stairs, four at a time. When Corinthia's trying to get somewhere fast, she'll usually take them in threes, like when she's escaping the gaze of speech team captain Swinta Folger, who sits behind her in Great Books class and whose disapproving eyes are like a pair of warm beetles crawling on the back of her neck, or when her stomach is funny from her thyroxine/anti-inflammatories cocktail and she has to get to her special second-floor bathroom like five minutes ago.

It takes her only a few strides to reach the first floor, where she bounds across the sun-stroked, locker-lined hallway toward the school's main entrance. She isn't aware of any pain in her knees, or in her feet or wrists or hips or lower back, for that matter. No, no, no, there is no pain anywhere in her body, none whatsoever.

She extends her stride, really opens up, digging the heels of her custom-ordered size 22 Pony low-tops into the marble floor, *woomf-woomf-woomf,* and bursts through the double doors of Lugo Memorial High School as if something's chasing her.

"Everything okay?" grounds supervisor Barrett Bacon, who the students call "The Milkman" because of his unusually waggly male breasts, calls to her from atop a loud, clattering riding mower. He's just completed a long row of mowed grass.

But Corinthia doesn't answer. She just charges ahead, shielding her eyes from the bright late-August sun.

2

August 26, 2015
First day of classes
Lugo Memorial High School

Dear Dave,

This is my first entry. Nice to meet you, Dave. My name is Billy Ball. William Eugene Ball, to be precise.

I am fourteen years old, five feet four inches tall, and weigh 125 pounds. I have brown hair and hazel eyes, which means greenish-brown, and I'm pretty pale. I'm right-handed, but I like to try to do things with my left hand, too, like comb my hair and button my shirts and write letters to my dad, who died a few months ago. I'm not good at sports or dancing. But in junior high I received a bronze medal in creative writing for a story I wrote about a mute digital cowboy who falls in love with an analog talking mare named Claribel. The story is set in space, but it's not about extra-terrestrial beings or asteroids or intergalactic warfare. It's about technology and love and the search for oxygen.

Another thing to know about me is that I have a severe gas problem, meaning I have to pass gas often. Today it was pretty bad, Dave. Nerves, nerves, nerves. The simethicone, which is the drug I take to combat this ailment, didn't kick in until just before lunch. I know that's a lot to tell you right off the bat, but Mr. Smock encouraged me not to hold anything back. In general, my nervous system and stomach and bowels have a complicated relationship. Most of the time everything down in that arena feels heavy and swampish, like I have fish swimming around inside me. I pass a lot of gas and catch a lot of shade for it. "Shade" is attitude, Dave. I'm not going to assume that you know slang words. That's one of the only slang words I use. If I start to use any other ones, I'll be sure to let you know.

It would appear that Lars Silence and Mark Maestro are planning to steal my Android Nexus 6. In English, while Mrs. Blanton was handing out the reading list, they kept whispering things about me. "Nerd" this and "nerd" that. And "Is that a Droid, Silence?" And "Is that supposed to be a haircut, Maestro?" I could feel them behind me the whole period, Dave. After class they waited for me in the hall, but thankfully Mr. Cuff was there, talking to a student, so they left me alone.

Lars Silence isn't any bigger than me, but I heard he studied at the Kuk Sool Won Martial Arts Academy in Peoria this summer. Mark Maestro is built like a box of baking soda, and he always has a toothpick in his mouth, which he uses to poke people with.

I'm considering blindness. Meaning maybe I'll try faking being blind for a while. Like I could just not blink and walk into desks and doors and reach for things like I'm forever lost in the dark. Or maybe I'll take a fork to my eyes and do it for real. Then they'd give me a cane and a German shepherd, and I'd get to wear sunglasses ad nauseam. "Ad nauseam" refers to something that has been done or repeated so often that it has become annoying or tiresome. It's a Latin phrase. I learned it in English class.

The rest of the day wasn't as bad as English.

The cafeteria at Lugo Memorial is clean, and the food is pretty good. This Mexican girl was serving chicken cutlets. She has a face like a sad Bible person. Like someone who cried at Christ's feet. Big faraway eyes and hardly any mouth. She's the youngest server, and her hands are soft-looking and tan. When we spied each other, it felt like slow tingly thunder rolling through my chest. I'm sure there are poems about this feeling, and I will have to find them. Poems about love and blindness and Mexico. I imagine she smells good and spicy. But not spicy in a burrito way. Spicy in a hot-blooded cholo way.

Before she served me my chicken cutlet, she took off her hairnet and reached into her pocket and put another one on. It was pretty graceful, and I think she did it for my sexual entertainment. Her hair fell to her shoulders like a dark river. . . . What I just wrote could be lyrics to a song, Dave. I could be a blind singer with sunglasses and a devoted German shepherd at my side. When she wasn't looking, I reached over the service station and took the discarded hairnet, which she'd left balled up next to the green beans. I'm small but I have long arms. Plus I'm double-jointed. You will learn many details about me, Dave the Diary. Like about my double-jointedness and my gas problems and the various items I keep in my school locker. The girl in line next to me saw me take the hairnet and squinted.

"What?" I said.

She called me a weirdo.

She said, "Fucking bug-eyed weirdo."

I told her to stop throwing me shade and then she told me I stank.

"You stink," she said, and then squinted again and added, "Did you just shit your pants or something?"

And I'll admit that I passed gas, Dave, and yes, it was pretty bad, but I still wanted to punch her, I really did, with my right fist, not my left. But I stopped myself because Camila was there, and I don't want her to think I'm a violent person. That girl who was throwing me shade's name is Cinthia Hauk, and she is the first name on The List. I have to educate you about The List, Dave. It's too complicated to go into right now, but I'll tell you more about it soon enough. The List has been on my mind a lot lately, and when I actually saw it take shape in my head, I got so excited that my stomach went funny. Thank God the simethicone finally kicked in. Sometimes I can feel when it starts working. It's like a switch gets turned on and all the swampishness stops. When I thought about putting Cinthia Hauk on The List, I got so excited I also almost urinated in my pants, but I didn't. The List has powers.

I wound up eating at a table with two other kids: a boy with a deformed arm named Durdin Royko and this chubby Asian girl, Keiko Cho, who brings her own lunch and never looks up. Keiko Cho eats cucumber sandwiches with the crusts cut off and balls of popcorn. She pretty much acts like a cat that gets stuck in a room with weird plants, meaning she sort of slinks around and doesn't speak. Durdin Royko makes clicking noises like there's a little machine inside him counting stuff. His deformed arm is more like a tool than an arm. The three of us ate in total silence. You could see the muscles in Durdin Royko's jaws bulging as he chewed. Keiko Cho's smooth Asian face hardly moved while she ate her sandwich. Everyone else in the cafeteria was throwing shade at us, particularly Lars Silence and Mark Maestro, who were sitting three tables away and ribbitting like frogs every time Keiko Cho took a bite of her popcorn ball.

I guess we are officially the Freshman Frogs.

3

At home, Corinthia is met with a look of delicate consternation.

Marlene Bledsoe is some twenty inches shorter and 140 pounds lighter than her daughter. Marlene's hairdo, whose actual hue is difficult to decipher these days, might be mistaken for a world-class breakfast pastry. She is using a bristly kitchen blob to scrub potatoes with short, firm strokes. It seems like she's punishing tiny limbless children.

Corinthia is sitting on the kitchen floor with an ice pack on her head. A silence has been expanding between them like a giant mushroom in a damp fungal forest.

"You left your special desk," Marlene finally says.

Yes, Corinthia finds herself in yet another room with another adult—her own mother this time.

"It's not that special," Corinthia replies.

"Of course it's special," Marlene retorts, really digging into the skin of a particularly dirty potato. "It took you *days* to make that desk. *Days*."

"It's a few hunks of carefully arranged wood."

"But you were so *proud* of it. The first time you brought it home, you showed it off like it was the greatest thing you'd ever *done*."

Corinthia has the sudden sensation that her mother is on a small pontoon boat, slowly drifting away. A pontoon boat with a working sink and a bucket of brown Idaho potatoes, no less, but an actual pontoon boat.

Marlene Bledsoe's butt jiggles while she works. Recently she's been trying to get back into shape, and for the past three weeks she's been spending an hour and ten minutes a day dancing in place in the living room to a middle-aged workout celebrity who instructs Marlene while flitting about on the high-definition forty-two-inch flat-screen. This woman, whose name is Stacey or Lacy or Traci Something-or-other, has the same exact hairstyle that Marlene does and supposedly changed Madonna's body and Miley Cyrus's body and Barbra Streisand's body and J.Lo's body like at some unfathomable cellular, subatomic level, and this fitness guru appears to have more energy than three small children after eating ultraviolet breakfast cereal.

Yesterday Marlene added a Hula-Hoop to the regimen. She doesn't actually spin it, though; she simply sets it on the floor and dances inside and outside its perimeter. From her upstairs bathroom, Corinthia can often hear Marlene wheezing through the workout like some veteran truck driver.

"Would you care for more ice?" Marlene asks her daughter from the sink.

"I'm fine," Corinthia replies, briefly closing her eyes, hoping for a kind of vast gray blankness or, more specifically, a freshly rained-upon natural slate wall. When overwhelmed, Corinthia does her best to summon this wall, this indefinable monolith. She imagines placing her hands on it, inviting its cool, stolid permanence to calm her. But after a few seconds, she finds that she has to open her eyes, fearing another visit from those tornadoes.

Over the running water, Marlene says, "Mr. Smock spoke as if you'd *abandoned* your desk."

"Dogs are abandoned," Corinthia replies. "Dogs and busted bikes."

"Don't be smart, Cori."

"And dirty children at interstate truck stops."

It's cooler here in the kitchen. Sometimes, in the middle of the night, Corinthia will sneak out of her room, descend the stairs, and lie on the smooth Mexican tiles. There are fewer mosquitoes down here. In her room they disappear into the Sheetrock and wait for her to fall asleep. They particularly love her big, fleshy knees, which are so bitten up, it looks as if she suffers from a skin condition.

"Do we need to schedule an appointment with Dr. Flung?" Marlene says.

Dr. Flung is the psychologist whom Corinthia stopped seeing some months ago. Dr. Nene Flung, a small Filipina with a gentle voice and drawn-on eyebrows, who bought a pair of leather beanbag chairs especially for Corinthia because her office sofa was too small. During sessions they would each sit on a beanbag, Dr. Flung perched on top of hers like a little wooden bird. She would ask Corinthia the strangest questions.

Questions like: "If you were to draw yourself twenty years from now, what kind of hair might you have?"

And: "When I say the word *porcupine,* what's the first thing that comes to mind besides a porcupine?"

Hanging out with her for forty-five minutes was like visiting someone in their parents' refinished basement. Corinthia always got the feeling that after twenty minutes of discussing physical ailments, mild family dramas, and the general anxieties of high school, they might eat cookie dough and play video games.

Dr. Flung mainly led Corinthia through meaningless, childish exercises and acted supportive. But she did teach Corinthia about summoning her wall; she took her through the entire imaginative process, and for this Corinthia will always be grateful.

"I think a visit with Dr. Flung might be a good idea," Marlene offers.

"Can't I just lie here?" Corinthia says, adjusting the ice pack on her head. The peaks of her tented knees almost rise above the horizon of the kitchen table.

Marlene Bledsoe, mother of two, sighs mightily and continues washing the bejesus out of her potatoes. Wife to Brill, and former bookkeeper of Lugo's only nail salon, Nails and Everything Else ("Everything Else" referring to eyebrow threading, bikini waxing, and anal bleaching), Marlene is a professional sigher. Or at least it seems that way to Corinthia. She certainly can sigh with the best of them.

Once petite and downright smoking hot, Marlene is now a tad doughy in that strange fleshy way of middle-aged male fast-food managers. Prone to serial purchases from the FirmaMall catalog (eight-inch stone gnomes, electrolysis devices disguised as oral hygiene utensils, and a large triangular corduroy sleeping pillow the color of a popular indigestion medicine designed to rest on the coach-class seatback tray), Marlene likes to eat Haribo Gold Bears and has a hard time standing still. There's always a slight tremor in her hands and a pinched quality about her hips and glutes that makes her look as if she's constantly doing everything she can not to suddenly break into an exit sprint.

Sometimes Marlene Bledsoe, whose maiden name is Ottinger, looks at her daughter with the astonishing thought, *This THING came out of ME.* Or, more specifically, *This GIANT* BURST FORTH *from my VAGINA,* and when encountering Corinthia, though blithely unaware, she'll invariably plant a fist in front of her plum terry-cloth relax slacks (she also owns peach and mauve) as if to ward off any possible further birthing trauma.

"You're doing it again," Corinthia will tell her mother.

Marlene will then place her hands behind her back, clasping them together with a forced stoicism that would rival an army general's.

"I promise I'm not going back in," Corinthia will joke assuredly. Because humor is the salve to sadness, after all, especially when that sadness is most tenaciously experienced in the spaces shared between mother and daughter.

Although at birth Corinthia was a normal eight pounds seven ounces, the span of the past five years— since the arrival of that storied tumor—has seemingly wiped away the "standard" childhood anecdotes from her mother's memory. Marlene has somehow forgotten all those beautiful firsts. Corinthia's first words, which happened to be "big girl," echoed her mother's, who was praising her for using a spoon for the first time. Who would've thought that these two syllables would gain an ironic, almost poetic meaning?

Other firsts that have been deleted from Marlene's memory are her daughter's first steps, her virgin bike ride without training wheels, and the first time she hid underneath the dining-room table with all seventeen of her stuffed FirmaMall dogs, proclaiming to the world that she was running away to Menomonee Falls, Wisconsin, which happened to be the name of the town stitched into all the manufacturing tags found under the tails of her dogs. Corinthia obviously thought this was a place of magical deliverance (not to mention more stuffed dogs).

So the memories are gone, and now there's this GIANT IN MARLENE'S HOUSE, this medical-physiological MIRACLE. It's as if Corinthia has always been this way. She might as well have arrived on the Bledsoe premises five years ago, after disembarking from some fateful southern Illinois bus containing Midwestern Freaks.

And then again, when a mother is confronted with such a dramatic deformity of progeny every day of her life, perhaps she must live in the hyper-present tense.

It undoubtedly involves a certain amount of terror. Who knows how much larger her Corinthia's hands will grow? Those fish-belly white slabs with the creepy funeral-home-director fingers and Alpine-peaked knuckles. And how quickly? Will the plates of her skull ever stop expanding? And what about that chin? At some point will horsehair begin sprouting from it?

There were a few months when it seemed to Marlene like every time Corinthia lumbered through the front door, there was something more grotesque to behold. If it wasn't the blotchy cheeks (a reaction to the thyroxine), it was the flaking, inflamed eczema ringing her mouth, or the hellish dandruff, or the outbreak of unexplained bloody noses that made it look as if her enormous daughter's face were violently *menstruating*.

Marlene has turned to God more and more lately, fearing that she is losing connection to her youngest child. The Bledsoes have never been an outwardly religious family — they attend the local Lutheran church only on Christmas Eve and Easter Sunday, but God can find his way into the hopes and dreams of even the most marginally faithful. In addition to sneaking into First Lutheran during afternoons after she's finished the food shopping, Marlene has started praying.

Dear God, she'll implore quietly while kneeling beside her and Brill's brushed-steel four-poster bed (one of her early, most resolute FirmaMall purchases), *please give me the strength to be a Good Mother, to love my Baby Girl. Please grant me the serenity to see her on the* Inside, *to cherish her* Honesty and Goodness, *to love her* unconditionally, *to do my best not to watch her eat those enormous helpings of my creamy burrito casseroles or listen to her mouth-breathe at night, which sometimes sounds like a felled, lung-torn wildebeest snuffling for its life in the sun-blighted, dung-clogged earth of some violent, puma-saturated, Sudanese grassland.*

Please let me not take strange pleasure in enumerating her visits to the basement where her private bathroom is and where she will sometimes stay for upward of forty minutes. Is she voiding her bowels, God? Is she urinating? Is her bladder that big? I've seen camels urinate on wildlife cable shows, and it just comes and comes and comes like some kind of industrial faucet that won't turn off! Is it like that for Corinthia, too, God? Or is she doing something strange down there, like looking at herself naked in the mirror or comparing her breasts or picking at a constellation of moles that I don't know about, like seven raised moles forming the face of that awful villain in the first Die Hard *movie, or is she starting to get skin tags, because her father certainly has a few of those and I hear you can just pull them off, but if one were to do that, would it cause another one to grow, or would some leaky intestinal noise commence and never cease, or is she down there studying the water stains that have inexplicably been forming on the gypsum ceiling we installed last year? Maybe she's just sitting on that enormous commode, just sitting there in the dark because this is the only place where she genuinely feels like she isn't being ogled by everyone. Yes, I ogle her too, Precious God of Thunder and Light. I ogle and ogle and ogle, but how can I not? Help me, God. Help me to* help *Corinthia Lee. Please bless her and keep her . . .*

But despite Marlene Bledsoe's desperate overtures to God, the nightmares come.

Which include:

Corinthia eating the local Lugo children, feasting on their limbs like drumsticks, her mouth a horror-movie rictus of saliva and innocent, half-chewed flesh, her eyes pinned and cougarlike, her nostrils flaring ludicrously.

Or the one where the knobs of Corinthia's spine are pressing through her skin, and she's cackling madly while protoplasm-slathered pterodactyl wings are bursting through the flesh between her shoulder blades.

Or the other one, where Corinthia opens her mouth and the sound of the universe screams forth, which is sort of like an infinite chorus of lost hysterical children mixed with the sounds of earthmovers, and then thousands of bats fly out of her throat and blacken the sky.

On Tuesday nights, Marlene has started to frequent a support group across the Ohio River, in Louisville, Kentucky, to be exact, where, not far from the city's beloved Yum! Center, in a fluorescently lit, wood-paneled church basement that smells a little like damp, moldy curtains, she gathers with a dozen or so other Parents of Grotesquely Disfigured Children, the PGDC.

One African-American man, Sturm Fullilove, has a daughter, Opal, who was born with no mouth. Opal is four now, and in addition to being mouthless, she has a nose that runs incessantly, and according to the pictures Sturm brings to Group, there seems to be a permanent rime of dry mucus caking the area where her upper lip would be. The word for having no oral cavity is *astomatous*—Sturm likes to use this word a lot. The first time he passed around a framed portrait of Opal to the other Parents of Grotesquely Disfigured Children, Marlene Bledsoe almost vomited into her own perfectly normal mouth.

In an effort to provide her with another orifice through which to draw oxygen (her nose is often severely congested), a small spout has been surgically created just below Opal Fullilove's chin. Of course, this spout is simply and exactly that—a spout. There are no teeth. There is no tongue or salivary system and thus no way to break down and ingest food orally, so her nourishment is all fluid-based. The poor girl has been attached to some intravenous system or other since birth.

Then there were many weeks when, through the most delicate forms of physical therapy, Opal Fullilove had to learn to use this spout, much like a porpoise does. In fact, that's exactly what Sturm said while showing the photo to the rest of the group.

"She breathes through that little hole there, just like porpoises do."

Sturm Fullilove often brings Krispy Kreme doughnuts to the Tuesday-night meetings. Doughnuts topped with icing and jelly beans and multicolored sprinkles.

Clinette and Spinner Sloper, also African Americans, who parent six-hundred-pound DeMarcus, bring fat-free muffins. But every once in a while they'll bring hot browns in a box instead. The hot brown, Marlene has learned, is a traditional Louisville sandwich made with turkey and bacon on toasted white bread and smothered with a mysterious condiment called Mornay sauce.

Then there's Chauncey Shore, a white man whose daughter, Pru, was born with two left arms (in addition to a right arm). Chauncey brings a big bag of sea-salt-and-vinegar potato chips to meetings. Daughter Pru's pair of left arms is totally normal, but the right one is really small and sort of looks like a turtle leg. The hand at the end of the arm doesn't *quite* have fingers, but instead the blunt, melted hint of them.

Chauncey is the only one who eats the sea-salt-and-vinegar potato chips, probably because he doesn't actually distribute them but holds them in his lap and pretty much lords over them as if his life depends on it. Marlene has a mind to snatch them out of his lap and give them to a homeless man who always solicits her where she parks her car in the garage across from the Yum! Center.

And what does Marlene bring to the meetings?

Marlene Bledsoe, whose fellow suffering parents have come to accidentally call her *May*lene, brings miniature bottles of Poland Spring water that she buys from the Sheetz on the Kentucky side of the Ohio River. If she were to buy them at the Sheetz on the Illinois side, she fears she might be spotted by someone, like her husband's barber, Willis Brunch, for instance, or her daughter's physical therapist, the kindhearted, always-smiling Carole Pie, or Hakeem Maybe, the ageless West Indian man with the ancient, minty-smelling dreadlocks, who manages the Better Burger on Tango Drive. Then there's Dora Momadora, her former employer and owner of the nail salon, who seems to be *everywhere* at *all times*. Or Zumba enthusiast Shoshone Candeleria and her yippy little schnauzer that has a face like a bitter third-world dictator.

While crossing the Ohio, Marlene Bledsoe often experiences the feeling that she can get away with just about anything. The thrill of possibility tingles in her kidneys and makes her feel sort of like she has to pee, but in a good way.

Oh, crossing the Ohio River and its dirty little thrill!

And speaking of tingling, the person Marlene likes the most at PGDC is Lemon Tidwell, a tranquil white man with an FM radio deejay voice, who brings bags of individually wrapped pastel-colored blobs of salt-water taffy.

Lemon Tidwell's son, Cecil, has a football-size benign but inoperable tumor growing out of the left side of his skull. Benign because it's about as malignant as a wooden shoe but inoperable because it's managed to house itself too dangerously close to Cecil's anterior cerebral artery. During the colder seasons, Cecil is forced to don two knit caps: one that he wears over the expanse of his slightly lunch box–shaped head, into which a hole is cut to accommodate the Sputnik-like tumor; and another for the tumor itself, which doesn't grow hair but pulses with enough nerve life to register extreme temperatures.

Lemon will often break out his compact slide-show device, which attaches to his smartphone through some mini-USB-cord-port arrangement and projects images onto a white sheet that he duct-tapes to one of the church basement's slightly warped wood-paneled walls. The lighthearted photos, curated with the hope of injecting humor into each meeting, are captured by Lemon Tidwell himself through the user-friendly but sophisticated technology afforded by his Nikon digital point-and-shoot. The subject is his son Cecil, of course, who, seven now, is featured outfitting the tumor with lamp shades, an empty KFC bucket, an orange traffic cone, various serving and mixing bowls, a broken cuckoo clock, an unfinished birdhouse, a giant cardinal-red LOUISVILLE IS #1 sponge hand, and the riffled, gutted remains of a piñata.

Marlene Bledsoe appreciates Lemon Tidwell's upbeat approach to Cecil's deformity, and his thick salt-and-pepper hair has grown on her in recent weeks (not literally). Marlene's husband, Brill, who is forty-three now, has very few grays—you can barely see them, in fact—and her former high-school prom date will likely continue to age this way, and it's his natural external youth and trim belly that make it easier for her to accept the blinding morning breath (like an old banana left in a mailbox), his strange intestinal warblings heard at the dinner table, and the recent sty and accompanying twitch that's emerged under his right eye. The sty is pearl-colored with just a hint of yellow crust, and she and Brill have never actually talked about it. And the not talking about it—this inviolable collusion—hangs in the air between them like some half-dead monkey dipped in corn oil and in intermittent spasms makes Marlene feel like she might just thrust her hand into the opening of the garbage disposal and turn the thing on! She practically makes a fist every time she walks past the sink just so she won't do it!

At the most recent PGDC meeting—last Tuesday, to be exact—Marlene learned that Lemon Tidwell is a widower. His wife, Nancy, died of a strange condition related to sleep apnea. Lemon is relatively new to the group—he started coming only a week or two before Marlene did—and when Clinette Sloper pointed to his wedding band and asked if his wife might attend, he simply stated, "My wife died in her sleep about a year ago." Then he smiled sweetly, his teeth just the least bit dim in that sexy cowboy sort of way, and offered a piece of salt-water taffy to Sturm Fullilove, whose face was racked with such grief that one might've thought Lemon Tidwell was talking about *Sturm's* dead wife.

The sleep apnea details were revealed a few weeks later when, during the twenty-minute break, while most everyone else was either outside bumming cigarettes or finding a more service-friendly area to check their smartphones, Marlene approached Lemon at the snacks table.

"Was your wife ill?" she half whispered.

Lemon Tidwell used his gentle cowboy voice to tell her about his wife's condition and how she stopped wearing the special mask prescribed by her doctor, one that helped battle the sleep apnea.

He said, "Nance didn't like the mask. Complained that it made her look like she was goin' deep-sea diving. So that was that."

Marlene loves that he calls his wife "Nance."

And she loves that he wears faded Lee jeans and smells like pipe tobacco.

And more than anything, she loves his reddish-brown mustache and sandpapery face.

As far as Marlene can tell, Lemon Tidwell is a man who doesn't succumb to the undertow of bad luck and sorrow. He keeps the bottom-feeders of bitterness at bay with a long spear of positivity and shows up at meetings with entertaining slide-show photos of his grossly deformed but good-spirited son.

And there's also this little tidbit:

Marlene has been hoarding his taffy.

She hides it all over the house: behind books, under the fine crystal in the living-room china cabinet, and inside the hollow belly of the ceramic elephant she brought back from the trip she and Brill took to Thailand before Channing was born.

She's even buried a few pieces in the depths of the flour bin.

Marlene Bledsoe has yet to share a picture of Corinthia with the group. Sharing is a big step, after all. It can take months. And there's no pressure; there really isn't. But everyone talks about how freeing it is.

Shepard Montrose, the leader of the PGDC, is always talking about how important it is to share, but also how one must come to this moment in one's own time.

Shepard, a gentle, passive man with thick white hair and a mouth like a letter opener, has a son who was born without limbs. Toby Montrose, seventeen now, recently left home to join a traveling freak show known as *The Beautiful Apocalypse,* which tours small colleges in the American South and Midwest. He is basically a head attached to a lumpy, formless, lightly furred torso, but he boasts a pair of impressive carotid arteries on either side of an extremely well-developed neck, a neck so well developed, in fact, that Marlene has found it almost erotic.

The concept of Toby's attraction is that he is "planted" in a Plexiglas terrarium of soil, among carefully arranged dandelions. This startling installation is billed as "Plato the Potato Boy." Bored into each of the four panels of Plexiglas are fist-size holes, designed for either airflow or feeding, though it's not entirely clear, because Toby Montrose is prone to hunger strikes.

Apparently there is a lavaliere microphone taped

to his cheek, and Toby, who has officially changed his name to Plato, likes to sing anti-consumer songs, a cappella, over a P.A. "Fling Your Smartphone at a Drone" is his favorite one; that and "App-Happy Babylon," which is actually more of a spoken-word piece than a classic song in that it trades conventional melody for a kind of demonic, incantatory chant that is downright disturbing.

Occasionally, overcome with the need to rant about the hypocrisy and evils of professional baseball, particularly those associated with the St. Louis Cardinals post–Albert Pujols, Toby/Plato will stop singing and unleash long, heavily embroidered monologues.

Shepard Montrose shares pix of Toby performing as Plato the Potato Boy in his Plexiglas box. He doesn't project them like Lemon Tidwell; he simply passes around three-by-five snapshots.

Regarding his son's dark turn, Shepard's demeanor is quietly accepting, if not resigned. Last spring he spent some time following *The Beautiful Apocalypse.* After visiting Shorter University in Rome, Georgia, and Coker College in Hartsville, South Carolina, he ended his trip at Rust College, an African-American liberal arts institution in Holly Springs, Mississippi, after his son started spouting invective over the P.A. while using an infrared laser device that was attached to his forehead to point out his "asshole father" to the students gathered around his box. The laser beam's red point danced invasively around Shepard's left eye until he was forced to turn away.

"STOP FOLLOWING ME!" Toby/Plato screamed, red-faced and seething. He then told everyone how at the age of sixteen, he had legally divorced his parents (which is true) because he was tired of being objectified as a "thing" to be "carried around" and "shown" to people, like an "exhibit." (The profound irony of course being that this is precisely what he has become.) Then Toby/Plato led the students in an Ebonical chant of "PEACE OUT, POPS. PEACE THE FUCK OUT! PEACE OUT, POPS. PEACE THE FUCK OUT!" until, humiliated, Shepard made his exit to thunderous undergraduate African-American applause and so much hissing, he thought snakes were slithering after him.

The whole thing just got to be too painful.

At the last PGDC meeting, Shepard handed out four-color programs from *The Beautiful Apocalypse*. The cover featured his son, Toby, aka "Plato the Potato Boy," preaching to hundreds of undergraduate students from his terrarium. Marlene took the program home, along with Lemon Tidwell's taffy, and hid it at the bottom of her sock drawer. She has since taken it out three times and studied the cover along with several other freak-show attractions. One woman has a face like a crocodile. There is a set of Siamese twins joined at the head called Tito the Two-Headed Boy. The back of the program lists the many colleges that comprise the tour, as well as a website and contact information.

Brill Bledsoe knows nothing of his wife's Tuesday-evening trips into Kentucky to attend these support group meetings. Marlene takes the second car, a 2009 Chianti-colored Hyundai, which she drives a few miles per hour slower than the speed limit, bracing for the oncoming bridge-crossing kidney tingle, clutching the steering wheel so tightly, her wrists are often fatigued by the time she arrives in Louisville.

Brill thinks she's eating Mexican food over in Kaskaskia with her former coworkers from the nail salon.

During the early part of the week, Brill Bledsoe has to stay late at the administrative office of Bazoo Meatpacking, where he's worked for the past twenty-one years, to process weekend back orders and other shipping and slaughtering particulars. His quiet dedication to the meat business is like that of a great small-town high-school football coach who gracefully deflects all praise and glory onto his players.

But it's Thursday now, not Tuesday at all, and unfortunately Marlene will have to wait five more days before she can be with her fellow PGDCers and wolf down Sturm Fullilove's doughnuts and look at photos of Grotesquely Disfigured Children and abscond with Lemon Tidwell's beloved taffy.

Five days is 120 hours from now, and that seemingly unassailable length of time makes Marlene's hands tremble so much, they might just burst. The first forty or so hours are doable, but after that, the time just seems like miles of interminable high-noon desert that she must cross in big clunky shoes.

Thus the need to busy herself with extreme potato scrubbing.

And lately Marlene absolutely *hates* falling asleep, because that's when The Beast comes. The Beast meaning daughter Corinthia, starring in an endlessly turning rotisserie of those unbearable nightmares. In the past few years, Marlene has taken on such pastimes as reading legal thrillers and surfing the Internet for home-improvement updates and finishing the local paper's daily word jumble. All this to distract herself from that tempting, dastardly, always-changing Firma-Mall collection!

Brill Bledsoe knows all too well his wife's tendency to make purchases from the storied miles-high catalog. The Black Forest Welcoming Gnome and the Cat Memorial Angel Stone (memorializing the cat they've never had) and the Plantar Fasciitis Night Splint (anticipating the imminent foot condition; someone's *bound* to get it, after all). The Hideaway Elliptical Trainer and Vivitar Digital Camera/Binoculars combo and the Shiatsu Leg Massager that looks like a urinal for Ewoks. The Tetris Lamp and the Northwest Stars Projector and Clock with Accompanying Soothing Lullabies. Brill understands that his wife might be bored since the onset of her early retirement from the nail salon. He has no idea that Marlene's constant need to make purchases is one great distraction from the impending nightmares about their daughter.

But in recent months, Marlene has exhausted herself trying to stay awake. It's just gotten to be so god-awful tiring, fretting about everything! She often wakes contorted into herself, as though she's been thrown from the back of a landscaping truck by surly gardeners, her shoulders and wrists aching, her eyes so puffy she looks as if she's been bitten all over by yellow jackets.

But for the past week, Marlene has adopted a new outlook, which is this: she's come to genuinely embrace the idea of insomnia! And it's actually been amazing! It's all about sneaking downstairs and making use of her Genio Single Serve Coffee Maker, which brews up a cup so quietly, one might think it was manufactured by and for ninjas! She will stay awake for the rest of her natural born life if it means never having to experience those horrible dreams about her daughter!

It's actually been three nights in a row now that she's managed to stay awake. If only she can make it all the way to Tuesday, when she will get to spend a few hours with Lemon Tidwell and her culturally diverse friends at Group!

You can make it till Tuesday, Marlene, she self-coaches, scrubbing her potatoes, clutching and unclutching her butt cheeks, an exercise she's recently learned that helps to keep her awake and connected to her pelvis and tailbone. *Keep that core engaged,* she tells herself, scrubbing, scrubbing, clutching, and unclutching. She engages these muscles with such fine, hardly discernible movements, it's almost impossible for anyone else to see. The "glute thrusts" have become her little fitness secret. They can be done at the dinner table, or while folding laundry, or even while seated in coach on a plane.

When Brill Bledsoe enters the kitchen, he kisses his wife of twenty years on the cheek. He kisses her and squeezes the fullness of her arm affectionately.

Marlene smiles and continues scrubbing, though she now abandons the glute thrusts.

Brill then pivots to his daughter, lifts the bag of ice, and kisses the crown of her cold, damp head.

"Hey, kiddo," he says.

"Hey," she replies, meeting his eyes, which are gray and loving.

After doubling back to the front door to hang his white BAZOO MEATPACKING jacket on the coatrack, to Corinthia, Brill says, "I understand you had a strange day."

She nods, adjusting the bag of ice.

"You left your desk there."

"And she broke a door," Marlene adds.

"The folks at Memorial probably have another door hidden away somewhere," Brill says lightheartedly, winking at his daughter. Despite her aching head, Corinthia musters a half smile, just enough to let her dad know she appreciates his going easy on her.

From her post at the sink, Marlene says, "All I know is when one starts destroying school property, it has a funny way of making its way onto one's permanent record."

Corinthia can suddenly feel how tender and sore her left shoulder is, the one she heaved into Bob Sluba's classroom door.

Marlene stops washing potatoes, awaiting a response from her daughter to what she said about permanent records. She even turns the water off and looks directly at Corinthia, her tweezed eyebrows forming perfect little arches.

Corinthia simply adjusts the bag of ice on her head.

"Do you feel no regret about what you did to that door?"

"I regret it, okay?" Corinthia finally says.

Marlene cranks the water back on and then to Brill adds, "According to Mr. Smock, she claimed to be having visions."

Scratching the back of his ankle, Brill says, "What kind of visions, Cori?"

"Tornadoes," Marlene offers before Corinthia can answer. "Of all things."

"Was there a warning?" Brill asks. "I don't recall hearing the horn."

Marlene scrubs a little and says, "They were *visions*, Brill. *Visions*. The kind of tornadoes that exist in one's *imagination*."

"I need to go take my medicine," Corinthia says, and heaves herself to her feet, which is usually a three- or four-part move, depending on the day — today she does it in two — and bounds up the stairs to her room.

Six months ago, the Bledsoes added four-inch extensions to the lip of each step because the standard step proved to be too shallow for Corinthia's foot. She was starting to have to negotiate the stairs pigeon-toed, knock-kneed, and even sideways, which, all told, caused more knee pain.

One Saturday, Brill's carpenter friend, Ron

Ricadonna, showed up with a bundle of precut wood and completed the job in four hours. He used graphite L brackets and topped off the extensions with a skin of grooved traction rubber.

Corinthia's brother, Channing, has been using the extended steps as a more challenging workout for his calf muscles. With the added few inches, he can really go deep on the heel raises and work those Achilles tendons. He'll sometimes do fifty on each foot, breathing sharply through his nose.

Brill seems to have no new relationship to the augmented stairs. Like most things in life, he's figured out a way to invisibly assimilate. He's always been a bastion of poise and graceful adaptability. His blood pressure rarely skyrockets. A former cross-country runner, he has a pulse that is often under sixty. If he hadn't gotten onto a career path in the meatpacking industry, he would probably have made a heck of an EMT.

Marlene, on the other hand, ascends the stairs as if she is walking barefoot on broken glass. Like everything else related to her daughter, the new stairs have only come to remind her of the various grotesqueries she must suffer. The level of difficulty seems to increase with each of the twelve steps. By step five, it's as if she's carrying loads of laundry. By step ten, she'll sometimes cry out as if she's come face-to-face with a coiled rattlesnake.

"You okay, honey?" Brill will call up to her from the living room.

"These dang stairs," she'll say, sighing. "Are you sure they're all the same size?"

"Sure as stones in a quarry," he'll reply, or something to that effect.

One night when the family had been encamped in front of the TV, Marlene announced that she was going to bed, and Corinthia offered to carry her up the stairs.

Marlene turned and cocked her head, her once supple, now slightly jowly face beset by a brief, lip-loosening look of wonder.

"Now, sweetheart, why would you say that?" she asked her daughter, who was sitting on the floor, reading *The Great Gatsby* for her American literature class, the paperback like a small wallet in her hand.

"I just had this urge to bundle you up and carry you like a baby," Corinthia replied, staring down at her book.

From his leather recliner, Brill chuckled.

Channing, however, who was at the threshold of the kitchen, completing a set of super-wide reps with his circular push-up mounts, was oblivious, as his ears were plugged with sweat-resistant, workout-friendly iPhone buds.

"Let her carry you," Brill offered brightly, dipping his glasses off the bridge of his nose.

"I'll carry *you*, Captain," Marlene retorted, though Brill Octavius Bledsoe has never been a military man, no, not even remotely, and then she headed up the stairs precariously, clutching the banister as if the extra-big steps might sprout monstrous spired teeth, start masticating, and swallow her whole.

After she takes her medication (all seventeen pills), Corinthia calls Cloris Honniotis, her best and only friend. Cloris is four feet nine. She is nineteen and works part-time at Lugo's small public library while attending night school at Lugo Community College (LCC), where she is taking core requirement classes toward a degree in library science. She also practices Brazilian jujitsu twice a week at the local community center. She is currently a purple belt but will be trying for her brown belt sometime next spring.

"What's up, Jabbar?" Cloris says.

She's nicknamed her best friend after the former NBA star Kareem Abdul-Jabbar, the legendary seven-foot-two-inch Los Angeles Laker.

"You reading?" Corinthia asks.

"The reading machine is indeed reading."

"Bivouacking in the bathroom?"

"My little sanctuary. Can you smell the Lysol? What about you?"

"I'm talking to you, Ewok."

"You sound depressed."

"Just exhausted."

"Were you crying? I detect a great loss of tears and the ensuing ophthalmic dehydration."

"I had sort of a weird day," Corinthia says.

"Bull Run?"

"Bull Run" is the pet name that Cloris Honniotis has assigned to Corinthia's period. Which makes sense, as the volume of blood that manifests during Cloris's best friend's menses is nothing less than extraordinary, and Cloris likes to assign pet names to extraordinary things. There were a few months when Corinthia had to resort to using an adult diaper. Even now she keeps a spare one in her school locker in case of an emergency. She's become adept at fashioning a Depends into a makeshift maxi pad, folding it into a triangle and using her father's silver duct tape to reinforce the corners. Twice Corinthia has bought a package of Depends at the local Target.

"They're for my grandpa," she told the extremely thin, petite checkout girl with the candy-red hair and violet eyeliner, who said absolutely nothing in response.

Corinthia's grandpa Earl has been dead for five years, and as far as she knows, he never suffered from incontinence. His resurrection delivered as a lie to the Target checkout girl made Corinthia feel like her very normal, non-dyed cinnamon-colored hair was falling out. After she swallowed this mouse of shame and brought the matter to her mother, the Internet was surfed and websites were visited, and following Marlene Bledsoe's extensive search, a not-for-profit company was discovered that features special hygienic and toiletry needs for "Enormous Individuals":

savethegiants.org

With fewer than twenty strokes and force-clicks of Marlene Bledsoe's touch pad, a year's supply of various Large Person's Sanitary Napkins was purchased and arrived via FedEx two days later. They're currently stored in a custom-made cupboard that Ron Ricadonna created with Home Depot plywood. The cupboard, complete with old-school leather suitcase handles to accommodate the largest hands possible, hangs over Corinthia's extra-wide bariatric commode in the basement.

Cloris Honniotis says, "So word on the crusty old Lugo dirt road is that you had a vision, and I know you don't want to discuss this matter with yours truly, but you know in that oversize heart of yours that I'm the only one, aside from God, the Devil, and the ghost of

Elvis, who might actually believe you, so lay it on me. What'd you see?"

"Three tornadoes," Corinthia replies.

The four syllables settle in her stomach with the certainty of iron. She goes on to describe the tornadoes in great detail: their scale against the yellow-gray sickly Illinois sky; their violent, tendril-like spirals; the torn rooftops and divulsed cornfields; the displaced cow at center court in the field house.

Cloris says, "Holy apocalypse, Showtime."

Cloris occasionally calls Corinthia "Showtime" because that was the media nickname assigned to the storied eighties Lakers team that featured Kareem Abdul-Jabbar, Magic Johnson, James Worthy, Byron Scott, and Kurt Rambis. Cloris can speak to the statistics, dynamics, and personalities of this team with great passion and accuracy. How Cloris Honniotis, at four feet nine, is not only a professional basketball enthusiast but also a downright encyclopedic roundball junkie is anyone's guess.

Though the two friends were never at Lugo Memorial together (Cloris graduated the year before Corinthia arrived), they became acquainted at the local public library, where Cloris curates a robust and provocative young adult section. Cloris happened upon Corinthia perusing her shelves, and they struck up a conversation about Lorcan Nutt, a reclusive young adult author whom they both admire. The library is the one place where Corinthia has always felt at ease. After all, the bookcases are eight feet tall, and it's one of the few settings in her life where her head isn't the closest thing to the ceiling.

Cloris says, "Have all those meds finally turned you into some kind of soothsayer?"

Corinthia grunts in a semi-agreeable, exasperated manner.

Cloris says, "Don't tell me . . . you're in your basement, chillin' on your gigantic toilet."

"You should be in your basement, too," Corinthia warns.

"Because of your dreaded twisters."

"They're really coming."

During the ensuing silence, Corinthia stares at the many pits and pockmarks in the gypsum tiles. Why her parents outfitted the basement with such a ceiling is anyone's guess. It makes her feel like she's going to the bathroom in the waiting area of the dentist's.

Cloris says, "My basement smells like old photo albums and kitty litter."

"So spray some Febreze."

"I'll take my chances hanging out on the first floor."

"Have fun turning into scrambled eggs like the rest of Lugo."

"Easy there, Chewy."

"Chewy" is the third nickname Cloris calls Corinthia — a direct response to "Ewok."

From the perch on her own standard-size, lowered toilet seat, Cloris says, "So, I hear you took it upon yourself to do the work of the tornado horn."

"Who told you?"

"Doris Dabaduda," Cloris says. "We librarians are a tight-knit bunch. She has a micro-tear in her hamstring, by the way. And you broke a door."

"I did, indeed," Corinthia corroborates.

"The Thin Door of Human Reason?"

"The life sciences classroom door, actually."

" 'Hoppin' Bob Sluba," Cloris says, "I can just see his ageless bald face absolutely racked with wonder. You really went Beef Burgundy."

Going "Beef Burgundy" means losing your shit.

Corinthia then asks Cloris if she has any weed.

"Does the White House got a president in it?"

Cloris Honniotis has a tenacious weed habit. Her dealer, former Lugo Memorial classmate Terence "Baby Arm" McAvery, has a weekly delivery arrangement whereby he and Cloris exchange little manila envelopes at the library's book returns bin. It's as simple as rice, really. Terence texts her as he's parking his car, and then she meets him at the bin, where they slide manila envelopes to each other across the Formica counter.

Corinthia asks her if she can come by her house, but Cloris says that she's booked for the next few hours.

"Doing what?"

"I may be having a phone conversation with Lorcan Nutt."

"Lorcan Nutt!" Corinthia blurts out. "What the—? *How?"*

Their aforementioned favorite author lives in an unincorporated town somewhere in the middle of Arkansas. He's written more than sixty young adult novels, most of which are out of print. Few titles are known, but his ability to articulate the hearts and minds of characters to whom Corinthia and Cloris relate is uncanny, if not borderline miraculous.

Take, for instance, his 1996 novel, *The Smallest Hands,* in which young children comprise the world's workforce because their hands are small enough to assemble the most minuscule manufacturing particulars of nanotechnology. Eventually, each child's hand size outgrows the required size limit, and the work is outsourced to a younger, less developed child, at which point the maturing, unneeded child mysteriously disappears. It's implied that the missing children are getting dispatched by the Human Resources department so as to guarantee not passing along nanotech secrets to rival companies. At the center of this manufacturing tragedy is Willa, whose hands start to grow—employee hand growth is monitored on a monthly basis—and who catches wind of her grisly fate and orchestrates her escape through rocky, mountainous terrain that is policed by corporate drone wolves.

Cloris discovered the book in a literary trade journal review that was neither hugely positive nor in any way negative. She felt it was a diamond in the rough and placed a modest order of three copies for the library. When it arrived, she read it, loved it, ordered five more copies, erected a mini-display in the young adult section, and started talking up the book to precocious junior-high-school students as well as to Lugo Memorial freshman Corinthia Bledsoe, who had read one of Lorcan Nutt's earlier novels, *Rocky River Makes Me Shiver*, which is about the struggles of a six-fingered boy who draws naked pictures of the citizens of his small town, exposing birthmarks, scars, and genital configurations. The pictures appear at the post office, the supermarket, and the entrance to the local Catholic church. The boy's father, embarrassed and ashamed, winds up cutting his son's extra finger off with a bowie knife after a naked picture of him (the father) is posted on telephone poles all over town, exposing a telephone number written across his chest in black Sharpie ink, which proves to be the number of a woman—the local pharmacist's wife, to be exact—with whom he's having an affair. After the boy's finger is cut off, he loses his ability to draw, and his father forces him to learn how to play classical piano.

Cloris Honniotis explains to Corinthia how she tracked down Lorcan Nutt detective-style, extracting clues to his whereabouts from his strange, self-written mini–author bios featured in the back of his books. Before Cloris starting working there, the Lugo Public Library carried only four of his sixty-some novels, and she's had to take it upon herself to hunt down used, rare, and remaindered copies of his books. It's been an act of literary archaeology, to say the least.

"Lorcan Nutt?" Corinthia cries.

"The man himself."

"You're shitting Jabbar."

"I would not shit Jabbar, Chewy."

Cloris snot-rockets into the sink. Sometimes her year-round allergies make it difficult for her to get through a full-fledged conversation without having to send mucus flying in one direction or another.

"But what to do about these tornadoes?" Cloris asks.

"If the horn starts blowing, at least promise me that you'll go down to your little smelly basement."

Cloris Honniotis lives by herself in a white clapboard ranch house that's not much bigger than a two-car garage. Despite her cluttered basement, she keeps the house nice, with a ceramic deer poised in the front yard and little flower boxes lining the windows.

"I promise," Cloris finally replies. And then adds, "What are we gonna do with you, Nostradamus?"

Suddenly there is a knock on Corinthia's special bathroom door: three knocks, their reports tentative and faint.

"Dinner's ready," Marlene Bledsoe's voice sings from the other side. It has a quality like a teakettle's whistle expiring; a four-syllable descent of exasperation.

"I could use a vision or two," Cloris adds. "Lucky giant."

4

August 26, 2015, part two

Dave,

I'm home now. It's quiet. I can hear the crickets in the backyard. They sound like the throbbing mind of a monster. A thing with glowing eyes circling the house. Sometimes I think it's the ghost of my dad looking for his watch, which he was always misplacing. The watch was a gift from my mom before they were married. There wasn't anything fancy about it — it was a Timex Expedition men's analog/digital combo watch with a brown band — but it was important to him, and he would always lose it and then go on these epic searches. Once he found it in the refrigerator's butter cubby. Another time it was actually on his wrist and he'd been looking for it for over an hour. I see him creeping around the lilac bushes in Mom's garden, picking the slugs out of the mulch and looking for his watch. Mom's been pruning the older branches so new lilac bushes will grow. But no matter how much time she spends back there, it doesn't do any good. It seems like her lilac bushes will never get as tall as she wants them to be. Sometimes I get this feeling that they're going to start growing in the house. I'll come down to the kitchen and they'll be creeping through the floor and crawling up the walls like they have a strategy. But they won't grow in the garden. Not until my dad finds his watch.

Mom is in her room, reading and crying. I think she still misses Dad. Twice a week she goes to Belleville to talk to this woman about grief, but it only seems to be making things worse. Sometimes her crying sounds like laughing and sometimes it sounds like birds. I keep thinking I should buy her an ant farm, just to give her something to do besides pruning her lilac bushes.

One more thing about Mom: I think her hair is falling out. I saw a clump of it on the bathroom floor. I'm going to start gathering it for her, just in case she wants it back some-day. When you look at it up close, you can see how some of it is a little gray and some of it is sort of red, too. I'm storing it in a shoe box under my bed.

Tomorrow is gym. I DO NOT WANT TO TAKE A SHOWER, DAVE. That is the last thing I want to do, because I bet I'm the only boy in class who doesn't possess pubic hair. I might Scotch tape some of my mom's dead hair to my upper junk area. I think I could pull that off if I execute it with excellence. The hair on my head is dark brown, Dave, and, like I told you already, my mom's has gray in it and it's also a little red, but once I found one of my dad's old *Playboy* magazines, and the centerfold had blond hair on her head but her vagina bush was black like a cat with no face.

God, I hope Lars Silence and Mark Maestro aren't in my gym class. I hope we never play dodgeball, and I hope they aren't on the opposite team. I have practiced dodgeball in my mind. My guidance counselor, Mr. Smock, says that visualizing being good at sports can sometimes make you better. I close my eyes and perform deep-breathing exercises, and then I visualize myself doing incredible things. I catch all the dodgeballs — even the fastest ones coming at my head. I can throw with both arms — left and right equally — and the other team doesn't have an answer for me. I am the last one standing, and my classmates see something in me that they didn't know was there. But sometimes other things happen at the end of these visualizations, Dave. Like things I can't tell you about yet.

Dave, I know in my bones that at some point, Lars Silence and Mark Maestro will come at me. I know it the way you know there are slugs in Mom's garden. They will have weapons, and they will break me open and cut my foot off with a saw or a high-end serrated kitchen knife and bury it in the football field, and in the spring, grass won't grow there, only mushrooms, like the poisonous kind that make you spit up black oil.

Dave, I know you can't see me, but do you think it's weird that I'm wearing Camila's hairnet? I've been wearing it for a few hours, since like 6 p.m., and I can feel my heart beating faster. And I can also feel my hands filling with blood. I would wrestle a wolf for Camila, Dave. I would break a bottle over someone's head and then stab his thuggish partner in the neck with the weaponish shards.

Camila Camila Camila Camila Camila
Camila Camila Camila Camila Camila Camila
Camila Camila Camila Camila Camila Camila
Camila Camila Camila . . .

Saying her name over and over makes me
feel huge, like my bedroom is too small for me.

So, as an assignment from Mr. Smock, I'm
supposed to tell you about five things that I
care about. Here they are:

> 1. Mom.
> 2. My dad, who died at the kitchen
> table for no apparent reason — he
> just fell face-first into his brussels
> sprouts and then he made a clucking
> noise and then his heart stopped.
> 3. Camila the Mexican cafeteria
> worker.
> 4. The Freshman Frogs.
> 5. I can't think of a fifth thing
> right now.

And here is the beginning of The List:

> 1. Cinthia Hauk.
> 2. Mark Maestro.
> 3. Lars Silence.

5

At dinner, a small planet of some sort of stew with meatballs, celery, peas, and carrots has been plopped onto Corinthia's plate. It appears to be infinitesimally trembling beside a serving of Marlene Bledsoe's scrubbed potatoes, which have now been skinned, mashed, and whipped into spiraling mounds not unlike the arrangement of her hair.

Brother Channing sits across from Corinthia. He wears a tight-fitting Lugo Memorial Varsity Football sweatshirt, its sleeves pulled up mid-forearm. The veins in his hands and wrists are practically bursting. His hairless skin is like taut designer calfskin gloves. When he chews his food, he breathes through his nose in a measured, controlled manner. During most meals, Channing rarely looks up, because he is so consumed with "visioning" all the incredible feats he will pull off during football games. A few weeks ago, at the dinner table, when asked by his mother to explain the concept of visioning to the rest of the family, he told them that he closes his eyes and imagines running his routes, changing speeds, and executing tight 180 buttonhooks and sharp turns. He also visions a variety of catches: mediocre two-handed grabs for short yardage; elite one-handed snatches while falling out of bounds; effortless over-the-shoulder snags for long yardage; across-the-middle receptions in heavy traffic; and downright jaw-dropping Hail Mary end-zone miracle catches. He visions his body's acceleration toward the goalposts and his all-business, almost nonchalant consignation of the football to the end-zone turf, as if he is dropping off an important package at the post office in a responsible, timely fashion. He has already set Lugo Memorial career records for receiving yards, touchdown receptions, and punt returns. Friday night's game versus Clinton Academy is no doubt at the forefront of his mind.

It suddenly occurs to Corinthia that today she also had one of these visions, but perhaps hers was far less useful to herself, to her high school, and even to her community. No one wants to be associated with the bearer of bad news, after all. That became clear to her in her freshman ancient literature class, where she learned about the origins of the concept of the phrase "Don't shoot the messenger" while reading Sophocles's tragedy *Oedipus the King.*

Have she and her brother inherited this talent from their parents? Does Marlene secretly vision, too? Does her dad?

Marlene sits at the foot of the table, her back facing the archway to the living room, while Brill mans the head. This has been the arrangement for years now. Marlene, Brill, and Channing sit on matching high-back dining-room chairs, while Corinthia, whose knees haven't fit under the table for going on four years now, is set back some three feet from the table and sits on an old piano bench whose joints have been reinforced with titanium brackets. She'll often hold her plate in her lap when she eats, and the effect is prayerful, as if she's some penitent martyr forced to stare down at the tops of her thighs while the other members of her family attack their plates with forks and knives.

As soon as Corinthia fills her glass with the Bledsoe soft drink alternative — Hi-C Flashin' Fruit Punch — her father passes her something. It's a neon-yellow origami crane fashioned from a Bazoo Meatpacking Post-it Note. He places it on her knee. It's as weightless as a fruit fly. Corinthia has no idea how her father knows how to make origami, but she enjoys the occasional miniature crane, elephant, or municipal backhoe.

She opens it with her long, slow fingers. In very small all-caps print it reads:

IF YOU WANT TO TALK TORNADOES . . .
OR NOT.
UP TO YOU.

Brill Bledsoe winks at Corinthia, and she smiles.

In addition to eating his food, Channing drinks a creatine-rich, time-release, whey-protein shake. Brill and Marlene allow this dietary supplement on Thursdays during football season. Channing won't look at his sister. He is clearly embarrassed by what happened today, as the news spread through their small three-story high school like so many ants on a paper plate of cold cuts.

Or is the sudden emergence of Corinthia's ability to vision disturbing to Channing? Is he somehow threatened by his sister's newfound talent? Sickened by it?

Sometimes Corinthia thinks her brother is so handsome that it physically hurts her to look at him. It can be piercing, like stepping on a thumbtack in socked feet. He is a B+ student and will definitely be playing football somewhere in college, as he is already fielding several offers from Division I schools throughout the Midwest, including Illinois State, Northern Illinois, and Missouri.

As of late, Channing has been speaking to his only sibling less and less frequently. This started weeks ago, well before Corinthia's outburst at school, and she can't for the life of her figure out what's caused his distance. There was a time when they were close. This was before her enormous growth spurt. They would play video games and stream Netflix movies and compete in best-four-out-of-seven basement Ping-Pong matches. But after she grew, their friendship drifted apart, and it's been painful for Corinthia. The truth is that she pities her brother's weakness. To her, Channing is a boy-man trapped by his own beauty. The other day she caught him touching himself while gazing at his reflection in the bathroom mirror, tracing a finger along one of his biceps, his ribs, his perfect hairless chest. Despite his breathtaking good looks and athletic prowess, Corinthia finds him to be strangely asexual. When she imagines him intimately arranged with another, invariably Channing's partner is a large Nerf puppet named Yvonne, and he's not actually fornicating with it but, rather, spooning with it the way a four-year-old might embrace a beloved fire truck under the Christmas tree. Sure, it's well known throughout the Lugo community that he's been dating senior cheerleader Winter Hornacek for the past three years, and they cling to each other in the hallways with a tenacity that would rival a pair of blind people trying to cross a frozen lake during an ice storm, but Corinthia has always felt that there was something false in their relationship, something performed. Despite Winter Hornacek's outward good cheer toward big little sister Corinthia, there has always been something oddly vacant in her perfectly round, cervine homecoming-queen eyes.

After a long silence marked by a score of utensils clinking on dinner plates, Marlene says to Channing, "So, how was practice?"

With a tight, serious mouth, Channing replies that practice was "utilitarian" and gulps his shake. A worm of gray protein slop settles on his upper lip. He can't be bothered right now, and the Bledsoes know and respect this. He is no doubt scrolling through the details of the varsity playbook in his head, seeing his routes like lines on a graph, feeling the hard cuts contracting in his thighs, his hamstrings, his calves, the arches in his sinewy feet.

"Were you in pads today?" Brill asks.

"No pads," Channing replies, his voice congested with whey and taurine and L-arginine.

To Corinthia it looks as if he's drinking wet cement, and she briefly imagines Channing as a concrete statue, waking up in bed this way, skipping the glory of his final year of high school, college, and professional football, and simply becoming the inevitable monument of himself. Brill and Marlene hiring movers to have him transported over to Lugo Memorial, where he will be erected on a marble dais beside the flagpole.

Corinthia feels a wicked delight, imagining her and Cloris Honniotis tagging the statue with black spray paint, smiting out the eyes with a hammer, adding a mock Chicago gang symbol or two.

Corinthia always wonders where Channing is at school when the shit hits the fan, like when Coach Task and Mr. Hauser are wrestling her to the ground, for instance, or when students are thumping ominously on the door of her private bathroom when she's simply trying to have a good, clean pee. Where is her heroic older brother during these crucial moments?

He's nowhere, is where he is.

Her brother lives in the Land of Nowhere.

"Well, we're all excited for the game tomorrow night," Marlene says.

"Clinton Academy," Brill adds for good measure. "It's a big one."

"We'll all be there," Marlene continues. "Right, Cori?"

"Yep," Corinthia manages to utter in between spoonfuls of mashed potatoes. Tonight she feels like she could eat everything in the house: all the contents of the refrigerator and the pantry, all the canned goods that are stacked in the cupboard over the microwave, all those pieces of salt-water taffy her mother hides in the flour bin, even Channing's protein powder. The family would wake up and they'd be without food.

Channing makes a face that's almost a smile. Corinthia thinks he puts far too much pressure on himself, so much so that even when he intends to express appreciation facially, it comes off flat; not forced, just flat. There is an undeniable stoicism at play, one that might befit a much older man. A cowboy, for instance. Or a black-sheep drifter in a train-robbery movie. Perhaps it's the burden of sacrifice for one's community. Striving for excellence day in and day out has to really make it hard to muster a smile. It's like a man who is hungry rather than happy. Channing has become too hungry to enjoy the taste of a good meal.

That night, Corinthia rereads the first twenty pages of Lorcan Nutt's *The Smallest Hands*. Just as she is about to drift off to sleep with the book tucked under her chin, there is a knock on her door.

"Come in," she says.

The door is opened, and Channing stands there. He's still wearing his gray varsity football sweats, and it's hard to make out his face because he's backlit by the soft yellow hallway light.

"Hey," Corinthia says.

"Hey," he says back, mostly in silhouette.

It's unlike Channing to knock on her door like this. She can't even remember the last time it happened.

"Come in," she says. "Close the door."

"I'm good here," he offers.

"So, stay there, then," she says, trying to make out his face. "What's up?"

"If you sit still enough in the presence of a wolf," he explains, "it'll talk to you."

"A wolf?"

"Yeah," he says, "a wolf. But it won't say anything unless you're absolutely still."

"Oh," Corinthia replies, a little thrown. "Will it talk to you in English?"

He nods. Or at least she thinks he does.

"With any particular dialect?"

He shakes his head. Again, his face is mostly in shadow, but she can make out its general movement.

"What kind of a wolf?"

He doesn't answer.

"Like a lone wolf?" she asks after a long pause.

"Any wolf," he finally replies. "But you have to sit really, really still."

Another silence. Only the sound of the grand-father clock clipping time in the hallway, the steady ticktock that can be heard most distinctly only after hours when everyone's gone to bed. Brill had the hourly gong mechanism dismantled two years ago, when Marlene started struggling with her insomnia. The ambient noises of the house — the low burbling of the plumbing; the central air's preprogrammed, gently whirring cycles; and the grandfather clock's tiny, mechanical persistence — seem to sharpen and reveal their hidden mysteries at night.

Channing's silhouette barely stirs.

"What exactly are you sitting on during this encounter with the wolf?" Corinthia asks. "Like a woodland stump?"

"Sure," he replies, "a woodland stump. Whatever's utilitarian."

There's that word again — *utilitarian:* "designed to be useful or practical rather than attractive." Corinthia wonders if this is a word he learned in the SAT prep class that he takes during his free period in an effort to improve his vocabulary. His test scores as a junior, though respectable, weren't as good as everyone had hoped, especially the reading portion.

"Channing," Corinthia says, "are you talking about Clinton Academy?"

The Clinton Academy Timberwolves are Lugo Memorial's opponent tomorrow. It's been a long-standing intra-county rivalry. Perhaps first-game-of-the-season jitters are responsible for her brother's weird behavior.

But Channing doesn't answer. Instead, he reaches toward her. His hand passes through a blade of moonlight that cuts into Corinthia's room from the gap in her curtains. His hand looks ghostly, lifeless, a thing completely separate from his well-conditioned body. He grabs the doorknob and pulls.

Then the door closes and he is gone.

Corinthia dreams of beautiful dollhouses that she and her shop teacher, the one-eared Dolan Yorn-Pamutmut, have been building for thousands of years. The attention to detail is stunning, as precise as frost. She knows that the creation of these dollhouses has been an act of faith spanning a millennium because Dolan Yorn-Pamutmut has a long white wizard's beard and he uses an ancient walking staff with an assured, balletic wisdom.

Inside the dollhouses are the smallest, most intricate pieces of furniture one can imagine: bookshelves and cabinetry; settees and sideboards; claw-footed tables. French doors and winding staircases; chandeliers and credenzas; fireplace mantels; lamps and bone-china candy dishes. Corinthia can see how each individual piece was labored over, the years it took to hone the most minute details, the decades of artistry.

She has the distinct feeling that *she* made this

furniture, that *she* whittled and forged and carved those lamps and candy dishes.

In the dream, she feels great purpose. A warmth spreads throughout her limbs.

Is this love, this feeling?

Is it grace?

In the dream, she looks at her hands. They are thin and important. She possesses the wrists of a child pianist. Her fingers are fluted, beautiful. She is a great prodigy with hands as delicate as birds.

At five o'clock the next morning, with a great intake of breath, Corinthia Bledsoe launches out of her custom-made, seven-by-ten-foot bed on the second floor of the Bledsoe home, precisely at the moment that a family of three tornadoes comes raging into town from the northwest—from the Belleville/Freeburg/Venedy area, to be exact—well ahead of the tornado horn, and pulls the roof off Lugo Memorial High School's legendary Connie and Dillard Deet Field House, which is located a few hundred feet from the limestone school building.

The gymnasium had recently been refurbished, thanks to the generosity of a local proctologist and his wife, Dr. Alton and Dorothy Bartizal, but even the state-of-the-art materials and top-of-the-line construction couldn't keep the roof on.

The roof is almost surgically lifted away, like the lid from a shoe box, and when local police, firefighters, and other civic officials arrive just before dawn — squibs of siren beams dancing through the half-light — a lone 850-pound Holstein cow, white with black spots, of prominent udder; dark, soulful eyes; and the contemplative, poised face reminiscent of any number of nineteenth-century U.S. presidents, is discovered at midcourt, in handsome if not downright competitive county-fair condition, almost perfectly centered in the cream-and-crimson jump-ball circle, as if the Hand of God had placed it there for all to see.

PART 2

6

The late morning in Lugo is greeted by one of the finest blue skies in recent memory: a cloudless, chromium blue that seems to extend far beyond the firmament.

Despite the astonishing fact that all of the tornado damage occurred at Lugo Memorial High School, police cars, fire trucks, and other municipal vehicles have been stationed throughout the community. Although the structure of Lugo Memorial's stalwart limestone building was not compromised in any major way, several windows have been blown out, the electricity systems were mangled, and countless desks, computers, and cafeteria tables were reduced to rubble. The flagpole was sent javelin-like through the air and was later discovered in the middle of the Shelby McSwinton Little League diamond, two miles away, off the frontage road. It now sticks out of center field at roughly 45 degrees, the American flag buried deep in the soil. Fortunately no one was injured.

Oddly enough, aside from Guidance Counselor Smock's basement office, the one well-trafficked space in the building left relatively untouched was the library, probably because of its central second-floor location. But when it comes to the chaotic, unpredictable nature of tornadoes, one can never be sure about such things.

At one o'clock, despite the devastation, an all-school assembly is called in the roofless field house, where Gaylord Yost, a dairy farmer from nearby Kaskaskia, had come by to claim one of his cows only minutes before. As he escorted Daisy into his aluminum cattle trailer, the gentle, confused creature looked like the prize from a beloved annual cakewalk.

The Lugo Memorial school buses fire up their engines, and some 420 teenagers are brought to the Connie and Dillard Deet Field House. While the shell-shocked student body files into the bleachers, weatherproof tarpaulins are being arranged to cover the field house. The clods of earth, heaps of cotton-candy-pink insulation, and clusters of conduits have been swept away, and the long, glossy floorboards of Lugo Memorial's beloved basketball court still gleam as if nothing happened.

But, oh, the missing roof makes the field house look like a toy that some gigantic, whimsical toddler pulled the top off of.

Apparently one major part of the roof was found in nearby Murphysboro, some twelve miles away.

There is talk of bringing this section back to Lugo — all twenty by thirty-two feet of it — as a kind of nostalgic totem to surviving disaster and to civic fidelity, and also as an extra-large symbol of resiliency in the ongoing battle of "Us versus Them" in the tornado belt.

As the student body awaits public address, while homeroom teachers and coaches and department heads nervously mill about the court-level row of bleachers, Facilities Manager Shoreland Splitz quietly confers with Principal Margo Ticonderoga and Vice Principal Doogan Mejerus, pointing skyward to the all-weather tarpaulins, where, on a trio of thirty-foot scaffolding, several men wearing state-issued blue jumpsuits are working at securing the makeshift roof.

The students peer up at these men, confused, as if they are strange uniformed angels who've not climbed the scaffoldings but rather descended upon them from some mysterious rift in the sky.

Once everyone has settled, Principal Ticonderoga approaches a lectern — one that obviously survived the calamity — and adjusts a microphone that is powered by a small, battery-operated public-address unit arranged on a table several feet off to her left. Without the aid of amplification, Vice Principal Doogan Mejerus, using his calmest, wettest, most benevolent voice, greets the student body and leads the Pledge of Allegiance, placing his hand over the fleshy breast that contains his bursting heart.

"Let's all face the field-house flag, please," he says, and everyone pivots accordingly, sending a rumble under the bleachers.

Following the Pledge of Allegiance, everyone pivots back to face the podium, and Vice Principal Mejerus asks the assembly to link hands. Though awkward, the student body, faculty, and staff do so, and then Vice Principal Mejerus, once a divinity student, leads the assembly in a short prayer, beseeching God to please pay special attention to the men, women, and children of Lugo, Illinois. He thrusts his face Heavenward—projecting his humble thoughts well beyond the temporary tarpaulins being secured by those men in blue jumpsuits—and closes his eyes, really connecting his heart and soul to his words.

After a choral "Amen," Vice Principal Mejerus opens his little piglet eyes, takes a step back, and stands beside Principal Ticonderoga, placing his hands behind his back, the ever-supportive acolyte. Hemispheres of sweat are now visible under his arms. There is no longer central air, after all, certainly not today. Vice Principal Mejerus bows his head deferentially, the crown of his bald skull reflecting a halo of light coming from the temporary fluorescents attached to the scaffolding.

Principal Ticonderoga stands before the lectern, turns the microphone on, and tests the sound: "One-two . . . one-two . . . one-two-three—"

A sharp squeal of feedback has many grabbing for their ears. Principal Ticonderoga turns to Vice Principal Doogan Mejerus for help, and the diligent V.P. hustles over to the table containing the temporary P.A. system and lowers a fader.

"Try now," he says.

Principal Ticonderoga checks the microphone yet again, counting a few times, and then goes on to greet the assembly.

"Good afternoon," her voice calls out.

"Good afternoon," everyone replies in unison.

No more awful feedback, thank God.

Despite the rough events of the early dawn, Principal Ticonderoga hasn't skimped on her wardrobe, and she wears one of her many smart-fitting outfits and her high-end penny loafers. A statement of leadership, perhaps. This day will be no different, and she will lead the community of Lugo Memorial beyond this catastrophe and into the future, and she will do so while sporting her lightweight, cornflower-blue twill pantsuit and cream-colored silk blouse.

Principal Ticonderoga starts out somberly, speaking to the sadness of destruction and loss, how helpless it feels when one wake up to chaos. She cites the great fortune that no deaths have been reported in Lugo, that no homes were destroyed. Despite the field house's missing roof and the damage to the interior of the school building, it was a lucky morning for Lugonites.

And somehow, she suggests, perhaps by an act of God, the varsity boys' football equipment was spared by the tornadoes! This good news brings heartfelt cheers from the assembly.

Go, Mastodons!

Principal Ticonderoga goes on to report that tonight's game against Clinton Academy, however, has been canceled because both the home and away locker rooms are "no longer affiliated with our current space-time continuum," she gently jokes. "It's amazing how delicately discerning a family of tornadoes can be," she adds to scattered laughter. "They take the roof off our beloved field house, destroy the home and away locker rooms, but spare all the football equipment. Go figure . . ."

She seems to project her voice above their heads, even those seated in the uppermost bleachers, as though she is also addressing God, or at least His more horizon-bound minions, like maybe a few of the Apostles who were at the Last Supper—those hungry-looking bearded men in flowing pastel robes, at least as interpreted in Leonardo da Vinci's painting, which is a main staple of Rightor Ruggiano's senior art history class. And there he is, by the way, rarely seen Rightor Ruggiano, sitting between consistent-as-a-mailbox science department guru "Hoppin'" Bob Sluba and the health teacher, Kim "Endless Summer" Linwood, who appears to have a black eye today, at which she keeps dabbing with a tissue.

Principal Margo Ticonderoga speaks eloquently and with admirable resolve about the *unity* in *community* and how students and families of Lugo, Illinois, should not look at the near destruction of their beloved high school and field house—"this legendary athletic cathedral"—as a tragedy but, rather, as an opportunity to come together, to pick one another up by their collective post-disaster bootstraps and embrace new-found civic purpose.

While the music of her resonant, assuring voice calms the hearts and minds of Lugo Memorial's student body, faculty, and staff, Corinthia Bledsoe, who woke with a splitting headache, one that might even be classified as a migraine, scans the bleachers. The inflamed, puffy-eyed, tear-smeared faces of her fellow students, teachers, coaches, and cafeteria workers seem to coalesce in a kind of damp, epic Lugo

Memorial turkey loaf. . . . She searches until she finds Guidance Counselor Denton Smock . . . third row center, looking sharp as ever with his pristinely combed hair, Clark Kent glasses, and pin-striped skinny rockabilly pants. He's even wearing a tie today. He is listening to Principal Ticonderoga's speech with a kind of detached clinical intensity, as if he is a medical student observing surgery being performed on a dying child.

Corinthia fixes her gaze on him and will not look away. She musters all her available brainpower — whatever has been spared by the pounding headache — and wills Guidance Counselor Smock to turn and face her. She can feel her recent extreme body heat travel from her solar plexus up her throat and spread through her sinuses. She can smell coal and bacon grease.

A full minute passes.

The men on the scaffolding continue securing the all-weather tarpaulins, reaching, hoisting, working in teams of twos and threes, braiding and knotting ropes, silent as monks. One of them has eyes like a shark. Another looks like Jesus if Jesus wore a silk rag on his head. Even from a distance one can see the little tattoo of a tear sliding down his cheek.

Look at me, Smock, Corinthia quietly bellows at Denton Smock with the voice in her mind. *Look this way, you ignoramus!*

Principal Ticonderoga's speech seems to be getting

more and more impassioned. There is the sense that an anthemic song is forming. Words like *altruism* and *benevolence* and the newly coined hyphenate *super-neighbor* become musical notes being struck on, say, a really high-end xylophone or, better yet, one of the two retired glockenspiels that survived in the third-floor music room storage closet.

Phrases like "Community starts with the individual" and "There is no *i* in *teamwork*" and "Let's not let these tornadoes tell us who we are!" form a loose but tenacious chorus. At one point, Principal Ticonderoga, whose usually sallow, somewhat inanimate face starts to redden with the fervor of a Pentecostal preacher, initiates a call and response between her and the student body/faculty/staff crowd in front of her. Phrases like:

COMMUNITY HAS PEOPLE,
COMMUNITY HAS PIE.
COMMUNITY HAS ALSO
A "YOU" AND AN "I"!

And

THREE TORNADOES THIS,
THREE TORNADOES THAT.
LUGO MEMORIAL,
THAT'S WHERE IT'S AT!

And

**PEANUT BUTTER SUFFERS
WHEN THERE IS NO JAM.
WE CAN DO THIS, LUGONITES,
YES, WE CAN!**

It somehow feels like she's taken the call to duty beyond the realm of the high school and is now enlisting *all* citizens of Lugo, Illinois. Is she running for office? Laying track for a mayoral bid? Principal Ticonderoga pumps her fist and shouts these Seussian quatrains a good five feet from behind the lectern, without the aid of the microphone, so that her unamplified, natural voice is doing the work now, because when it comes right down to it, she — Principal Margo Ticonderoga, former Lugo Memorial student herself — is no more important than anyone else; at least this is what the gesture seems to imply. Everyone in the bleachers echoes her clever rhyming arrangements.

In the midst of this call-and-response game, at the height of the choral esprit de corps, Guidance Counselor Denton Smock finally turns to Corinthia, rotating his head so that his chin is now resting on his right shoulder. He finds her up in the ninth row — she's not easy to miss, after all. Corinthia's return look must be one of bowel-shuddering intensity, because once they find each other, Denton Smock has to remove his glasses. His eyes are like buttons on a snowman, at once full and vacant. Corinthia and the Lugo Memorial guidance counselor stare at each other for a full twenty seconds. Denton Smock knows this because he measures such things. He checks his digital wristwatch and chants.

Then, all of a sudden, he stops chanting with the assembly and, to Corinthia, mouths the following words:

I
HAVE
YOUR
DESK

And just like that, Corinthia is standing. The two students seated beside her, sophomores Lucas Blondheim and Natasha Sumpter-Fisk, are surprised, to say the least. Natasha Sumpter-Fisk even loses hold of the banana clip that she was planning to arrange in her hair after the assembly, but now, like so many things taken by the tornadoes, it feels unfathomably lost — in its case, in the dark cavern under the bleachers.

Corinthia teeters a bit, and the unexpected act of her standing and the peril of her brief teetering create a sudden anxious hush in Lugo Memorial's Connie and Dillard Deet Field House. Principal Ticonderoga's fervent chant-along has ceased. The only thing that can be heard is the toiling of the blue-jumpsuited workers securing the many all-weather tarpaulins.

"What is it, Corinthia?" Principal Ticonderoga asks.

For the briefest moment, Corinthia Bledsoe's eyes roll into the back of her head. Her hands reach high above her, spastically, as if they suddenly possess their own lunatic intelligence. There is a collective intake of breath. Even Coach Task and his assistant coach, the rhino-faced Roy Toscas, are completely agog, their mouths hanging open as if they are suddenly starving.

Corinthia's hands fall to rest at her sides, and she simply says, "There will be birds."

"Birds?" Principal Ticonderoga replies, sort of bewildered, understandably so.

"Birds will eat the football field," Corinthia says.

"What kind of birds?" Vice Principal Doogan Mejerus interjects, his high voice tooting.

"Important birds," Corinthia hears herself say.

"Well, thank you for the information, Ms. Bledsoe," Principal Ticonderoga says, still off mic.

"It'll be the greatest flock of birds anyone in Lugo's ever seen."

There is nothing threatening in Corinthia's voice. Nothing obnoxious. In fact, if anything, her voice carries with it a calm certainty, a resolve one possesses when one has grasped something truly remarkable.

"Again, thank you," Principal Ticonderoga says, directly into the microphone this time, sending a blade of feedback into the proceedings. While all assembled squint and paw at their ears, Vice Principal Doogan Mejerus performs a little jig of assistance and adjusts the grooved flexible neck of the microphone holder for her.

"Please sit down, Ms. Bledsoe," Principal Ticonderoga adds.

Corinthia waits a few moments, casting her large, round, haunted eyes out over the entire assembly.

Where is my brother? she suddenly wonders.

She can't find Channing anywhere. Usually he's within arm's reach of Winter Hornacek or clustered with his football buddies—they're all wearing their game-day varsity letterman jackets today—but Channing's not with them either.

Where is the senior class's most cherished varsity athlete?

Has he shrunk down to the size of an ant? Corinthia wonders. *Does he have the ability to do* that, *too? Has he so mastered his body that he can actually change shape like a superhero? Has he lowered himself under the bleachers, where he is snapping off a fast set of fifty push-ups?*

Corinthia gazes up at the men on the scaffolding.

They've ceased working now and simply stare down at her as the long blue tarpaulins flutter and pop high above the assembly.

"Do I need to have you removed from the assembly, Ms. Bledsoe?"

Principal Ticonderoga's voice is kind, forthright, maternal. Its arrangement of even, mellifluous notes drifts through the field house like the sound of an oboe. It almost makes Corinthia sleepy, this sound. It's a long way down for her to sit, but Corinthia manages it in a three-part move, finding the wooden surface of the bleachers with her hands, lowering her hips, and easing herself down.

Nothing else is said for close to twenty seconds. Guidance Counselor Denton Smock engages the stopwatch feature on his digital Timex and copies the exact interval of seconds (19.55) in his little notebook, which obviously survived the tornadoes, as did his clown fish, Rodney, and his aquarium that pulses with pastel brain light.

Principal Ticonderoga details the immediate plans for classes while the cleanup team gets the main school building back in order. Specifically, the high school will be leasing a fleet of Airstream trailers from nearby Ketchum, which will be parked at close proximity to the main school building. Temporary classrooms as a kind of utopian campsite.

"Things are going to be a bit creative for a while," she warns lovingly, "so I expect everyone to be on their best behavior. It's time to be more than simply a member of the student body or a member of the faculty or the staff. Let's challenge ourselves to come together as dynamic citizens of *Lugo*!"

The applause is thunderous and heartfelt. Head Librarian Doris Dabaduda practically lifts up off her first-row pinewood bleacher — leg brace, cane, and all.

Larry "Oh, for Pete's Sake!" Ambromitis, the putty-faced band leader and JV cross-country coach who is rumored to have an inoperable ganglion cyst on the back side of his left knee that bears an uncanny resemblance to Whoopi Goldberg, is so enthused that his arms rise up and he begins conducting a marching band that isn't even there.

Denton Smock presses the top of his most trusted mechanical pencil, extending the filament of soft lead, and duly notes all the necessary information. He is particularly drawn to one new student, Billy Ball, a prepubescent freshman loner seated in the center of the bleachers, so diminutive that, in the crush of normal-size students, he looks puppetlike. Over the summer break, Billy Ball's father, the owner of a local potato chips distributor, collapsed and died at his dining-room table, and his widow, Kitty Ball, called the Lugo Memorial guidance counselor a few days after the funeral to see if Mr. Smock would begin seeing her son the week before school began. She told him that Billy had been acting extremely withdrawn and that his obsession with Native American culture was starting to border on disturbing. One night, for instance, Billy came to the dinner table and sat in his father's seat with several arrowheads arranged in his hair as well as a stroke of red face paint splitting his eyebrows. It frightened Kitty Ball, and she hasn't since been able to shake the image.

"Dan used to take him canoeing and arrowhead hunting," she explained. "But it wasn't anything serious."

A week before classes, Billy Ball and the Lugo Memorial guidance counselor met in the little basement office with the orange clown fish, and after thirty minutes of intermittent chatting about this and that, Denton Smock thought it would be a good idea for Billy Ball to start writing in a journal, to essay his private thoughts.

"Don't think of it as an assignment," he urged Billy. "It's a place where you can tell things to yourself. A safe place. These are things you might not *even* tell me."

Denton Smock unlocked a special drawer and produced a new thick notebook of green graph paper, exactly like the one he keeps his statistics logged in. He then slid it across his desk to Billy and could've sworn that his new friend took it in his small, pale hands and regarded the notebook with a kind of awe, that perhaps the very idea of writing in a diary opened up a whole new world for this young, grieving teen.

In general, Denton Smock was struck by Billy Ball's quiet stillness, his large hazel eyes that rarely seemed to blink, and a subtle self-possession that belied his physical stature. He found he could make no explicit assessment about the boy's psychological well-being, and when asked about his father's death, Billy Ball seemed neither grief-stricken nor particularly interested in the subject. In Denton Smock's estimation, he was a fascinating but somewhat inaccessible boy.

Denton Smock looks forward to their next session—he's seen Billy Ball four times thus far—and with this thought, he locates his new counselee, who is seated beside ginger-haired sophomore Ben Krabbenhoff. Denton Smock even gently waves to get Billy Ball's attention—a simple extension of the right hand, palm facing out, as if in benediction—but the boy's large hazel eyes seem to be focused on a point somewhere between the fiberglass backboards and the blue-jumpsuited workers maneuvering on the scaffolding high overhead. Billy Ball is "somewhere else," as Denton Smock likes to say. He is outside of his young, unformed body, perhaps roaming some ethereal rolling meadow where dad death, peer pressure, and the greedy-eyed hoarders of puberty aren't looming behind every corner.

During their second meeting, Billy Ball confirmed that, yes, he had begun writing in this notebook. He pulled it out of his backpack and held it up so Mr. Smock could see. Billy Ball had written DAVE across the front cover with black Sharpie.

"Who's Dave?" Denton Smock asked.

"Dave the Diary," Billy Ball replied, and then returned the notebook to his backpack as if it were as insignificant as an unbreakable comb. Then the high-pitched three-second tone signifying the end of the period sounded, and that was that. Billy rose and exited with an odd, almost vacant look of bemusement that reminded Denton Smock of Merlin Whitehawk, a fellow altar boy from his youth. Merlin Whitehawk, also large-eyed, quiet, and pale, so fascinated Denton Smock that he would follow him home after Sunday Mass, all the way to the Whitehawks' unremarkable clapboard ranch house, where Merlin would enter through the slim front door that would open and close behind him as if by its own will.

The winter of eighth grade, during Christmas break, Merlin Whitehawk fell through the ice and drowned in Big Bear Lake, and there is always a moment in the late fall, just as the temperature grows too chilly for sweaters and thin jackets, when Denton Smock is reminded of this loss.

At the end of Principal Ticonderoga's tornado assembly, everyone is released and sent home. As instructed, classes will commence tomorrow, and the rest of the day will be spent getting those Airstreams up and running.

Just as Corinthia is about to exit the field house, Principal Ticonderoga stops her. In her calm, controlled voice, she says, "Can I have a word with you, Ms. Bledsoe?"

Corinthia nods, and Principal Ticonderoga guides her toward the corner, just under a pull-up bar, to be exact, which Corinthia has to negotiate her head underneath and then up, so that her face is now positioned between the iron pull-up bar and the field house's unforgiving brick wall.

Vice Principal Doogan Mejerus stands a few feet away now, hands behind his back, his bald head gleaming, his always-smiling eyes cast down deferentially.

"Corinthia, I think you should take a few days at home," Principal Ticonderoga begins. "Some time away from school will be good for you."

"Because of what I said about the birds?"

The pull-up bar is now abutting the little fleshy valley between her lower teeth and chin.

Principal Ticonderoga makes a strained face — her liver-colored lips sort of curl into her teeth, and her eyes go small in a reptilian way. She says, "You've obviously been under considerable strain. Sometimes it's best to take a step back. Think of it as an opportunity to get some perspective."

Corinthia says, "But what about my perfect attendance?"

"I'll make sure your student record isn't compromised in any significant way. Vice Principal Mejerus spoke to your mother just a moment ago. And he also left word for your father at work. Right, Doogan?"

Corinthia looks down and over at Vice Principal Mejerus, who is nodding so animatedly, he might be mistaken for some overly eager cartoon platypus.

"The Airstreams are gonna be pretty cramped," he offers in his congested soprano.

"This is true," Principal Ticonderoga agrees. "Many of them are only six and a half feet tall."

"Seventy-five inches, actually," Vice Principal Mejerus confirms. "The standard exterior height is a hundred inches, but we can't very well put you on *top* of one of those puppies."

"But we'll eventually solve that," Principal

Ticonderoga says. "In the meantime, take this time. We'll make sure your class assignments are delivered to you via e-mail. The important thing is that you get some rest. And try to clear your mind of these apocalyptic thoughts."

"They're not just thoughts," Corinthia says, her lips grazing the cold, indifferent, molecular surface of the pull-up bar.

"Bad thoughts are what usually does a person in," Vice Principal Mejerus offers obliquely, inching closer to his boss, his hands still clasped behind his back.

"One more thing," Principal Ticonderoga adds, again conspicuously not contending with Corinthia's comment about her apocalyptic thoughts. "Your brother didn't attend the assembly."

"Yeah, Channing wasn't here, was he?" Vice Principal Mejerus says.

"Any idea where he might be?" Principal Ticonderoga asks. "I understand he wasn't on your bus this morning."

"On game days he walks to school," Corinthia says.

"Well, today *was* supposed to be a game day," Vice Principal Mejerus offers. "I wonder if Coach Task has any idea where he might be."

Corinthia tells them that the last time she saw him was at last night's dinner.

"You didn't see him this morning?" Vice Principal Mejerus asks.

Corinthia shakes her head, grazing the pull-up bar with a cheek.

"Huh," Principal Ticonderoga offers. A simple "Huh." As if she turned the light on in a room and a man she's never met before is sitting at a table, carving an apple.

Corinthia stops by her locker to retrieve her spiral notebook binder and the rest of her textbooks. Someone has scrawled FUM across the face of her locker in black Sharpie, the ink so freshly applied that she can smell its quick chemical odor. The letters have been composed with long, stilt-like elegance and are pristinely framed by the tall, thin rectangle of her locker door, just below the three grooved ventilation slats. She goes down on a knee to confirm the careful arrangement of the sloping middle vowel and two terminal consonants. FUM. *As in fee-fi fo . . . ?* Whoever tagged her locker did it recently, most likely after the assembly, while she was being cornered. Did Principal Ticonderoga and Vice Principal Mejerus sense something like this would happen? Is this why they've asked her to stay away from school? What would be next, more explicit graffiti? A scarier message? A beat-down? A death threat? But the tornadoes weren't her fault! She wasn't *responsible* for their arrival! She can't control Mother Nature!

After she gathers her things, Corinthia shuts her locker and takes in the single syllable once more.

FUM

It's the first time anyone's ever written on her locker. Once, when she was a freshman, a girl named Shawna Dabonis got her period for the first time in the middle of home ec and wound up running out of class with an embarrassing stain seeping through the seat of her white Dittos. A few hours later, after a visit to the school nurse, Shawna Dabonis was allowed to go home to change her clothes. When she returned to Lugo Memorial, someone had painted FIRST PERIOD in red nail polish across the face of her locker.

The second floor of Lugo Memorial is quiet. Per Principal Ticonderoga's instructions, the rest of the student body has gone home. The hall smells strange, like wet leaves and soil. The tornadoes have unleashed something in the air. Perhaps Mother Nature herself has been somehow perverted. Will there be earthworms in the water fountain? Baby birds in the wood shop cubbies? Grass growing in the cafeteria?

Down the hall, two men in blue jumpsuits are using push brooms to sweep up the scattered debris. Corinthia feels like she and this duo have survived an apocalypse, like they've emerged simultaneously from some underground bomb shelter. The men stop and stare at her, their brooms at rest at their sides, mouths agape, but she *is* a giant, after all. She's used to this.

"You okay, miss?" one of them asks. He is slim and pale. The other one is taller, darker, shaped like a kangaroo, and is wearing what appear to be safety goggles, which reflect squibs of light from the overhead fluorescents.

Corinthia nods to them.

"I'm fine," she says.

They return the nod and resume their work.

Before she heads out, she stops by her private bathroom, where she is greeted by the same word. FUM has been written with slasher-movie violence across the heavy blond-wood door. Corinthia takes in the dark, runny spray paint and starts to reach toward the letter F when she hears a voice.

"I wouldn't touch that."

Corinthia turns to face one of the blue-jumpsuited workers. He is African American, of average height, thin, and very dark-skinned. He holds a bucket containing a rag and a rectangular aluminum can of turpentine. His woolly hair is thinning at the crown of his head. His large brown eyes appear tired, the whites a bit dull.

"It's still wet," he adds. His voice is deep and dry. When he speaks, Corinthia notices that he's missing an incisor.

"Sorry," Corinthia says, retracting her hand.

He tells her that the girls' bathroom is empty.

"This one's mine," Corinthia says.

"You got your own personalized spot?" he says. "You must have juice around here."

"No, I just seem to keep breaking stuff," Corinthia explains. "Too unwieldy for standard utilities."

"Well, some dude with a clipboard just sent me up here to clean that word off the door."

"Go ahead," Corinthia says, and simply stands there. For the first time today, she feels her sleepless night catching up with her. A faint gaseous warmth passes through her brain. She'd like to slide down the wall and sit for a while. Though she tried to keep thoughts of the tornadoes at bay, the few times she closed her eyes, the funnels materialized.

"You okay?" the man asks.

"I'm fine," she says.

"You ain't gonna be sick, are you?"

"I'm just tired," she replies. "I didn't sleep much last night."

"I couldn't sleep neither," he says. "I think them

tornadoes was messin' with the equilibriums. Didn't nobody know they were comin'. Not even the weather-man on the news."

He douses his rag with turpentine.

"They sure did a number on your school," the man says, rubbing the rag over the surface of the door. "Whole first floor looks like wild dogs was let loose. All the windows are blown out. Glass everywhere. Cafeteria tables tossed this way and that. Third floor's even worse. All the locker doors got tore off. Y'all lucky this happened at night; otherwise there'd be a lotta hurt people."

Corinthia watches the back of the man's neck, where the sinews pulse up and down his shoulders as he pushes the rag through the spray-painted letters.

"Strangest thing about it," he continues, driving the heel of his hand into the rag, "is that those tornadoes didn't hardly touch nothin' else. No cars. No houses. No trees or telephone poles. Only this high school. Like they were *aimin'* for it. Like they were seekin' revenge."

Last year, when they read George Orwell's *Animal Farm* in her sophomore Great Books class, Corinthia learned that the word for attributing human characteristics to animals is *anthropomorphizing*. Corinthia wonders if this word can be applied to tornadoes, too.

"Doggone gymnasium caught the worst of it," the man adds, gently laughing.

"You think weather has human powers?" Corinthia asks.

"I'm not sayin' tornadoes are like people," he replies. "But don't you think it's strange how they didn't touch nothin' else? Not the church. Not the libary. Not one thing. It's like them three tornadoes got their own mind to do stuff. Like they're straight-up willful." He stops, takes a step back, and adds, "Listen to me. This turpentine's makin' me run my mouth. . . ." He breathes through his nostrils a few times.

For a brief moment, Corinthia considers the impossible: Did she somehow *summon* the twisters? Was it a vision or an act of will? But why would she want to bring such calamity to Lugo Memorial? Does some part of her hate her school, her community? Sure, she's had dark thoughts here and there, but the worst of them are akin to forcing Rinna Buss into her locker or mushing a handful of mashed potatoes in Skyler Montreal's face.

"Fum," the man continues. "Is that what they call you?"

"Apparently," she says.

"So what's *Fum*?"

"I'm pretty sure it's from *Jack and the Beanstalk*," she explains. "The giant says it: 'Fee-fi-fo-fum.'"

How she's managed to avoid this English-fairy-tale reference until now is practically miraculous. Are her fellow students finally turning on her? Were these instances of graffiti executed by an individual, or is it announcing the advent of some kind of revolt against Corinthia Bledsoe? Or does it have an opposite meaning? Were yesterday's proclamations about the tornadoes now being appreciated? Is *Fum* an acknowledgment of respect?

"So, some fool's tryin' to be slick," the man says. He soaks his rag with more turpentine and continues working on the door. "Messin' with a person just 'cause she's tall."

Corinthia notices his hands, which seem large for his size, the palms bright and cracked. She has an urge to take one of them in hers—she doesn't know why—but she lets it pass.

"What's your name?" she asks, as he uses the rag to wipe away the last few slashes of paint.

"Lavert," he says. "But you didn't hear that from me."

"Who'd I hear it from," she says playfully, "the turpentine can?"

"I'm not s'posed to be talkin' to you kids," he replies.

"How come?"

"I'm just not," he says quietly. "So please don't tell nobody."

"I won't," she says.

"Oh, God," he says. "If they find out I'm talkin' to one of you, they'll send my butt back down."

"Back down where?" she asks.

"Where I don't want to be," he answers, glancing over his shoulder.

Corinthia says, "There's all kinds of places where people don't want to be."

After a brief silence, through the side of his mouth, he says, "Du Quoin."

Corinthia tries to see what he's looking at down the hall, but there's only a drift of debris.

"What's Du Quoin?" she asks.

"Du Quoin's Du Quoin," he replies, clearly setting a boundary. He forces his tongue through the space in his teeth, perhaps a nervous habit. Though she is curious, she doesn't want to push him about whatever Du Quoin is.

"What's your last name?" Corinthia asks, deftly changing the subject.

"Why?" he asks. "You some kind of detective?"

"Can't a girl be curious?"

"Birdsong," he says quietly, as if he's unscrewed the top of a jam jar, uttered his name into it, and screwed the cap back on.

"Nice to meet you, Lavert Birdsong," Corinthia says, extending her hand.

"Nice to meet you," he says, setting down the

rag in the bucket, wiping his hand on the thigh of his jumpsuit, then taking hers in his. His hand is warm and strong and dry. "What about you?" he asks.

"Corinthia," she says.

"No last name?"

"Bledsoe."

He looks up at her, but not in some astonished way. To Corinthia's surprise, for once, it doesn't feel like someone is beholding a freak, a beast, or something *apocryphal,* which is a word she had to spell during an early round at last year's school-wide spelling bee. Sometimes strangers regard Corinthia with such disbelief that she gets the sense they think there are two smaller people stacked one on top of the other, operating her like some colossal school mascot.

"Corinthia Bledsoe," he says.

Her name sounds like music coming out of his mouth. Like soulful, time-soaked, bluesy music. After a breath, he adds, "You might be the tallest person I've ever seen in my life, Corinthia Bledsoe."

He stares up at her, almost smiling.

"What?" she says, sensing the faintest bit of mischief in his eyes, which slide a bit as he leans back and peers down the hall yet again. When he sees that they're still alone, he adds, "Let's just say you definitely ain't no storybook monster."

There is something about this man, Corinthia thinks,

something about his quiet, deep voice; his slow, warm hands; and the intensity of his gaze.

The three letters are gone now.

"Thanks for cleaning my door," she says.

"My pleasure," Lavert replies.

She opens the door with her key, ducks her head under the upper casing, and enters her bathroom.

7

It's a two-mile walk home, and instead of taking the shortcut through the modest neighborhoods of Lugo, Corinthia decides to tack along Lugo's frontage road, "No-Name Road," as it's come to be known over the years.

No-Name Road is marked with shaggy, grassy ditches, gravel shoulders, and a few miles of forest where, last spring, a small pack of gray wolves was discovered, along with untold mutilated carcasses of deer. The wolves were written about in the local paper just this morning. "More Wolves Spotted in Lugo," read the headline. The story was also reported on the news.

"Where there are deer, there may also be wolves," the anchorwoman in pancake makeup said, looking directly into the camera.

The citizens of Lugo were advised to stay out of the forest and to "let nature take its course." But yesterday in Mr. Sluba's class, before the marine-world subjects of phytoplankton and krill were introduced, he brought up the wolves. On Thursday, as a way to kick things off, he spent the first few minutes of class posing questions relating to local life-science issues.

"After their food supply runs out, where do you think these wolves will turn?" Mr. Sluba asked.

No one raised their hand—it was early in the quarter, after all, and that slippery business of sycophants and class participation hadn't yet been established.

"Will they become vegetarian?" Mr. Sluba continued rhetorically. "Will they turn on themselves and practice cannibalism? Will they leave the forest and start hunting the yards and porches of our neighborhoods?"

This final question settled in the room like an early winter chill. Corinthia imagined all the slain cats and dogs in her neighborhood, the wolves being confused by ceramic deer, stone rabbits, and the many statues of garden gnomes in red wizard caps.

The Bledsoes have a ceramic Dalmatian in their yard, which guards the mailbox. It arrived in a FirmaMall shipping container over a year ago, and more than once Corinthia has seen her mother speaking to it and patting it on the head as if it were real. Marlene named it Chet and will sometimes tease Abel, the Latino mailman, saying things like, "Careful, Abel, Chet hasn't been walked yet," and "I'm teaching Chet Spanish. Soon he'll be able to say hello."

What would those gray wolves make of Chet?

Corinthia suddenly recalls Channing's strange visit before she went to sleep last night.

"If you sit still enough in the presence of a wolf . . ."

Is Channing in the forest? she wonders.

Corinthia stops walking, crosses the gravel shoulder, hops over the grassy ditch, and takes a few steps toward the tree line. But something makes her stop. A strange feeling passes over her. Her arms are suddenly plagued with gooseflesh. She has the strong sense that something very bad will happen if she continues.

"CHAN!" she calls out to the trees. "CHANNING BLEDSOE!"

She waits a moment, but there is no response, so she moves away from the tree line, jumps back over the ditch, and continues walking on the gravel.

The sun is bright and warm, and the air feels somehow thinned. It's as if the tornadoes stole the late-August humidity and plan to unleash it on some heartland town farther east. Corinthia walks along the shoulder, her long, heavy feet trudging through the gravel. She can feel fatigue radiating outward from her lower back. It's starting to seep into her hips, but she knows if she stops to rest, she will fall asleep in the tall grass and turn into potential wolf meat. The following morning, they'll find her picked clean in the ditch, all those humongous bones looking more like some weird shipwreck of ancient timbers and scrimshaw than a human skeleton.

The clean, ripe smell of dirt, pollen, and the dolomite from the sunbaked gravel floods her nostrils. In the distant farmlands, she can see a pair of grain elevators, an ancient, scarred barn listing to the left, a half-empty corncrib with a tin conical hat. Part of her wants to venture beyond Eagle Ridge Road, where she normally turns left and heads for home on the final stretch. Corinthia sees herself walking west for hundreds of miles, crossing the Mississippi River into the wheat-colored expanse of Missouri on foot, and into Kansas, where she will find some other small town and start her life over. She could get a job at a local bookstore, arranging new titles — she's certainly tall enough to reach the higher shelves without a ladder — or find work on a farm, baling hay or feeding baby goats.

A few cars pass along the two-lane road. When the aspirin-shaped Lugo water tower comes into view, she can see that, on its face, beneath the town's namesake, the same word has been written that appeared on her locker and on the door to her bathroom. In black capital letters, there it is again:

FUM

Who is this graffiti artist?, she thinks. *Is it a boy? A girl? A faceless, genderless ninja enshrouded in black?* She feels her stomach give way to cold emptiness. It's as if she's swallowed a chilled metal plate. This is what shock feels like, she thinks: like swallowing cold dinnerware.

She mentally scrolls through everyone she knows at Lugo Memorial and can't think of a single person who might actually *hate* her.

Corinthia finally comes upon Eagle Ridge Road. She stops for a moment and again considers the world to the west. She looks in that direction, but all she can see is the timberline of that long forest. It almost seems like the trees are growing themselves, extending their reign over the land, in cahoots with the gray wolves. She imagines the wolves strategizing, communicating telepathically, outsmarting the world.

At home, Corinthia is greeted by her mother and a pudgy blond man in a light-blue cotton suit, gray tie, and black orthopedic shoes.

"This is Detective Moon," Marlene Bledsoe says. "He works for the Bureau of Missing Persons."

"Dick Moon," he says, offering his thick, stubby hand. "Hello, Corinthia."

At a glance, Corinthia thinks he looks like a fat, sick baby. She sets her book bag on the floor, shakes his hand, and just stands there. It's clear that Detective Moon has been briefed about Marlene Bledsoe's daughter's extraordinary size, as he appears to make nothing of it. He holds a small moleskin notebook and a ballpoint pen.

"Take a seat, honey," Marlene says to her daughter.

Corinthia does so — on her repurposed piano bench — but Detective Dick Moon remains standing. Marlene, who is wearing lemon-colored yoga slacks and a T-shirt that features artwork from the first Indiana Jones movie, stands as well. Her small, tense hands are wedged into her armpits.

"Corinthia," Detective Moon says, "you may already be aware of this, but since the tornadoes touched down, your brother is the only member of this community who hasn't been accounted for."

She nods.

How is it possible that Channing is the only one of Lugo's four thousand some-odd citizens to have gone missing?

"When was the last time you saw him?" Dick Moon asks.

"Last night at dinner," she says.

"You didn't see him after that?"

"I went to bed early."

"As I told you," Marlene interjects, "Corinthia had sort of a rough day."

Detective Moon jiggles some coins in his pants pocket.

"Well, it's been a rough morning, too, I'm sure. For all of us."

Corinthia decides that he is an oversize thumb with a face and arms.

Her mother has been doing dishes. Corinthia wonders if she sometimes washes them, dries them, and then washes them again, just to give herself something to do.

"Where's Dad?" Corinthia asks her mother.

"At work," she answers. "He couldn't get anyone to cover his shift."

"Corinthia," Detective Moon says, "did Channing give you any indication that he was planning on taking a trip?"

"Detective Moon thinks he might have used the tornadoes as a distraction to run away," Marlene says.

"At this point it's just a theory," he says. "But we have to consider all possibilities."

"He barely speaks to me anymore," Corinthia says.

"He's been under a lot of pressure with football," Marlene tells Detective Moon. "Football and SAT prep. When the season gets under way, he tends to keep to himself."

Detective Moon asks Corinthia if she's noticed anything different about her brother lately.

Again, she recalls Channing's strange late-night visit to her room, their conversation about stillness.

"All he does is work out and study," Corinthia offers.

"The night before football games, he hardly even speaks to his girlfriend," Marlene adds.

Detective Moon says, "Winter, right?"

"Winter Hornacek, yes," Marlene confirms for him.

"And we know for a fact that Ms. Hornacek is at home with her family?"

"I spoke with her a few minutes before you arrived," Marlene replies.

"You might want to talk to Drake Sirocco, too," Corinthia offers.

"Drake is the quarterback on the football team," Marlene explains. "They spend a lot of time together, too."

"Drake . . . Sirocco . . ." he echoes, writing in his little notebook.

"The Siroccos live over on Log Drive," Marlene adds.

"Thanks," Detective Moon says, returning the notebook and pen to the interior of his suit jacket. He then thrusts his hands into his pockets and starts jiggling that change again.

"Well," he says to Corinthia, "if anything occurs to you that might help us get a lead on the whereabouts of your brother, please call me. I gave my card to your mother."

Corinthia nods.

"I better go check if there's any new information over at the office," he adds, then nods to Marlene.

While exiting, he tells both women how lovely it was to meet them and he pledges to do everything in his power to find Channing.

Corinthia and her mother remain in the kitchen, Marlene's face inflamed. Per usual, Corinthia gets the sense that her mother is having a hard time looking at her.

Marlene turns away from her daughter and peers dramatically out the window, as if she might start singing a melancholic ballad.

"Your vice principal called," she starts in, a bitter weariness clotting her voice. "Mr. Mejerus. I understand you'll be staying home from school for an undetermined period of time. That he'll be sending along your homework assignments via e-mail."

Corinthia has an urge to walk over to the clean dishes, grab a coffee mug, and hurl it to the floor.

But instead she tells her mother not to worry.

"You'll hardly know I'm here," she says. "Don't worry."

And then she excuses herself from the table.

In the basement, Corinthia is washing her hands in the extra-large sink of her customized bathroom when she is seized by the image of geese — thousands of geese peppering the sky, their black, wavering mass like some terrible thought sprung from the mind of an all-powerful deity beset by madness. Though the word that came out of her mouth during the school-wide assembly was *birds*, it was only a word, and now she's seen that they're *geese*. She is certain of this because of their long, dark necks, gray wings, and the white stripes marking their faces. They fly through the milky-gray, cloudless sky of her mind. And now she can hear the cacophony of their collective honking. It's an inconsistent, mind-boggling sound. Corinthia brings her hands to her ears.

And then, just like that, the geese are gone and Corinthia comes back to herself.

She finds that she is down on a knee. She is breathing hard, suddenly starved for oxygen, genuflecting in her bathroom. She grabs the edge of the sink and pulls herself up. In the mirror she can see that her face is flushed. The whites of her eyes have gone pink. Her nostrils are flaring. She can feel a knot forming where her left knee met the floor, and she kneads at it.

First tornadoes and now geese? she thinks.

Why geese?

What could they possibly mean?

In her bedroom, she uses her landline to call the Lugo district library. She asks for Cloris Honniotis, but the head librarian, Norma Klondike, tells Corinthia that Cloris is currently unavailable. Corinthia asks her to please, please, please ask Cloris to call her and leaves her name and number.

"Ms. Bledsoe, I believe you have an overdue book," Norma Klondike says after she writes the message down. "Lorcan Nutt's *The Smallest Hands.*"

"I'm rereading it," Corinthia tells her.

"According to our system, it was due back here over two weeks ago. We're going to have to fine you."

"I'll bring it by soon," Corinthia promises, and hangs up.

Corinthia's breath is still shallow. She feels lightheaded, as if tiny bubbles are swirling around her eyeballs. Should she call her guidance counselor? Her former therapist, Dr. Flung?

She resets the phone, picks it up again, and calls information, looking for a "Birdsong" in Lugo.

"There's no Birdsong listed in Lugo," the operator tells Corinthia, "but there's a Florida Birdsong in Wigwam."

Corinthia asks to be connected to Florida Birdsong in nearby Wigwam, and after a few rings, an elderly lady with a voice like dry tissue paper answers.

"Hello?" she says.

Corinthia says hello and tells the woman that she's sorry to bother her but was wondering if a Lavert Birdsong might live there.

"Lavert's my grandson," the old woman says. "But he isn't here right now."

"Does he live with you?" Corinthia asks.

"Who wants to know?" the old woman asks, understandably suspicious.

Corinthia tells the old woman her name.

"Corinthia *who*?" she says.

"Bledsoe."

"You from the hospital?"

"No," Corinthia replies. "I met your grandson earlier this afternoon."

"At his therapy?"

"At the high school. We were both part of the tornado cleanup crew," Corinthia lies.

"You with the church?"

"The Red Cross," Corinthia lies. She can feel her

temples throbbing. "We've had quite a day over at Lugo Memorial. The roof of the field house was damaged pretty badly."

"Y'all have a program with the work farm, too?"

"We do," Corinthia hears herself say, pushing the lie.

"Well, Lavert was real happy to help out," the old woman says. "You got more work for him?"

"I just might," Corinthia continues, braiding her lie into a long, winding serpent.

The old woman tells Corinthia that she'd be happy to pass along a message to her grandson, and Corinthia leaves her phone number.

September 2, 2015

Dave,

Hello.

It's been a few days. You wouldn't believe what happened. Lugo Memorial got attacked by tornadoes! Three of them! That's like getting bum-rushed by some gangstas at a Dunkin' Donuts! The roof of the field house got torn off and many parts of the main building were damaged. They wouldn't even let us go into the classrooms. We were only allowed to go to our lockers to get our books, and you could see these huge piles of glass and fiberglass insulation and pieces of bulletin board getting broomed into the corners by these guys from some nearby prison.

Authentic criminals in our school, Dave! And they weren't throwing shade at anyone;

they were just minding their own business and trying to help!

There was this big assembly at which Principal Ticonderoga delivered a speech about coming together as a community, and she rallied everyone to hang tough while the school building and field house and the flag-pole were being repaired.

I kept looking for Camila, that Mexican cafeteria server I was telling you about — the one whose hairnet I stole — but I couldn't find her. I started to worry that maybe she got sucked into the sky by one of the torna-does and that I'll never see her again, and this was painful, Dave. I actually punched myself in the thigh twice, like really hard, and this tall guy with a huge Adam's apple looked at me and shook his head. I have a bruise where I punched myself, and I'm hoping it'll turn into the face of Camila. If that were to happen, I would stroke it so much she'd come back from the sky. She'd float down through the clouds with little white birds chirping in her hair.

Oh, yeah, I forgot to tell you: Before Principal Ticonderoga gave that speech, Vice Principal Mejerus led us in a prayer and made everyone hold hands. I wished it was Camila's hand I had to take, but this was not the case, Dave. I had to hold hands with this redheaded kid named Ben Krabbenhoff. Krabbenhoff is a sophomore. He plays clarinet in the band, and a lot of people say he was born in a test tube and that he stuffs his clarinet with Bumble Bee tuna and has sex with it, and as I'm sure you can imagine, Dave, many individuals get quite freaked out by this kind of behavior, particularly Lars Silence and Mark Maestro, who treat anyone who's a little different like they're a cat carrying a disease and must be set on fire.

Even though I was sitting in the middle of a row, Krabbenhoff was the only person close enough to hold hands with. The girl to my left was sitting several feet away from me and wouldn't look in my direction when we were instructed by Vice Principal Mejerus to hold hands.

Krabbenhoff's hand was cold and clammy. It was sort of like holding a dead frog, which I have done. I've held several, in fact. On canoe trips in Michigan. Frogs and salamanders and catfish, although you have to be careful with catfish because they'll stick you with their whiskers.

Vice Principal Mejerus led us in prayer, during which he asked God to look after everyone in the Lugo community and bring us safe skies and bless us with his countenance. I think Vice Principal Mejerus used to be some kind of priest-in-training, or maybe he was a high-ranking official in the Boy Scouts. He's pretty good at leading prayers. He stores a lot of emotions in his voice and makes this pained expression, like his heart is aching or he has love cramps, which I can relate to. . . . By the way, Dave, I just looked up the word *countenance,* and according to the dictionary app on my Android, it means "face," so I'm not exactly sure what Vice Principal Mejerus was asking God to do. I imagine God taking his face off and rubbing it all over the Lugo Memorial parking lot or something. Or like we have to all line up and take our clothes off and then there's this little room with God in it, and, one by one, we enter the room and he speaks in code and takes his face off and rubs it all over our bodies, like on our armpits and over our hearts and where our junk resides. In that scenario, I imagine God wearing skintight jeans and Google glasses, and

every time he speaks, he speaks in code, and
when he takes his face off, he has to remove
his Google glasses and set them on this little
desk where he keeps his iPhone, and he has
one that's from the future, like an iPhone 47,
and maybe he also uses a little Bluetooth ear-
piece that looks like a miniature spaceship. I
also imagine him not wearing a shirt and his
bare chest is old and saggy, with little clear
moles all over it, and each mole, if you look
really close, contains the face of Jesus Christ,
who sort of looks like that actor Jared Leto.
That's what I imagine, Dave, and I know this
is really specific, but that's what my freshman
composition teacher, Mrs. Plano, encourages:
specificity. Like if you're going to describe
something, then really describe it in painstaking detail. She actually used the word "painstaking," which means thorough. And that's
what I'm attempting to do for you, Dave. I'm
really trying to be painstaking and not hold
anything back, just like Mr. Smock advised at
my last counseling session.

After the prayer, Ben Krabbenhoff took
his hand back and wiped it on his pants like I
had some kind of infection. I used to feel bad

for him. I would see him carrying his clarinet around and think about how lonely that must be — practicing an instrument in your basement or your bathroom or your garage all the time — but after he wiped his hand like that, I'm tempted to put Krabbenhoff on The List. And I want to also add that it's NOT because he might be stuffing his clarinet with Bumble Bee tuna and having sex with it. I'm tempted to put him on The List strictly because of the way he looked at me when he wiped his hand on his pants. Should I give him another chance, Dave? Once a person goes on The List, it's a permanent situation.

Speaking of The List, during the entire assembly, I was looking around for Lars Silence and Mark Maestro. Part of me was hoping that they'd been killed by the tornadoes. I kept seeing their bodies flying through the air, hurtling end-over-end, like when you throw a cat off a roof. I saw Cinthia Hauk right away, who was sitting exactly one row in front of me. She was wearing her hair up, and I couldn't stop looking at her neck, where I could see this little vein throbbing. She has these wispy blond hairs. I have a plan to get some of those hairs.

A plan, a plan, a plan. I'm a man with a plan . . .

You see, Dave, I have recently purchased a pair of scissors from Target. They're small ones. I think they're supposed to be used for eyebrows and nostril and mole hairs. When the time is right, I will sneak up behind Cinthia Hauk, quiet as a warrior from the Nez Percé tribe. The members of this particular tribe were especially good at hunting and killing because they were so quiet. I will go straight-up Nez Percé on Cinthia Hauk, Dave. She won't even know, because I'll do it without feeling. It'll be as easy as putting your hand on a window.

And when I get my feet good and quiet, I'll sneak up behind Lars Silence and Mark Maestro and get their hair, too. It won't be easy with Lars Silence, because his hair's cut in a flattop. I might have to use some sort of razor on him. My dad used to use this old-school straight razor. His shaving kit is still in the cupboard under the sink. I'll probably have to sharpen it, but I learned how to sharpen knives in Cub Scouts. What you do is, you use this thing called a whetstone, Dave. It makes a pretty mysterious sound when you sharpen a blade on it, too, like the world is whispering a secret to you, like it has plans that you're suddenly a part of.

Plans, plans, plans . . .

That's what we're all looking for, right, Dave? A plan?

This is what I'm thinking:

Everyone who winds up on The List will have to part with a little hair. I'll keep it all in that shoe box under my bed, the one that contains my mom's hair and my arrowhead collection. I'll be sure to separate all the hair samples with rubber bands. The Mohicans were really into hair, Dave. They would scalp their enemies, meaning if someone threw shade at them or committed a crime on their particular tribe, they would cut the tops of their heads off and keep the scalp flap containing the hair as a trophy. The Mohicans were quite eccentric.

After the Crow Creek Massacre, which dates all the way back to 1325 AD, 90 percent of the skulls that were found showed evidence of scalping. Dave, couldn't you just imagine the Lugo Memorial trophy case being full of scalps instead of championship trophies?

There is one more person that I'm adding

to The List, but I'm not going to talk about that right now, Dave. Let's just say that there's this very tall girl in school, and her name is Corinthia Bledsoe. I think she might be some kind of prophet. Anyway, she stood up during the assembly and told Principal Ticonderoga that all these birds were coming, and while she was standing, this individual who I am adding to The List pointed their finger at her like it was a gun and shot her three times. This person was sitting behind Corinthia Bledsoe and I think I might've been the only one who saw this unjust business. This person's name is Ward Newbury, and he is a junior with an intimidating muscular build, and I will be keeping a close eye on him. I've seen him in the cafeteria, drinking protein shakes. He brings little packets from home and mixes them into his milk, and he makes sure everyone is watching him when he does it.

Dave, the thing about Corinthia Bledsoe is she's the one who predicted the tornadoes, but everyone just thought she was trying to get attention. But they came, Dave! The three tornadoes came, and she tried to warn us! She is someone I want to get to know. I heard she got suspended from school for her outburst about the birds. I do not want to cut any of Corinthia Bledsoe's hair off and put it in that box under my bed. Someday I would like to be her friend and have her tell me things.

They brought, like, twelve of these huge mobile homes to serve as temporary classrooms, and after the assembly, Principal Ticonderoga let us go home so the silent criminals in the blue jumpsuits could finish cleaning the school and get the mobile homes ready.

One of those men in the blue jumpsuits was really pale and had a face like a melting snowman. He might have been burned in a fire. Or maybe he'd had acid thrown in his face or something like that. Criminals deal with a lot of shade, Dave. Anyway, we met eyes! We met eyes, Dave! His were really clear and pale blue. That happened during the Pledge of Allegiance, and during that part about the Republic for which it stands, our eyes met. He was squatting on one of the lower parts of the scaffolding, and he looked at me, and I looked back at him, and I felt a wobble inside like a little slippery animal was running in my stomach, and then I urinated a little, Dave, just a tiny little bit like when you squeeze a grape, and then the very pale man with the face like a melting snowman in the blue jumpsuit nodded at me twice. It was like we both knew something really, really, really extremely important at exactly the same time, and his two nods confirmed this, Dave.

Can you understand what I'm saying, Dave? It was spooky.

Lucky for me, there's been no gym class yet. But I was prepared anyway. I got up extra early and used some superglue to attach a select portion of my mom's hair that I collected from off the bathroom floor to my junk area. I have to say, it looks pretty good. Like sort of bushy and unbushy at the same time. I'm not sure if *unbushy* is a word, but you get the idea.

Dave, I should also tell you, and this is embarrassing . . . When I saw myself in the mirror with my bush wig, I got an erection. It was very stiff and curved upward like a bratwurst. And then I masturbated. I'm still at this place in my sexual development where nothing comes out, but I do have an orgasm. It's like this little shudder of pleasure that feels like I'm falling backward through a bright, warm sky and getting tickled with a thousand feathers at the same time. And then my muscles go all weak and I get still and sleepy and I start sighing like an animal that has felt all the pleasure that is possible to feel.

My mom just called for me, so I have to go, Dave.

I can't wait to start using those little scissors, Dave.

I will get my feet quiet.

I will become a human whisper with scissors.

They won't know I'm there.

They'll be like, *Whoa, was someone just behind me?* but then they'll look and I won't be there, and they won't even know I have their hair.

I can't wait, I can't wait, I can't wait.

9

Two days later, Corinthia enters her brother's bedroom, whose paneled walls are covered with posters of various NFL wide receivers: the Dallas Cowboys' Terrance Williams; the Indianapolis Colts' T.Y. Hilton; and Antonio Brown of the Pittsburgh Steelers. Corinthia hasn't ventured into her brother's room in what seems like years. The two other bedrooms in the Bledsoe home feel like the interior of a dollhouse. Cornelia's furniture is custom-made to accommodate her size, after all. Even her parents' king-size bed seems far away from her, smaller than it truly is, almost like from a fable, as if it's more suited for a sick child than two standard-size adults.

The faint smell of Channing's sweat socks and his Irish Spring deodorant taints the air. The smells of an athlete seem to always prevail, no matter how neat and hygienic he might be. His desk is so organized, it could be mistaken for an art installation, an exhibit of young American male achievement in a museum. His textbooks are perfectly stacked, largest to smallest, his writing utensils vertically aligned, the pencils meticulously sharpened. Several trophies line his windowsill, including his two Lugo Memorial Most Valuable Player varsity football plaques. His laptop is centered on his desk, but when Corinthia powers it on, it's of no use because she doesn't know his password. She can't even get to the computer's desktop, so she lowers the lid and puts it to sleep.

She looks under his bed. . . . Nothing, not even a dust bunny. She opens his closet. . . . Only clothes and sneakers, a few cotton-blend suits handed down from their father, a pair of football cleats, and a pair of penny loafers. On the long shelf above the closet's hanging rod are several pairs of neatly folded gray workout sweats. Beside them are his circular push-up mounts, a can of athlete's foot spray, and a stack of V-necked sweaters. Wherever he might be, it doesn't appear that he's taken anything with him. Even his gym bag is in the corner, unzipped, revealing his leather weight-lifting belt and a towel.

Corinthia sits on the edge of his bed, which has been impeccably made. Channing has always been the consummate neat freak, putting his dirty clothes in the hamper in a timely fashion, keeping his room picked up, making his bed before breakfast, and he's downright obsessive about smoothing the wrinkles out of his

"Big Ben" Roethlisberger Pittsburgh Steelers quilt that he's had since the fifth grade. But the current attention to detail—the crispness of the top sheet, the glasslike smoothness of his quilt, the stiff squared corners—is even more noticeable than usual, almost military-like in its execution. Corinthia wonders if her mother came up here and made everything more presentable for Detective Moon.

She feels under Channing's pillow. . . . Again, nothing. She pulls his quilt and top sheet down to see if he left some clue tucked between the sheets, but it reveals only a cool expanse of linen, so she remakes the bed, doing her best to duplicate its perfection.

She can hear her mother working out to one of her DVDs in the living room. Marlene Bledsoe's squeals of failure periodically spike over the dance music.

Corinthia closes her eyes for a moment and simply breathes, half expecting to see all those geese again, or another family of tornadoes, or whatever else might be out there in the world beyond Lugo. Killer bees? Locusts? Giant worms? A scourge of Midwestern crocodiles? Flying monkeys circling, gathering force, homing in?

Instead she sees her tall, cool, slate-colored wall. As she learned from Dr. Flung, once the wall is success-fully conjured, it's important to keep it there as long as possible and to expect nothing else, to simply suspend all expectations, anxieties, and desires. The wall is so vivid, Corinthia can see its tiny pits and fissures, the moisture starting to gather on its dense surface, the sun reflecting off it, its sheer vertical power, a ladybug descending . . .

She opens her eyes, brings her attention back to her brother's room. The light from his window seems weak, doleful. There is nothing wrong, not a single thing that is unexpected or out of the ordinary. It might be the most orderly, most boring room she's ever been in. Everything about Channing's life until now has been prescribed, well executed, expectant.

And then she sees it: On his bedside table, next to the digital alarm clock, rests a tiny wooden wolf, the size of a walnut, carved with great detail, its snout facing Channing's pillow.

Corinthia picks it up, places it in the center of her broad palm. It's heavier than expected. There's a density to the wood. She taps it against the corner of the bedside table. It's solid through and through.

She replays the last thing her brother said to her, the evening before the tornadoes came:

If you sit still enough in the presence of a wolf, it'll talk to you. . . .

She makes herself as still as she possibly can, and simply stares into its eyes.

"Talk to me," she tells it with her mind. "Talk to me, little wolf."

That evening, Marlene Bledsoe finds herself in Louisville, Kentucky, at Lynn's Paradise Café, a colorful kitsch diner on Barret Avenue with a gift shop that sells giant gummy worms, kooky T-shirts featuring phrases like I'M THE ONE WEARING THIS KOOKY T-SHIRT and MY DOG TALKS TO ME IN SPANISH, as well as the brand of salt-water taffy that Lemon Tidwell brings to their Tuesday-night Group meetings over by the Yum! Center.

She left a note on the refrigerator for Brill. A simple note composed in blue ballpoint ink:

Brill,

Hi, sweetheart!
I'm off to run a few errands. If you hear
anything about Channing, please call my cell.
Love,
Marlene

Out front, set beside the entrance to Lynn's Paradise Café, is a life-size polished aluminum horse with an enormous slice of white bread rising out of a rectangular channel where its spine would be. This is the legendary Thoroughbred Toaster. Marlene is so tickled by it that she purchases five bags of assorted taffy and a cat calendar entitled *Cats Rule the Kitchen,* which features various species of cats commandeering can openers and espresso makers, as well as baking tuna casseroles and grilling Chilean sea bass. Sometimes crossing the Ohio River gets her so excited, she just wants to buy things. She stands beside the horse, finds a good angle with her iPhone camera, and snaps a selfie. After she crops it to her liking and applies a flattering filter, she posts the picture on Instagram and waits for the appropriate cue, which is for it to be "liked" by a particular person.

Brill Bledsoe has no idea that his wife has an Instagram account or that she'll sometimes post photos on it to let a friend know that she's around the corner or on her way to a rendezvous. Regarding Brill's smartphone, beyond utilizing its most conventional function — as an actual telephone — he barely even *uses* it. He's not much of a tech person. At home he prefers the landline to his cell phone. He also favors cooking soup in a pot on the stove top to using the microwave. And don't even get him started about popcorn.

As of late, Marlene has found that her husband of twenty years' telephone persona has grown tiresome. Sometimes she'll call him at work to ask him what kind of vegetable he'd like for dinner, and he'll utter

"Green beans" or "Spinach" or even "Up to you" with such indifference, it makes her feel like she's talking to a bored billing assistant from the electric company. At times he comes off as downright uncaring. His stoicism is what originally attracted her to him—he was so quiet and mysterious in high school—but after all these years, it's starting to feel like apathy, even bloodlessness.

Not thirty seconds after her selfie post, her iPhone chirps, notifying her that her photo has been "liked" by the appropriate party, and she crosses the Lynn's Paradise Café parking lot, double-checking that her car is power-locked, and scoots in her newly purchased Mark Lemp open-toe flats a few blocks east and onto Bardstown Road, where she anxiously waits for a traffic light to give her the pedestrian walk signal. She looks down at her toes, which peek through the front of her flats. She is pleased with the tuxedo-red polish she applied only a few hours before. *My feet are still good,* she thinks. *I've always had the feet of a dancer from the Copacabana.*

While she stands there, even through the fits of two-way traffic—Bardstown Road is a busy thoroughfare, after all—she can see him seated at a booth inside the fast-food Mexican restaurant Burritos As Big As Your Head! The back of his full head of gray-brown hair gives way to his strong weathered neck and his broad shoulders.

Marlene feels a little wobble in her heart, and she quickly brings her hand to her mouth, cups it, and exhales, conducting a quick breath-freshness check. She's had lifelong anxiety about halitosis, and even though the family dentist, Dr. Linus Hyberger, always puts these fears to rest, assuring Marlene that, if anything, there is a subtle natural *spearmint* aroma tingeing her breath, her anxiety still persists, especially now that Marlene is forty-two and one of her rear molars zings whenever she drinks hot or cold liquids and she swears that there are instances throughout the day when she thinks she can smell an oddly vegetal odor leaking out of her mouth, like a pan that had been used for cooking broccoli.

The pedestrian walk signal finally flashes and Marlene crosses Bardstown Road and enters Burritos As Big As Your Head! She is greeted by the smell of, well, burritos. Tinny easy-listening rock plays. It's a Carpenters song, the one about being on top of the world and looking down on creation. To Marlene, Karen Carpenter always sounded so sad and soul-starved, even when she sang about love and happiness. If only the radio deejay would play some Michael McDonald or James Ingram. Or better yet, a song featuring *both* of them, like the 1983 hit "Yah-Mo Be

There." Or Luther Vandross would be the absolute *best*, but you can't just walk into a random fast-food place with a questionable name like Burritos As Big As Your Head! and expect to hear Luther Vandross. Luther is on a whole different level.

Lemon Tidwell is reading something on his iPhone when Marlene approaches.

"Is that the six or the six plus?" she asks.

"Believe it or not, I think I'm still using the five," he says. "Hey, Marlene."

"Hi, Lemon."

"Sit, sit," he says, placing his phone down.

She does so.

He is wearing a turquoise ring that she's never seen before. Despite being a widower, he still wears his wedding band, and this touches Marlene to no end. But the turquoise ring is new, and he's wearing it on his right hand. It has a thick silver band that Marlene briefly fantasizes about removing from his finger and putting in her mouth.

"Is that new?" she asks, pointing at the greenish-blue stone.

He says, "I've had this old thing for years."

"It's very nice," Marlene offers. "I've always liked turquoise."

"The stone fell out a few months ago, so I had to get it reset. Just got it back from the jeweler."

"Did your wife give it to you?"

"No, Nance didn't give me this."

"Sorry," Marlene says. "I didn't mean to assume that."

"I bought it down in New Mexico after I got out of the army," he says, easing the conversation away from the deceased. "I spent a coupla summers working on a rattlesnake farm."

"Rattlesnakes, wow!" Marlene says. "Was that dangerous?"

"Absolutely dangerous," Lemon replies. "But if you're smart and tape up your ankles and invest in a good pair of boots, it's not a death sentence. Plus they always kept a good amount of antivenin on the premises."

"Were you ever bitten?"

"Once. But it was a little one, and it barely penetrated my boot. They gave me a dose of antivenin and I was right as rain. All and all I enjoyed my time down in New Mexico. Learned a lot about myself. Good money in catchin' snakes."

She is suddenly taken with his mustache, which seems to pulse with a bristly intelligence. She almost feels powerless to it, as if *it* has seduced her, independent of its owner. Marlene has an impulse to reach across the table and touch it, but she sits on her hand instead.

"Hungry?" Lemon asks. "The burritos here really *are* as big as your head. Well, maybe not *my* head. Mine's the size of a bread truck."

Marlene chuckles at his self-deprecating humor.

"I ate over at Lynn's," she says.

"What'd you have?"

"An omelet."

"Oh, which one?" he asks.

"The Matador."

"The Matador's one mean sonuvagun," Lemon says. "The chorizo sneaks up on you. You got it with the chorizo, right?"

Marlene nods primly.

"Hot sauce?" he asks.

"I'm not exactly a hot sauce kind of person," Marlene replies.

"Not everyone is," he says. "Next time you gotta try their Paradise Pancakes. You might have to loosen your belt a notch or two afterward, but it's definitely worth it."

"Next time," she says, pleasantly surprised by his passionate knowledge of the menu over at Lynn's Paradise Café.

"And by the way," she adds, "your head's just fine."

"Well," he says, "it is larger than the head of your standard *Homo sapiens*, but you're kind for saying so."

Marlene chuckles again, perhaps a bit too excitedly this time — she can actually hear herself — so she bites her lower lip.

Lemon is wearing a blue denim shirt that brings out his eyes. Marlene can see that he doesn't bother wearing an undershirt, and the faintest hint of chest hair creeps through the opening of his collar.

Oh, the breakfasts they could have together!

Marlene would cook him omelets and pancakes and brew the best French-press coffee this side of the Ohio, and he would never want to leave the house. She imagines thrusting her face between the loaves of his furry chest, inhaling deeply, bathing in his manly musk. She almost audibly sighs.

"By the way, here," she adds, reaching into her purse and pushing a bag of sky-blue taffy across the table. "Just like you told me at Group: Lynn's Paradise Café offers an impressive selection of taffy."

"Blueberry!" Lemon beams. "My favorite! Thanks, Marlene!"

"I got some for myself, too!" she says excitedly. She has no idea why she just shared this with him, or why on earth she blurted it so loudly. She closes her eyes, hoping to restore what little poise she'd arrived with. She exhales, really trying to slow down her breathing. "I got the blueberry, too," she continues, opening her eyes, calmer now. "Plus a bag of the pink. Well, it says sour cherry on the label, but they look pretty pink to me. I also bought a bag of assorted flavors."

"You're set for the apocalypse," Lemon jokes.

"I always like it so much when you bring it to Group," she hears herself say.

"You gotta try the chocolate caramel mocha," Lemon offers. "But proceed with caution."

Marlene laughs in a schoolgirl fashion and wiggles a little in her seat. She is suddenly worried that she's worn too much makeup and touches her cheek self-consciously.

A young boy from behind the counter is now sweeping up beside them. He has a pasty, pale, acne-riddled face, and Marlene finds that he moves with a slowness that is all too common, clichéd even, in lazy, shiftless teens. His name tag says KYLE, and his proximity to them makes Marlene feel anxious.

She turns to him.

"Do we need to order something, Kyle?" she asks.

He touches his name tag, seemingly surprised that a customer would call him by his actual name.

"Whoa," he says, clearly amazed.

"Well, do we?" she asks again.

"No, you're cool to chill," he replies, loping along in his low-top Chuck Taylors, whose soles barely lift off the linoleum surface of the floor. He engages his flip-flopping dustpan and sweeps up some paper straw sleeves. When he is finished, he moves away and resumes his post behind the counter.

"So, can I ask you a question?" Lemon says.

"Of course," Marlene replies. "Ask away."

He strokes his mustache and says, "Why the Instagram thingy?"

"Oh, it's just a game I like to play when I meet a friend."

"Phone games," he says.

"Yeah," she says. "Phone games are fun. By the way, I really enjoy scrolling through your feed. Those posts of you and your son are just *wonderful.*"

"Cecil and I have a good time," Lemon says.

"The one where he's wearing the box of corn-flakes on his tumor. What a hoot!"

"Breakfast of champions," Lemon offers, smiling.

"That was such a good caption!" Marlene practically sings.

They both laugh, and Marlene sighs sort of uncontrollably and in a way that suggests she also might start to cry or even wail, but she doesn't—she holds it together, and after her sighs decay to something approaching silence, Lemon says, "So, what can I do for you, Marlene? What did you want to see me about?"

"I'm ready to share," Marlene says.

"About your daughter."

"Corinthia," she says. "Yes."

"Well, that's great," he says. "Are you sure?"

"I'm positive."

"That's a big step. An important one."

"And I'm ready to take it."

"Group meets in two days," he offers.

"I know," she says, "but I'd like to share with *you* first."

Lemon Tidwell smiles and strokes his mustache again.

"Well, I'm flattered, Marlene," he says. "I really am."

When he says her name, she feels something go weak within her, a sensation that her spine is dissolving, that she's turning to yogurt.

"I brought pictures," she says. "From when she was a little girl. And, of course, the more, well, *difficult* ones. They're on my phone here."

She starts to pull up the pictures on her iPhone.

"You really should save this moment for Group," Lemon offers.

But Marlene continues scrolling through her photos.

"The best results occur when everyone is present for your first share. And I think you know this, Marlene."

"Lemon, please," she says. "Can't I just show you now?"

"I'm sorry," he replies, "but if the process is going to work—if real healing is to occur—we all have to abide by the statutes that are put in place. The first share must be a Group share. Those are the rules."

She capitulates and sets her phone down, flips it over so the screen is facing the table.

"My son disappeared," Marlene then blurts desperately. "Channing."

"Oh, my God," Lemon says. "When?"

"The morning of the tornadoes."

"That's just awful."

"And no one's seen him since."

"I'm so sorry, Marlene."

Marlene's face starts to convulse. Her mouth and chin spasm and contort into a visage of grief and horror. She wants more than anything for Lemon Tidwell to take her hand—the one she hasn't been sitting on—in both of his. She just knows his hands would be so warm and dry and large and strong, and the very thought of them causes Marlene to burst into tears.

"Hey," Lemon Tidwell says. "None of that, now."

His slow, deep voice is like a healing hymn. And he doesn't smell like meat, no, not in the least bit, which is something she's had to deal with her entire life, it seems, the perpetual stench of slaughtered beef emanating from Brill. It's in his hair, his hands, the fibers of his clothes. And it's always been this way, even when Marlene bought him those special shampoos and detergents and the charcoal-and-lavender hand soap he used for more than a year.

Lemon Tidwell smells more like a man who makes campfires; Marlene Bledsoe knows this in her bones. He is a man who builds roaring campfires and sits beside them unflinchingly and maybe smokes a pipe with a spicy ship captain's tobacco, and then very nonchalantly he'll take out a pocketknife and whittle a piece of wood into, say, a panther's heart and then hand it across the fire to Marlene, who would then ask, "What's this?" and he'd answer, "A panther's heart," and then she'd scoot around the sawing flames to join him and lean her head on one of his extremely broad, denim-clad shoulders, and then the things they would do under the infinite starlight, in the great Wilderness of Love, the rich, sweet smoke of the campfire mingling in their hair, the shapes their bodies would make beside the crackling flames . . .

Marlene's sobs continue, so Lemon Tidwell gets up from his side of the booth and slides in beside her. He wraps his arm around her shoulder and pulls her close.

"There, there," he says. "Don't cry, now, Marlene. Your son'll turn up."

"You really think so?" she practically squeaks.

"I really think so," he assures her.

"I just pray to God he's not dead," she says, more of a beleaguered squeal this time, the words barely heard. "My . . . my baby boy . . ."

Marlene can smell Lemon Tidwell's musky after-shave.

There it is, she thinks.

His smell.

He smells like a man who knows how to camp and whittle panther hearts and handle horses . . .

And then Lemon Tidwell finally does it. He takes Marlene Bledsoe's hand with his free one, the one featuring the turquoise ring. His hand is surprisingly smooth, warm, virtually hairless. Prominent veins travel between the peaks of his knuckles.

On the radio, Captain and Tennille's "Muskrat Love" is now playing. Though she never really liked this particular song, Marlene finds herself falling through the ether of its melody, Toni Tennille's voice signaling a kind of mid-'70s promise that's being broadcast directly to Marlene Bledsoe's tender heart. During the love-happy chorus, she allows Lemon Tidwell's strong arm to comfort her.

Lemon Tidwell asks her if the authorities are looking for Channing, and she nods and sniffles and wipes some mucus from her nose with the back of her free hand, and then pulls a napkin from the dispenser on their table and manages to paw the mucus off her wrist without having to wrest her other hand from the warmth and comfort of his.

And then she cries some more, mostly because her nerves are just so completely shot, but also partly because she knows she likely just smudged the rouge and foundation that she'd spent over an hour so carefully applying.

"I'm sure he'll turn up," Lemon Tidwell says comfortingly. "I'm sure of it, Marlene. Here, take this," he adds, and passes her a piece of the aforementioned chocolate caramel mocha taffy, which seems to materialize out of nowhere.

"Oh, thank you, Lemon," Marlene says, gently wheezing.

"Eat that. It'll make you feel better."

"I will," she says. "I will eat it."

But she doesn't. Instead she simply clutches it with her free hand.

They stay this way—Lemon Tidwell's arm draped across the back of Marlene Bledsoe's shoulders, both of them facing Bardstown Road now, sitting beside each other in the far rear booth of Burritos As Big As Your Head!—for two more songs.

As Marlene Bledsoe swallows her mewls and whimpers, she basks in his aftershave. For the briefest moment, she feels the sandpaper of his beard. She imagines him shaving early in the morning, what his back might look like, that space between the shoulder blades . . .

Behind the counter, acne-riddled Kyle is busying himself with his smartphone, and only one person enters, who orders a burrito for takeout.

This is Heaven, Marlene thinks.

I have truly died and gone to Heaven.

They hardly move as Marlene fixes her gaze on the recently polished turquoise in Lemon Tidwell's ring.

"Hello?"

"Who's this?"

"Um, Corinthia Bledsoe."

"The tall girl."

"Is this Lavert?"

"Yes, it is."

"Lavert Birdsong?"

"This is he."

"So formal."

"Is this the tall girl or not?"

"It is. I am the tall girl. In fact, I might even be the *tallest* girl."

"I just like to know who I'm talkin' to."

"Hello, Lavert Birdsong."

"Hello, Corinthia Bledsoe."

"You remember me, right?"

"Yeah, I remember you. By the way, there was another one of them *Fum*s down in the band room. I had to clean it off the tuba."

"That's probably because I played tuba my freshman year."

"You played the *tuba*? That big, crazy thing?"

"For me it was more like playing the French horn."

"You don't play no more?"

"It's not so easy on the lips. Plus you get tired of carrying that thing around. And all that blowing makes you light-headed, too. Especially if you have to do an eight-bar solo, which is rare, but it does happen. I should've played the triangle."

"The triangle?"

"The triangle's a perfect instrument. Almost impossible to screw up. You just strike it with a little wand a few times a song."

"That itty-bitty little thing?"

"It'd certainly make for easy transport."

"You're funny."

"Lavert Birdsong."

"Speaking."

"I just like saying your name."

"Yeah, that Brasso stuff ain't no joke—that's what

I used to clean the tuba. I thought turpentine was strong. But anyway, my gramamma said you called."

"I'm glad she gave you the message."

"Yeah, Gramamma's good like that. Sometimes she's forgetful about takin' her medicine, but she's good about most things."

"She seemed nice."

"Don't get her started on the electric company. There ain't nothin' nice about her when she gets to carryin' on with those people. . . . So, what's up, Corinthia? Why are you callin' me?"

"What are you doing?"

"Right now?"

"Yeah, right now."

"Just chillin'. Why?"

"I was wondering if maybe you'd like to get something to eat."

"With *you*?"

"Yeah, with me."

"For real?"

"Sure."

"Oh, Lord."

"Oh, Lord, what?"

"I don't know, Corinthia."

"Why not?"

"Ain't you s'posed to be in high school?"

"So?"

"So, I'm a grown-ass man."

"Where's your sense of adventure?"

"*Adventure?* Adventure's the last thing my trouble-some butt needs."

"Your butt is troublesome?"

". . . When?"

"Now."

"I can't eat now."

"Why not?"

"'Cause I got a treatment in the morning."

"A treatment?"

"Yeah. And if I eat after a certain time, it'll make me sick to my stomach. . . . I mean, I'll *sit* with you. But I ain't gonna eat nothin'."

"Okay."

It's quiet at Uncle's 24-Hour Waffle House. Corinthia and Lavert Birdsong sit across from each other in a recently reupholstered red-pleather booth.

Before Corinthia walked the half mile to Main Street, she put on eyeliner—just a hint—and two dabs of her mother's Calvin Klein Euphoria behind each earlobe. She worries that she used too much, that the subtle notes of black violet as described on the Calvin Klein website aren't so subtle. She's also applied her favorite bubble-gum-flavored lip gloss. Her hair is pulled back into a ponytail, and she wears a baby-blue halter top featuring a crocheted rainbow.

Corinthia sits before a stack of classic syrup-and-butter-slathered waffles and a trio of sausage patties.

Lavert Birdsong, wearing pressed jeans and a short-sleeved red-knit polo shirt, his fingers interlaced around a mug of chamomile tea, watches Corinthia. Every few bites, Corinthia looks at him, and he meets her gaze for a second or two, his mouth barely open. And then he closes it, swallows, and looks down. There is no doubt in Corinthia's mind that this man is hungry.

After greeting each other with a formal handshake, during which Lavert Birdsong twice cleared his throat, they were seated by the man rumored to be Uncle himself (strangely, his first name is Cousin). Cousin, who knows Corinthia by name, led them to their booth without judgment or the least bit of circumspection, dealt them a pair of menus, and told them how all the booths on their side of the waffle house had recently been redone and that his daughter, Julie, would be by lickety-split to take their orders.

It took a minute for Corinthia to negotiate her legs into a comfortable position under the table, after which she and Lavert made some inconsequential small talk about Lavert's car (a silver Dodge Neon that he is leasing from a local dealership), the post-tornado weather (cloudless skies), and the surprising lack of mosquitoes, which usually hang around this part of Illinois well into September.

The conversation caught some momentum when Corinthia brought up the damage suffered at Lugo Memorial and how nice it was that Lavert and all the other men in blue jumpsuits helped clean up, but just as Lavert was about to comment on the workforce, which Corinthia was certainly more than a little curious about, Julie arrived with glasses of water and took their orders.

Corinthia ordered the waffles, sausage patties, and a large orange juice, and Lavert ordered his chamomile tea, and Julie was nice and, like her father, didn't appear to be freaked out by this unlikely duo.

"Uncle's Classic Triple Play Waffles with sausage patties, a large OJ, and a chamomile tea, coming right up," Julie said, and moved away.

Corinthia has frequented Uncle's several times, mainly because their booths have more legroom than most other places in town. In fact, she and Cloris Honniotis have spent hours at the very booth she's sharing with Lavert. They will sometimes each bring a book and drink the bottomless drip coffee and order the Classic Triple Play and read.

After Julie walked away, things got pretty quiet.

The low-playing music (Neil Diamond, Simply Red, Sade) filled the silence so effectively, it was as if someone had been stationed in the back of the waffle house for the sole purpose of turning up the radio during conversational lulls.

And now Corinthia Bledsoe and Lavert Birdsong are officially beyond the small talk.

Julie has delivered their food, and Cousin came by to make sure everything was okay, and now here they are, with no more interruptions.

Corinthia eats her waffles, luxuriates in their sweet, buttery warmth. Her sausage patties are bathed in maple syrup. She drinks from her large orange juice.

"You sure you don't want some?" she asks after a big swallow.

"I really can't," Lavert says.

"Because of your thing tomorrow."

"Yeah, I prolly won't eat anything substantial till the late afternoon."

"Don't you get hungry?"

"Sometimes it feels like cats are crawlin' around inside me. But I can't tell if it's hunger or my condition."

"Condition?" Corinthia says, cutting the first sausage patty in half with her fork.

"I got cancer," Lavert tells her. "In my pancreas."

Corinthia sets her fork down. She swallows.

Everything goes dry in her throat. She drinks from her water glass and swallows again.

"Tomorrow morning I have to do chemo," Lavert says.

"Oh," Corinthia says. "Oh."

"Another three-week cycle."

"Oh . . ." Corinthia says yet again. "I had no idea. . . ."

After a brief silence, Lavert goes on to tell her that the pancreas is a glandular organ in the digestive system that produces important hormones like insulin as well as special juices that help the body absorb nutrients in the small intestine.

"So mine is all messed up," he adds.

She looks at him for a moment, grabs her fork, and then sets it down.

Corinthia says, "And you still work . . . in your condition?"

"Only when I'm feeling up to it. I just can't climb no scaffolding. I mostly sweep up, paint walls, turpentine stupid words off of bathroom doors."

Corinthia musters a smile.

Lavert says, "Now I've gone and spoiled your appetite."

"I was finished anyway," she assures him.

"I normally don't go around talkin' about my medical problems."

They are quiet. The music can be heard again. A Phil Collins ballad from the eighties, "One More Night." It seems as if the deejay is playing a cruel joke, considering the circumstances.

"How bad is it?" Corinthia eventually asks.

"Stage three," he says.

Corinthia tells him she's sorry but that she doesn't know what "stage three" means.

"Stage three basically means it's spread to my lymph nodes," he explains. "My oncologist tells me that in rare cases it does get better. I'm hopin' I'm one of them rare cases."

Corinthia can feel a wad of sorrow forming deep in her throat. She wishes she could scoop it out with her spoon. She can feel it sinking into her heart.

"If they had Maalox on the menu, I mighta got that," Lavert says, attempting levity.

Corinthia asks him how long he's been dealing with the cancer.

"Got diagnosed two months ago," Lavert says. "Started treatments pretty quick after that. I was already stage three when they started me on the chemo." He drinks from his tea and adds, "I was down in Du Quoin up until about six weeks ago, so I had to start the first round of chemo there."

"What's Du Quoin?"

"A work farm."

"You're a farmer?"

"I was in prison," Lavert says. "I was up at Stateville for most of my sentence, but I've been at Du Quoin for the past four months. I got an early release for good behavior."

"Oh," Corinthia says again.

"Yeah, all them dudes in the blue jumpsuits? We used to be at the work farm. It's a program that helps transition former convicts back into society."

Corinthia nods.

"Yeah, you picked one real accomplished nigga to watch you eat pancakes."

"Waffles," she says.

"I mean waffles."

Phil Collins turns into Huey Lewis and the News. "I Want a New Drug."

Lavert says, "Man, this song sounds just like the song from *Ghostbusters*."

Corinthia smiles and wipes away a few waffle crumbs from the front of her crocheted rainbow halter top.

She says, "So, you got out early for good behavior."

"Kept my head down up in Joliet. Didn't do nothin' thuggish."

"That's where I was born," Corinthia offers. "Joliet."

"Don't know much about that place," he says. "Except they got them gamblin' boats."

"What'd you go to prison for?"

"Armed robbery. A friend and me hit up a gas station in Quincy."

"With a gun?"

"We had this little snub-nosed thirty-eight. My friend shot and killed the attendant. I don't even think he meant to do it. Knucklehead got amped and pulled the trigger. Judge gave him life."

This information hits Corinthia square between the eyes like a stone. She drinks from her water glass. She may be sitting with someone who was an accomplice in a murder.

"And you?" she says.

"I got twenty years," he says.

"And you got out early."

"Thirty-seven months early," he says. "Yep."

"So your friend's still in prison?" Corinthia asks.

"He's dead," Lavert says. "Killed himself at Cook County Jail the night he was sentenced. Hung himself. Apparently the guard on duty let him have his belt. Prolly felt sorry for his youthful ass."

"Do you miss him?" she asks.

"Yeah, I miss him. He was my boy. Hopefully he in a better place now."

"What was his name?"

"Demetrius Purvis, but he went by Dee."

"Dee," Corinthia says.

"Yeah, Dee."

Something in Lavert's face softens when he says his friend's name.

"How old were you when you got sent away?"

"I was eighteen. Dee was nineteen. The D.A. wanted to give Dee the death penalty, to set an example, but the judge gave him a break 'cause we were still kids. I don't think Dee could handle the idea of being put away with a bunch of grown men."

Lavert drinks from his tea, sets the mug down, and adds, "If you wanna go, you can go. I'll pay for this."

Corinthia says, "I'm not going anywhere."

He says, "What, you wanna write a paper on me?"

"I just like talking to you," Corinthia replies.

"Waffles with the ex-con," Lavert says. "Watch him sip on old-people tea and act like a good, rehabilitated nigga?"

"*Are* you rehabilitated?" she asks.

He says, "Do I seem like I am?"

"When I met you the other day, I thought you were just a nice guy cleaning some graffiti off my door. You seemed like a gentleman to me."

"Then the good system must be workin'," Lavert says, smiling, no doubt half joking—or to Corinthia, at least, it seems that he might be—revealing that missing incisor again. "I'm definitely on good behavior now," he adds. "Got no choice. I mess up once, and they'll send my butt back down. Cancer or no cancer. I can't even steal the crackers from this waffle house," he says, pointing to the little basket in the center of the table containing packages of individually wrapped Saltines.

"So then behave," Corinthia says.

"I plan to," Lavert replies, still smiling. "I have no idea what little bit of time I might have left, but the last way I wanna spend it is pickin' soybeans and recyclin' doggone cardboard in Du Quoin. Believe me, I plan on bein' a *saint.*"

"How old are you, anyway?" Corinthia asks.

"Old enough," he says.

"Old enough for what?"

"Old enough to know when I'm sittin' across from trouble."

Corinthia says, "You think I'm trouble?"

"Nah, you seem cool," he replies. "Maybe a little too sharp for your own good, but you straight."

Corinthia drinks her orange juice, sets it down.

"You don't look old," she offers, wiping her mouth, but careful not to ruin her lip gloss any more than her waffles already might have.

"Black don't crack," Lavert jokes, tapping his cheek playfully. "See?"

Through the opening of Lavert's polo shirt, Corinthia notices part of a thin gold chain snaking over his collarbone. She briefly wonders if he took a shower before coming to meet her, if he'd studied himself in the mirror and applied an unscented facial moisturizer like she had, if he'd Q-tipped his ears and checked for offensively long nose hairs. Offensively long nose hairs are one of Corinthia's greatest daily fears. She towers over everyone, after all, so her nostrils are on display for the rest of humanity.

"Do you feel bad about what you and Dee did?" she says.

"I feel bad about that boy that Dee shot. Just some kid mindin' his business, doin' his job, clockin' minimum."

"What was his name?"

"Dennis Foley."

"How old was he?"

"Sixteen."

"Was he white or black?"

"What do you think?"

Corinthia picks up her fork and starts on her second sausage patty. Her mind is suddenly flooded with questions. When Lavert committed the robbery, was he wearing a mask? Did he shout awful things at the boy after they burst through the doors of the gas station kiosk? Was it in fact a kiosk or more of a mini-mart? Did they have a specific goal? A dollar amount they wanted to run off with? Where did they get the thirty-eight? Did they *want* to get caught?

Corinthia swallows the rest of the sausage patty and says, "When you were up in Joliet, did Dennis Foley's family ever try to get in touch with you?"

"Why would they wanna do that?" Lavert asks.

"I don't know," she says. "I've heard about how a family will sometimes visit a convict."

In last year's government and justice class, when they studied capital punishment, they watched a Sean Penn movie in which he portrayed a death-row inmate convicted of killing a young teenage couple, and one of the victims' relatives came to visit him before he was put to death. Even though Sean Penn's character had changed and become a better person, the victim's visiting relative had nothing in her heart for him. Nothing but hate. The question of who was worse—the rehabilitated death-row man or the embittered relative—inspired a heated debate afterward. Mr. Noah, the government and justice teacher, had to separate Karl Moore and Felix Stinson, who almost went to blows in the back of the class.

"I wouldn't wanna have nothin' to do with some low-minded thugs who killed my son," Lavert offers after drinking from his mug of tea.

"But you didn't kill him."

"But I was there." He drums his fingers on the tabletop a few times. "All I'd want is revenge," he continues. "And there ain't nothin' good about revenge, except maybe the little bit of satisfaction you might feel. But that passes just like anything else."

Julie comes by to check on them, and Lavert asks for more hot water for his tea.

After the waitress refills his mug, Corinthia says, "Do you have kids?"

"Nah," Lavert replies. "No kids. Just me and my gramamma."

Corinthia finishes the last bite of her waffles, swallows, and sets her fork down. She looks at Lavert again, directly into his large brown eyes. Her gaze travels down to his full mouth, and then to the dark, smooth skin of his neck, which seems as if it would be warm to the touch.

"So what's chemo like?" she asks.

She surprises herself with the question. It comes out more trivially than she'd intended. She might have just as easily asked him what his favorite food was or whether or not he smoked cigarettes.

"Chemo?" he says. "It ain't no *Bourne Legacy*, I'll tell you that much." He wipes his mouth with his napkin. "It's mostly boring. You basically sit in this big La-Z-Boy–type chair, and they hook you up to this machine that puts the medicine in you."

"How long does it take?"

"Coupla hours."

"And all you do is sit there?"

"Sit there and let the chemo do its thing. You can read," he adds. "Listen to music. Some people watch movies on their iPads."

"Can you have visitors?"

"Why?" he says. "You wanna come sit with me? Watch me turn green and spit up on myself like a baby?"

"I'm a good babysitter," she says, and though she's joking, it's true. There was a brief time when she was the most affordable, most sought-after babysitter in her neighborhood. But at eleven, when the legendary tumor arrived and caused her epic growth spurt, the neighborhood children became terrified of the monster on Stained Glass Drive and, just like that, her babysitting career was cut short.

"I'd like to come tomorrow," she says to Lavert.

"You can't," he says.

"Why not?"

"'Cause it's at nine a.m. and you got school."

"I'm not in school," she says.

"Why not?"

"Because I got suspended."

"Suspended for what?"

"Let's just say I got a little excited about some bad news."

"You broke some shit?"

"How'd you know?"

"'Cause usually you only get suspended for fightin' or breakin' shit. You can be a straight-up gangbanger, but if you don't fight or break nothin', they'll leave you be."

She says, "Sounds like you have firsthand knowledge."

Lavert smiles, revealing that missing incisor.

"What was the bad news?" he asks, changing the subject.

"I found out my brother was missing."

"For real?" Lavert says.

"He just up and disappeared. No one knows where he is."

"So what'd you do?"

"I broke a door."

"You were mad."

"I guess I was," she says.

"You two are close?"

"Sort of."

"Well, I hope he comes back," Lavert offers.

She can feel the white lie sitting in her stomach like a coiled, indigestible rope. She is hesitant to tell

Lavert the truth about why she broke Bob Sluba's life sciences door. The last thing she wants is to give him an excuse to dismiss her as some depraved lunatic besieged by apocalyptic visions.

"Breakin' down doors?" Lavert says, attempting levity again. "You a straight-up gangsta."

"Ha!" she says, and laughs.

He laughs, too. His laugh is slow, and there's an ache in it.

"You got a pretty smile," Lavert tells her.

"I do?" she says. "Really?"

"Real pretty," he says. "But don't let it go to your head."

In Lavert's silver Dodge Neon, which smells like the pine-scented deodorizing tree hanging from his rear-view mirror, Corinthia Bledsoe pushes the passenger's-side seat back as far as it will go and utilizes its maximum recline. Nonetheless, her knees are still tented high above the dash.

After Lavert politely asks her to wear her seat belt (she does so), he turns on the radio to an R & B/soul station, on which some lovelorn man with a husky voice is singing a slow jam about how when he met the love of his life, the rain stopped and the sky went blue and how she was a downright revelation and the chance of a lifetime and one in a million, etc., etc.

During this song and the next (similarly themed, but performed by a female singer and with less "mamba" to its bass line), Lavert and Corinthia don't speak. They simply let the music play while they pass through the small neighborhoods of Lugo.

Corinthia is pretty certain she can feel something like fondness or affection or maybe even the slightest hint of romance mingling in the front cab of his fuel-efficient compact car. She has a thousand questions for Lavert, like, for instance, where exactly did he grow up, and did he finish high school or get his GED in prison, and before the robbery did he have any goals, and did he and Dee commit other crimes, and when he was up in Joliet at Stateville, did he have a girlfriend like a pen pal, and did anyone ever come and visit him or send him care packages, and on and on and on.

But as they drive through her hometown, with its low storefront buildings and the windowless post office and the Roman Catholic church (St. Joseph's), with its modest white steeple, crawling a few miles per hour below the speed limit, all of these questions remain lodged in her head and she decides not to push things.

It starts to rain just as Lavert turns onto Stained Glass Drive. Distant thunder bellows as heavy drops splat silently on the windshield. Corinthia directs him to her house, and he puts the car in park and keeps the engine running.

Lavert turns the wipers on and says, "So, this is you, huh?"

"This is me," Corinthia says.

Lavert studies the house, the front yard, the driveway. "You climb that big-ass tree?" he asks, pointing to the old sycamore.

"Used to," Corinthia replies. "As a kid."

She goes on to tell him how she fell out of it once and broke her wrist, and how when her brother, Channing, was a boy, he'd do pull-ups from its lowest branches.

"Your pops drives an Audi?"

"That's his, yeah."

"Pimpin' ride," he says.

"It was a gift he got himself for his fortieth birthday."

"What's he do?"

"He's a foreman at Bazoo Meatpacking."

"Y'all must get a lotta free steaks," Lavert says.

Corinthia smiles and says, "Twice a week."

"You like livin' with your parents?"

"At this point I don't really have a choice. Only one more year."

"And then what?"

"I go away to school."

"Where you gonna go?" Lavert asks.

"Not sure yet," she says. "Maybe this place up in northern Wisconsin."

"You must like cold weather."

"You've been up there?"

"Spent some time in Milwaukee. My moms had a job at a brewery for a few years. People talk about Chicago winters. Winter in Milwaukee was *mad* worse than Chicago. February felt like it lasted a dog-gone *year*. Can't even imagine what it's like way up north. . . ."

During a long pause in the conversation, Corinthia watches the wipers glide across the windshield. She almost gets lost in their perfect, hypnotic choreography.

"You a good student?" Lavert asks, finally breaking the silence.

"Pretty good," she replies, "yeah."

"As and Bs?"

"Straight As."

"Damn," he says, "Straight As? You got some future ahead of you, huh."

They look at each other. The rain patters on the roof of the car. Corinthia has the distinct feeling that she is slowly falling into his deep-brown irises, like they are pools of velveteen warmth she could bathe in. She has the strange sensation that she is breathing under-water.

"Can I ask you a question?" Lavert says.

"Anything," she says.

"How on earth did you get my phone number?"

"The old-fashioned way," Corinthia replies. "I called information."

He tells her that he'll pick her up in front of her house in the morning.

"Eight forty-five," he says.

"Bright and early," Corinthia says. "See you then."

After she undoes her seat belt, she leans over and kisses him on the cheek. His face is warm and smooth and emits a faint animal fragrance. The smell makes her feel like she's just acquired a great secret, a thing she will hoard for the rest of her life.

She lets herself out.

"'Night," she says, and closes the door.

She watches his car pull away down Stained Glass Drive and turn at the stop sign. As she crosses under the old sycamore, she has to duck to avoid its lower branches. When she arrives at her front door, she comes upon Chet, the ceramic FirmaMall Dalmatian guarding the mailbox. Corinthia lifts her fingers to her mouth, hoping to keep the taste of Lavert's cheek on her lips for a few more moments.

When she enters the house, her father is asleep at the kitchen table. As Corinthia crosses the threshold,

hoping to sneak by him and go down to the basement to use her private bathroom, he lifts his head off
his arm.

"Hey," he says, not quite sitting up.

"Hey," Corinthia replies, stopping.

"Out late."

"I was with Cloris," Corinthia lies. "We were at
Uncle's."

"Late-night waffles," he says.

Her father is wearing light-blue pajama bottoms
and an old white T-shirt.

"She says hi," Corinthia lies.

"Cloris," he says, rubbing his eyes. "How is Lugo's
favorite librarian?"

"She's good," Corinthia replies. "She still has to
get her muffler fixed. That poor station wagon's starting to sound like a runaway garbage truck."

"I'd be happy to fix it for her."

"I suspect she secretly likes it," Corinthia says. "It
makes her feel like she's getting away with something."

"Seriously," Brill says, "tell her I'll replace her muffler if she brings me the parts. Save her some money."

Brill's always been a good mechanic. He worked
in a garage the summer after junior year in high school,
so he knows his way around engines and exhaust
systems.

"I'll tell her," Corinthia says. "That's really sweet of you, Daddy."

They are quiet. Corinthia notices how tired and puffy his face looks. There are dark rings under his eyes. His lips look dry and chapped. His hair is matted on one side, and he needs a shave. His glasses have fallen onto the Spanish tiles.

"Your glasses," Corinthia says, pointing to them.

Brill reaches down and picks them up but doesn't bother putting them on.

"Thanks," he says, setting them on the table.

The rain can be heard hitting the roof. Through the window over the sink, Corinthia can see it detonating on the wet driveway, which reflects the sodium vapor light from the lamp hanging over the garage.

"It's really coming down out there," Brill says. "Maybe some of this heat'll lift."

"Why are you down here?" Corinthia asks.

"I keep tossing and turning," he says. "Can't get comfortable. Your poor mother's gonna have to start sleeping in full pads."

"You were sound asleep on your arm when I walked in."

"Yeah," he says, "I guess I was."

She asks him if he'd like her to go get him a pillow, but he declines the offer.

"I'll go back up soon," he says.

"You must be exhausted," she says, folding her arms in front of her.

Corinthia has always thought her father to be handsome, even as he ages, even when he's tired. Channing looks more and more like him, she thinks, especially lately.

Brill says, "I like your shirt."

She tells him how she found it at a thrift store in nearby Kaskaskia. This particular thrift store carries larger-size clothes, and the owner, a woman who calls herself Suzy Blue, e-mails Corinthia when new items come in that might be of interest to her.

"Pretty rainbow," Brill says.

It's rare that Corinthia will wear a halter top, and she feels suddenly exposed. She's always sensed that her father knows more about her than he's willing to let on.

"How was work?" she asks.

Brill says, "It wasn't easy having to be there."

"You going in tomorrow?"

"I might do half a day," he says. "Hopefully our friends over at Missing Persons'll have some information for us."

"I think Channing's okay," Corinthia offers.

Brill looks up. He puts his glasses on and sits up. He says, "What makes you say that, Cori? Do you know something?"

"Gut feeling," she says.

"You've been having a few of those lately, huh?"

Corinthia nods.

She can't bring herself to mention the little wooden figure she discovered beside her brother's alarm clock or Channing's visit to her room the night before the tornadoes came. Even though she and Channing have grown apart in recent months, she somehow feels that sharing this information with her dad would be a betrayal. Something deep inside her knows Channing *wanted* to disappear.

From above, the sound of Marlene Bledsoe's feet can be heard padding down the hall. A door creaks open and closes.

"Mom's obviously not sleeping either," Corinthia says.

"She's likely running a bath."

"The house that never sleeps."

"I think we're all just a little on edge."

Corinthia uncrosses her arms and opens her mouth, intending to say something.

"What?" Brill says.

"Do you ever have visions?" she asks.

He thinks for a moment. He says, "Like you with those tornadoes?"

Corinthia nods.

"Once I had a dream that I fell off the garage roof of your grandmother's house, and then a few months later it happened. But that was me just being stupid with your uncle Kurt."

"Did you get hurt?"

"Broke my left wrist. I had to wear a cast for a few weeks, which got me a lot of attention from the girls in my eighth-grade class, so that was a perk."

"Was Mom in that class?"

"I didn't meet your mother till we were freshmen."

Corinthia already knew this, but she doesn't have a clue about their first encounter at Lugo Memorial. Did they pass each other in the hallway? Did they sit beside each other in a class? Was he behind her in line at the water fountain? Did she strategically drop her books so he'd offer to help her pick them up?

Was it love at first sight?

Lately Corinthia finds herself searching her parents' faces for a trace of her own identity. Sometimes she thinks she and her father share the same wide nose, the same slow, deliberate wrists. The only thing of her mother that she recognizes is when Marlene uncorks a laugh. She and her mother laugh with the same measured cadence, three or four loud reports — squawks, really — and then it's over. When Corinthia hears this, she feels a tinge of shame. She's been trying to transform her laugh for the past few years. She'd prefer one more like Cloris Honniotis's, a low, demonic snigger, a sound Corinthia has tried to appropriate to her best abilities, but when she least suspects it, her mother's laugh always creeps back in.

"I really did see those tornadoes," Corinthia tells her father.

"Well," he says, "I highly doubt you'd lie about something like that."

"I'm not a liar."

"No, you're not," Brill says.

"I saw three of them, and that's how many there were."

"I'm not denying any of this, Cori."

"I just hate that people think I'm crazy."

"You're not crazy."

"You're just saying that because you're my dad."

"I'm too tired to pretend right now. I believe you."

"Promise?"

"I promise," he says.

"Good," Corinthia replies.

He sits up a little straighter now.

"And what's this business I heard about from Vice Principal Mejerus? Apparently you interrupted the assembly with some 'absurd' announcement — something about penguins?"

"It wasn't absurd."

"Those were his words," Brill says. "'She assailed the assembly with an absurd notion.' I'm just quoting what he said."

Corinthia says, "They weren't penguins; they were geese."

"Geese, huh?"

"I said *birds* were coming, but I saw them the other day, and they're geese."

"You saw them where?"

"In my head."

"Another vision."

"Yes."

"How many?"

"Thousands."

"And what are these geese gonna do, Cori?"

"I don't know," she says, "but they're coming."

This new subject seems to have weakened Brill Bledsoe, worn him down even more. He hunches again, then gently forces the heels of his hands under his brows and presses upward.

"You okay?" Corinthia asks.

"My left arm's all fulla sand," he says, ceasing the pressure on his eyes, now jiggling his hand. "Pins and needles."

"I'll let you sleep," Corinthia offers.

"If I'm lucky," he says.

"Maybe you should put the kitchen table in your bedroom," Corinthia offers, half joking.

"Prolly not such a bad idea."

"'Night," she tells her father, taking a step toward him and kissing the crown of his head.

"'Night, sweetheart," he says, squeezing her hand.

After she uses her basement bathroom, Corinthia lurches up the two flights of stairs to her bedroom, where she takes off all her clothes and puts on her noise-canceling headphones.

She cues up Ariel Pink's "Put Your Number in My Phone" and lies there, on top of her covers, letting the air cool her.

She imagines dancing with Lavert Birdsong. Even though the Ariel Pink track emits a poppy jubilance, she envisions them slow-dancing at Homecoming, in the Lugo Memorial Connie and Dillard Deet Field House. A disco ball refracts spinning discs of silver light, and they are at center court, embracing, barely swaying, Lavert Birdsong's slightly balding head pulled close, just below Corinthia's breasts.

Corinthia wears a peach dress that fits her perfectly, and Lavert sports a handsome powder-blue tuxedo with frills and flourishes, and everyone encircles them, looking on, in less unique attire, their mouths agape, their classic tuxes and gowns appearing stiff and uninhabited. Her Lugo Memorial peers can only wish they could feel what she and Lavert are feeling.

She plays the song five times in a row, basking in her Homecoming fantasy, relishing the slow revolutions she and Lavert Birdsong make at center court of the Connie and Dillard Deet Field House, and then she falls asleep, her heart full, all her aches and pains far, far away.

She sleeps as deeply as she has in months and doesn't dream of tornadoes, geese, or other apocalyptic phenomena.

10

The thunderstorm ceases just before dawn. Birds chirp in the damp trees. The last slicks of rainwater skirl through gutters and drain into mounds of gravel and soil and landscaping mulch. Dogs relieve themselves throughout the neighborhoods of Lugo. As the sun rises up the eastern sky, its new light silvers the faces of the ceramic deer, rabbits, and garden gnomes populating the yards, pathways, and vegetable gardens of Stained Glass Drive.

Chet, the Bledsoes' FirmaMall Dalmatian, almost seems to change expression as his face slowly brightens out of the darkness.

On the kitchen radio, which was left on by Brill Bledsoe, the local news report says that four more deer carcasses have been discovered in the woods along the frontage road.

"Those gray wolves appear to be at it again," the newswoman says.

In sports, the St. Louis Cardinals are six games out of the Central Division lead and had to place one of their starting pitchers on the fifteen-day disabled list. The weather forecast promises bright-blue skies and temperatures in the mid-seventies.

Not quite an hour later, Corinthia sits on the floor across from Lavert Birdsong as he attempts to relax in a latte-colored pleather recliner. Before she was allowed past the reception area of the modest chemotherapy center in nearby Belleville, she was asked to fill out a visitor's form. One of the questions asked that, if necessary, would she be prepared to drive the patient home. Corinthia checked the "Yes" box even though she had no idea how she might negotiate her legs under the dash in order to properly operate Lavert's compact car. Another question asked about her relationship to the patient. In the blank answer space, in all capital letters, after some deliberation, Corinthia wrote FRIEND.

The bright little room smells faintly of a chemical burn, something perhaps more appropriate on the outskirts of a power plant than in the interior of a medical facility. The floor that she sits on is so immaculate that she can practically see her reflection in its linoleum surface. There is lemon-colored vinyl wallpaper, and a cat calendar on the wall features an orange kitten staring into a fishbowl containing an equally orange goldfish. A dehydrated spider plant hangs from the ceiling. Next to the recliner is an iPod dock centered on a Salvation Army–quality side table with no apparent power source. There is also a visitor's metal folding chair with a cracked and faded St. Louis Cardinals seat cushion that's been mended here and there with bits of silver duct tape. The lone window provides a view of the parking lot, which is filled to capacity with fuel-efficient compact cars not unlike Lavert Birdsong's Dodge Neon.

For obvious reasons, Corinthia elects not to sit on the metal folding chair and instead chooses the floor.

An intravenous tube connected to a medical port has been attached to the back of Lavert's hand, just below the peaks of his knuckles. Its insertion was executed by a quiet middle-aged nurse named Mary, whose kindness reminded Corinthia of Sister Josephine, a nun from Dubuque, Iowa, who came to speak to her junior high Community Service Club about volunteer work in Africa.

Even though Corinthia was still standing, Nurse Mary didn't flinch encountering her as she entered the room. She simply smiled and said hello and introduced herself and went about her business. She's obviously seen much worse than your run-of-the-mill local giant, and Corinthia appreciated the normal treatment.

After Nurse Mary attached the tubing to Lavert's chemotherapy system she injected a clear substance directly into Lavert's port with a hypodermic needle that seemed to materialize out of thin air. She then quietly asked him how his stomach was feeling, and he said, "Fine," and then she pressed a few buttons and asked him if he'd like a deck of cards, per usual, and he said no, that he was getting tired of solitaire, and then she smiled and told him to hit the assistance button if he needed anything, and he thanked her and she left.

Lavert is wearing a generic gray sweatshirt and old-school Adidas tracksuit bottoms — black with gold stripes. He's taken his low-top Nike Air Force I's off to reveal bright-white athletic socks. He rubs his hand over his thinning woolly hair. As he told Corinthia during the short drive to Belleville, this will be his sixth chemotherapy session, the final one of his second cycle.

"This'll all be gone soon," he says from his recliner, pointing to his hair. "I'm surprised it lasted this long."

"You should shave it," Corinthia offers.

"Maybe I should," he says. "Like my boy. Tupac."

During the three-hour session, they talk about many things. They talk about his dwindling appetite and how his grandmother usually brings him to his treatments but doesn't dare remain in the room with him while the chemo is being administered anymore because she just gets too upset and downright mad at God, and how she'll usually just stay in the car for the three hours and listen to the radio and pray on her rosary despite her recent feelings about the Almighty Father, and how the idea of going to a movie at the nearby Cineplex is just too hard because she wouldn't be able to focus on some big goofy actor's face anyway or going to eat ice cream or looking at puppies in that little store in the mall either, so she just hunkers down in the car for the whole three hours and when she comes up to get him at the end of his sessions, she cries anyway, even though she swears to Jesus on the Cross that she won't and her crying is really more like the inconsolable wailing of Italian matriarchs in overly serious early eighties mafia movies and invariably Nurse Mary has to come in and give Florida Birdsong a hug and provide her with aloe-rich tissues and help her sit in that metal folding chair with the St. Louis Cardinals seat cushion while a male nurse known as Steady Eddie Always Ready has to come in and take over and remove Lavert's IV and extract his port and help him to the toilet because Lavert usually has to go pretty bad immediately after a treatment and sometimes he also has to change into another shirt because he'll get sick to his stomach before the session is over, and, yes, he does receive medication for the nausea and his body temperature changes so often and so extremely that he's taken to mostly wearing sweat suits lately because they make for easy layering and the convenient shedding of garments and sometimes after a session he'll sleep for so many consecutive hours that he forgets what day of the week it is and he apologizes to Corinthia in advance if he should start to say something but not be able to complete the thought and then there's this moment where his face twitches just the slightest bit like an invisible fishhook has snagged the corner of his mouth and Corinthia gets the sense that this "medicine" that is mingling with his bloodstream — this mysterious chemotherapy substance — is an indiscriminate force of such serious power that it could break down even the mightiest lion king of the greatest jungle and when Corinthia asks him about his mother, the one who used to work for that brewery in Milwaukee, and about his father, whom he's said nothing about thus far, Lavert simply replies, "They ain't around no more," and when Corinthia asks him if they're dead, he says, "They might as well be," but he says it without pride and without asking for pity and the very absence of these two qualities makes her heart fill with so much love for this man who sits before her that she would like to reach behind herself and force her hand into the flesh of her back and remove her own non-cancer-riddled sixteen-year-old pancreas and offer it to him.

But instead she takes his hand in hers; his left hand, the one that isn't attached to the chemotherapy delivery system. She covers it with both of hers and stares into Lavert's eyes, and he stares back. They simply look at each other. For a brief moment, it feels as if the entire world has gone away. There is no sound. There is no treatment room. There is only the two of them. And then it happens. A inevitable feeling as certain as sunlight overtakes Corinthia. She can feel it filling her entire being. It's the first clear, absolutely unimpeachable thought she's had in a long time, and it's this:

Sometime very soon, Lavert Birdsong is going to ask me to help him die.

In an aluminum-bodied Airstream Classic, just beyond the fringes of the Cornelius Harlow Football Stadium, where three other Airstreams have been arranged, Guidance Counselor Denton Smock sits across from freshman Billy Ball. They are comfortably arranged on Naugahyde banquettes, a small Formica dinette table between them.

It's the final period of the day, and the temporary student–guidance counselor meeting space is nothing like Mr. Smock's office in the basement of the main school building, where Facilities Manager Shoreland

Splitz has been allowing Mr. Smock to go feed his favorite clown fish (Rodney) a few times a day.

A quiet oscillating fan, which has been set in a small kitchen nook, blows warm air around the thirty-one-foot-long, nine-and-a-half-foot-wide recreational vehicle, which, if Denton Smock's sweat-stained light-blue oxford-cloth shirt is any indication, offers little relief.

It's the last day of classes before Labor Day weekend, and since the Airstreams have been brought in, there is the general sense that Lugo Memorial High School has been transformed into a kind of utopian campsite, where teachers, students, and staff are somewhat adrift, overly smiley, and confused about their relationship to the main school building, which is still in the process of being brought up to standard operating level by scores of electricians, contractors, plumbers, supply vendors, and a small team of pot-bellied, tobacco-chewing, sunburnt window glaziers in tie-dyed T-shirts.

All lunches still take place in the cafeteria, one of the few sections of Lugo Memorial that's been deemed safe by Shoreland Splitz, Principal Ticonderoga, and various municipal leaders, but a rigid particleboard hallway has been erected, which is accessed through a pair of side-entrance fire doors and extends some seventy feet or so, directly to the cafeteria. It's believed by the powers that be that the corridor limits the amount of student curiosity and unproductive sneaking around during this all-important phase of repair. Principal Ticonderoga has assured faculty, students, and staff that the temporary Airstream system will be necessary for only a few more weeks.

All twelve aluminum trailers have been enumerated with handsome crimson-and-cream stencils, as well as a decal of the beloved Lugo Memorial Fighting Mastodon. The one that Denton Smock has been given for this particular period is Airstream number four. He is armed with his trusted notebook and mechanical pencil as well as a portable cardboard box containing student files. The physical relationship between guidance counselor and student—the small Formica table bisecting the two banquettes—isn't *that* much different from the one that exists in his basement office. But the sessions aren't the same. The conversational focus—the simple level of student concentration—just isn't up to snuff. And in all fairness, Denton Smock has found that he's also been guilty of being easily distracted. During recent sessions, he often catches himself staring out one of the three vista windows overlooking the football field's south end zone, where students are allowed to mingle, talk on their cell phones, and sit in the grass.

Speckled throughout the football field are wreaths, colorful signs, bouquets, and myriad handcrafted missives that say BRING HOME THE HEAT and COME BACK, CHANNING! and WE LOVE YOU, HEATSTER! The expanse of the football field, end zone to end zone, has been transformed into a kind of visual prayer for Channing Bledsoe's safe deliverance back to Lugo. This was, of course, approved by Principal Ticonderoga, Shoreland Splitz, and Head Football Coach Virgil Task, the only stipulation being that the various "Channing" pieces be portable enough to be easily struck from the field on game days and not damage the turf. The football team practices on the nearby practice field, after all, almost a mile away, just off Route 14B.

Denton Smock has been trying to talk to Billy Ball about the current cafeteria situation and how, earlier at lunch, he noticed him sitting with Durdin Royko and Keiko Cho.

"Have you made friends with them?" Denton Smock asks.

"We're civil," Billy replies, "but I wouldn't say we're friends, exactly."

"How often do the three of you eat together?"

"Every day."

"So it's become a ritual."

"The Sioux were really into rituals," Billy offers.

Denton Smock adjusts his glasses, and although

he's somewhat frustrated with Billy's continued obsession and romanticization of Native American culture, he asks him if he would say more about this.

"They would do these things called ghost dances," Billy explains. "Enacted to reunite the living with the spirits of the dead and protect them from the white man's bullets."

"Protect *whom* from the white man's bullets?"

"The living," Billy says. "The Sioux would dance in a circle and go into trance states."

"Interesting," Denton Smock says.

"They had a particularly fascinating relationship to death. The *nagi*'s journey to the spirit world involves a perilous test."

"The *nagi*?" Denton Smock says.

"The shadow of the Sioux," Billy Ball explains. "The spirit. He must cross a great mythical river on a very narrow log. If the *nagi* is afraid of this test, or fails it, he must return to our world and wander forever as a lost or forlorn ghost. There are few things they fear more than being lost in this world in the afterlife."

"Who is the *nagi* in your life?"

Billy Ball doesn't answer.

"Is it your father?"

The young man just stares at his guidance counselor.

"Do you see yourself as the *nagi*?" Denton Smock asks.

"I know where the log is," Billy Ball says.

"The log on the mythical river."

"Yes, that," Billy Ball says. "It's in the forest by the frontage road. The wolves are protecting it."

"What wolves are you talking about?"

"The wolves from the newspaper. The ones killing all the deer. They're protecting the log."

"But there's no river in that forest."

"It could be a river of dirt," Billy Ball says. "Or leaves. There's water in everything. You're mostly water."

"So are you," Denton Smock says.

"Maybe one of us is the river," Billy Ball says.

"What about your dad?" Denton Smock says. "Do you think he was able to cross the log? Do you think he was able to pass the test?"

"Sometimes I think he's still in my mom's garden," Billy Ball says.

"Doing what, exactly?"

"Looking for his watch," Billy Ball says. "In the lilac bushes."

"So he hasn't crossed the log yet."

Billy doesn't respond.

"Do you think your dad is having trouble finding the log?"

Again, Billy Ball doesn't respond. He is wearing a long-sleeved white T-shirt with a falling green leaves design on it. Denton Smock notices that the green in the leaves matches his hazel eyes.

"Tell me what you're thinking," Denton Smock says to Billy.

"I'm thinking that once he finds his watch, he'll be able to cross the log."

"Do you ever think about reuniting with the spirit of your father?"

Billy's pupils seem to momentarily surge. They overtake his irises. But the expression marking the rest of his face is one of blankness, the profound absence of thought or emotion.

"I'm going to help him find the log," Billy says.

"And how do you plan on doing that?"

Billy closes his eyes for a long moment.

Denton Smock depresses the stopwatch feature on his Timex. The digital numerals tumble away. It appears that Billy Ball has slipped into a brief state of meditation.

"I've been writing in my journal," Billy says, finally opening his eyes, some fourteen seconds later.

"To Dave."

"To Dave the Diary, yes."

"How is that going for you?"

"What?" Billy Ball replies indignantly, almost defensively.

"How are you finding it?" Denton Smock says. "The journaling. Are you enjoying it?"

"You said that it was for me, for my own private thoughts."

"It *is* for you," Denton Smock assures him. "It's solely for you."

"Then why do you want to know how it's going?"

"Just to get a general sense. I don't mean to pry, Billy. . . . Are you enjoying it?"

"That's between me and Dave."

"Okay," Denton Smock replies. "I'm glad you've found a confidant."

Some students pass by the Airstream. Two upper-classmen, Troy Aurora and a lineman on the football team, Nate Bluff, follow behind Rigby Nemtusiak, a tall, dark-haired sophomore girl with impressive breasts. Nate Bluff is wearing his letterman's sweater, even though it's 75 degrees outside and most of the other varsity football players have forgone the game-day tradition because tonight's contest, like last week's, has had to be rescheduled due to the damaged locker-room facilities.

Billy Ball, who has been watching them through the window, meets eyes with Troy Aurora, who flashes him a peace sign. Billy doesn't reciprocate the gesture but simply studies him, and then Troy Aurora rotates his hand and his peace sign transforms into a lone, extremely vertical middle finger—a blatant *fuck you*—and he and burly Nate Bluff, whose neck/shoulder relationship is sort of superhero-like, laugh and continue walking toward the south end zone, where they join a few other students who are milling about underneath the goalposts.

Denton Smock has witnessed all of this, but when Billy Ball turns his attention back to their session, the guidance counselor looks away.

"Let's just say that he knows stuff," Billy offers, his eyes still trained on the two upperclassmen.

"*Dave* knows stuff."

"Dave the Diary, yes."

"Do you have him with you now?"

"I always have him with me," Billy says.

Denton Smock finds that he is jealous of Dave, this invented diary persona. Here he thought he was introducing a forum in which Billy Ball might communicate his most personal thoughts and feelings and perhaps come to understand himself better, but he's only succeeded in creating more distance between himself and this special freshman.

He has an impulse to reach across the table and grasp one of the boy's forearms. It's a surprising impulse, to say the least, as intense as anything he's felt in the presence of a student since he was hired as a member of the faculty. But Denton Smock doesn't reach across the table and grab Billy Ball's thin, pale forearm. Instead, he asks him if he ever discusses his dad with Dave.

"Sometimes," the boy replies.

"What do you tell him?"

Billy Ball studies him for a moment.

"What?" Denton Smock says. "What's wrong?"

The way the boy is staring at him makes him want to turn around. It makes him want to turn the lights off.

Instead of answering the question, Billy says, "Why did you take your glasses off?"

It's true. Denton Smock didn't even realize it, but he's removed his glasses. And there they are, on the table between them, as plain as day. He rarely removes his glasses in front of any student. He has poor vision and can't afford to miss anything. He's caught off guard but resists his natural impulse to put them back on.

"Does it bother you?" he says. "My taking my glasses off?"

"Your face looks more bald," Billy replies.

"Oh," Denton Smock says. "I've never thought of a face as being bald."

"Do you even shave?" Billy asks.

"Of course I shave," Denton Smock replies. "I shave practically every day."

"Do you keep the whiskers in a box?"

"No," Denton Smock replies. "Why do you ask?"

Billy's attention seems to drift about the interior of the Airstream. Denton Smock tries to follow his gaze, but it never seems to settle on any one thing.

"Did your *father* shave?" he asks Billy.

Billy's head comes to rest.

"The Sioux pulled their facial hair out with their fingers," Billy says. "Their complexions were quite fascinating. They had the faces of old children."

"What an interesting turn of phrase," Denton Smock offers. " 'Old children.' An oxymoron."

"They were robust, yet smooth," Billy adds.

Denton Smock finds himself touching his own face. He can feel the faintest bit of sandpapery beard coming in.

"Would you like me to put my glasses back on?" he asks Billy.

"I'm making a list," Billy replies, yet again pivoting to another subject. "I'm calling it 'The List.' "

"What kind of a list is it?" Denton Smock asks.

"An important one," Billy replies.

"Have you told Dave about it?"

"He's the only one who knows."

"Is it a to-do list?"

"Sort of."

"A list of chores?"

Billy doesn't answer.

"Is your dad on the list?"

"My dad is dead," Billy says. "Will you please put your glasses back on?"

"If it will make you feel more comfortable."

"The Sioux believed they could see more clearly with their minds. They ate a special cactus that turned them into hawks and buffalo."

"What cactus is that?"

"It's called peyote."

"Peyote is a psychedelic drug," Mr. Smock says. "It's like LSD. I'm pretty sure the Sioux *thought* they were transforming into animals, but in fact, they were simply imagining it."

"They flew like hawks and ran wild like buffalo," Billy says. "I've seen pictures on the Internet."

Denton Smock arranges the arms of his Clark Kent–style glasses over his ears, pushes the bridge snug to his nasal bones. Billy's face comes into sharper focus. Those hazel eyes again, the color now almost completely overtaken by the blackness of his pupils.

"Billy," Denton Smock says, "I'd like you to show

me your diary. I'm not going to look inside. I'd just like to see it. Would that be okay?"

"Why?" Billy asks.

"Because I'm curious about it. You showed it to me before, but it happened so quickly, I really didn't get a good look. I'm just really glad you're putting your thoughts down. It's a healthy step in sharing your feelings."

Billy Ball says, "But don't open it."

"I promise I won't."

Billy Ball searches Denton Smock's face. Sometimes the smallest twitch will give someone away. He sees this twitch in almost everyone he knows. He's seen it in his mother when she kisses him good night. Sometimes he thinks she wishes it were he who died, not his father. She wishes it were he who fell face-first into his dinner and never woke up. He can see this thought tugging at the soft flesh under her left eye when she kisses him good night or when she watches him do his homework at the coffee table.

"What's wrong, Mom?" he'll ask.

"Nothing, sweetheart," she'll say.

But he knows she's harboring this terrible thought, which is trapped in the twitch on her face.

Billy Ball unzips his backpack. He reaches into it and produces the notebook. He slowly places it on the surface of the table, almost perfectly centered between them. He clutches both sides of it, his knuckles meeting the Formica surface of the table.

DAVE is written across the cover in black Sharpie.

Denton Smock ever so gently lifts his right hand and places it on the cover, partly obscuring the assigned name.

"May I?" he asks.

Just as Billy Ball is about to let go of his diary— he can actually feel his hands begin to release it—the surprising, absurd sound of scattered honking can be heard. It almost sounds like hundreds of people squeezing old-fashioned bicycle horns in a faraway parade. The sound is faint at first, but then it escalates in volume and, in a matter of seconds, grows to be cacophonous.

Denton Smock quickly stands and faces the window. He pushes his glasses higher up on his nose.

The sound is thunderous now.

"What is that?" Billy Ball asks.

From Denton Smock's view, he can see that the sky over the football field is suddenly dark. It appears that a wavering sea of black pepper is descending on the Cornelius Harlow Football Field.

The students who've been socializing under the south goalposts are now running for cover. Most of them have fled toward the entrance of Airstream number five and are pounding on its front door, its aluminum sidewall, its windows.

"It's geese," Denton Smock says, transfixed, his mouth hanging open.

The honking is almost ludicrously loud now, lunatic in its music, as if all the madness of the world were being violently, chaotically voiced.

And although neither of them can hear anything else, Denton Smock says it again, truly stunned.

"Geese."

In her master bathroom, with the pad of her thumb, Marlene Bledsoe is stroking the waxy wrapper covering the piece of chocolate caramel mocha taffy that Lemon Tidwell gave her at Burritos As Big As Your Head! when she hears a loud thud from downstairs. She stuffs the taffy in the front pocket of her DKNY cranberry capri pants and rushes downstairs, careful not to trip down the augmented steps, where, in the middle of the living room, her giant daughter has fallen to the floor.

"Cori!" she cries. "Cori!"

Corinthia Bledsoe's body shudders with violent spasms, her eyes rolled back in her head, her mouth open. Her body dwarfs the living room, and it looks as if toy furniture has been arranged around her in some attempt to reenact a children's fable.

"Cori!" Marlene Bledsoe screams again. "Cori!"

Aside from the murmur of the TV, the only sounds that can be heard are Corinthia's fists and heels pummeling the carpet, their reports like bombs detonating in a nearby war zone.

It takes everything in her power for Marlene Bledsoe to remain on her feet as the living room trembles and quakes all around her.

PART

3

11

A nurse wearing taupe scrubs and white cross-trainers enters a room in the Intensive Care Unit of St. Anthony's Hospital, approximately ten miles north of Lugo, Illinois.

Corinthia Bledsoe is resting in a makeshift hospital bed that bisects the room diagonally. The staff at St. Anthony's has taken it upon themselves to improvise beyond the normal amenities offered in the ICU and have managed to add some three feet to one of their standard-size beds by bringing up a table from the cafeteria and attaching it to the foot of the existing bed with large amounts of medical, duct, and electrical tape and then affixing many pillows to the surface of the table with strips of Velcro, and then covering the hodgepodge of padding with a folded hospital sheet.

So far the arrangement has worked out and Corinthia is comfortable, if not downright cozy.

After almost twenty-four hours of unconsciousness, and having been administered a large dose of

Valium, Corinthia is resting well and has been exhibiting strong vital signs. The Valium makes her feel loopy, as if she has bits of milkweed floating through her brain, but it's sort of like being on vacation. It makes her want to stretch out and quietly giggle, which she's been doing a lot of for the past hour or so.

It's the day after Labor Day, September 8, to be exact, and now that her mood has stabilized, although still being administered intravenous fluids, she's been okayed to eat regular cafeteria food and even get out of bed to move her bowels and release her bladder as long as she's willing to take her IV stand along for the ride and the large male nurse in training, Luke, is around to help her in case she gets lightheaded or slips and falls. "Luke the Fluke," as the other nurses call him, has been very polite to Corinthia, and despite the fact that she's easily six to eight years younger than him, he calls her "ma'am," as in "I got you, ma'am," and "There you go, ma'am," and "I'm right out here on the other side of this door if you need anything, ma'am."

When Luke the Fluke isn't working, the ICU staff has deemed it necessary that two nurses be on hand to help Corinthia traverse the small room in order to reach the facilities.

The nurse who enters — her name tag reads REGAN — is carrying a small gift-wrapped box.

"Someone left this for you at the front desk," Regan says, handing it to Corinthia. Regan has a face like a Siamese cat. She uses black eyeliner to accentuate the corners of her eyes. Despite the eye makeup, she is oddly inexpressive.

The box is about the size of a fast-food hamburger container and the gift-wrapping is of the thin white tissue-paper variety, decorated with little purple stars and crescent moons. Corinthia elects to deposit it in the large depression between her neck and collarbone.

"Thanks," she says to Regan.

As Regan takes her vitals, Corinthia says, "Still no TV privileges, huh?"

"Strict orders from on high," Regan replies, plugging Corinthia's ear with a digital thermometer. "No TV and no Internet."

The TV, which looms above in the corner, has been unplugged, and a plastic device has been placed over the plug's tongs so that it can't be inserted into any socket. It's the one time she wishes she had her smartphone, but it's been retired to that shoe box on the dresser in her bedroom.

Corinthia says, "'On high' meaning the doctor, or 'on high' meaning my parents?"

"Who do you think?" Regan says. "Dr. Neboshik's never had a problem with patients watching TV."

"How 'bout a newspaper?" Corinthia asks.

"How's that appetite?" Regan asks, changing the subject, then assessing Corinthia's bag of fluid.

"I could *eat* a TV," Corinthia says.

"Well, that's a good sign. We got a hot meal scheduled for you. Should be up in a little bit."

Regan goes into the closet and returns with a fresh pillow.

"Lift up . . ."

Corinthia elevates her head and Regan replaces the old pillow with the new one.

"Not even the local paper?" Corinthia says.

Regan places her fists on her hips and says, "Drink that," pointing to the Styrofoam cup of water set on the table beside her. "Hydrate, hydrate, hydrate."

"Hydrate, hydrate, hydrate," Corinthia echoes. "The key to life."

Regan exits with the old pillow.

Corinthia holds the gift in front of her face and shakes it. She peels away the tissue paper to reveal a white gift box with a lid. She lifts the lid. Inside the box is a blue velvet pouch, cinched at the top. Inside the pouch are a brass triangle and an accompanying wand. There is a leather loop attached to the apex of the triangle, and a matching leather grip, not even a half inch wide, capping the base of the wand.

Also in the velvet pouch is a note on a small piece of card stock. It reads:

Corinthia,
I heard you fell and bumped your head.
I hope you're feeling better. Thinking of you . . .
Lavert

Corinthia feels the muscles in her jaws soften, and her face blooms into a smile. She doesn't even bother hiding her teeth. It's the most unabashed smile she's unleashed for as long as she can remember. She begins to giggle.

Marlene Bledsoe enters the room wearing a peach velour tracksuit that highlights her camel-toe/bulging-inner-thigh arrangement, and this is precisely what Corinthia can see coming toward her: her mother's camel toe!

"You're up!" Marlene squawks.

Corinthia giggles and sends her a thumbs-up. She can smell her mother's post-shower all-over-body talcum. Like lilacs in a bowl of vanilla pudding. Her hair is different. She's lightened it.

"What's that?" Marlene asks, pointing to the triangle.

"A triangle," Corinthia replies. She has to concentrate hard not to slur her words.

Marlene is doing her best to *not look away* from her daughter, whose enormous pale head on the white pillow is like the rimy bust of some ancient Greek statue wrested from the bottom of the Aegean. But Marlene Bledsoe will not look away, no matter how much mucus she sees collecting in the caves of her daughter's nostrils, or the amount of milky drool pooling at the corners of her extra-wide mouth, or how oily her hair is, or, perhaps worst of all, how downright *mountainous* that godforsaken *chin* appears at the moment! Has it gotten even *bigger* in the past twenty-four hours?

My baby girl isn't well, she tells herself, *and I will not look away!*

"Is that velvet?" Corinthia asks of her mother's tracksuit.

"It's velour," Marlene replies. "But it's thick like velvet. Do you approve?"

"The color makes me think that at any minute a spry and ribald hobbit is gonna appear, wearing a matching tracksuit, and then you'll fist-bump, and like, a wall will open to another dimension, and then you'll both disappear into a rainbow of butterflies."

Corinthia unleashes a giggle that turns into mock machine-gun fire. She aims a finger gun right at her mother's vagina.

"Look who's feeling better," Marlene says. "What's 'ribald,' anyway?"

"'Ribald,'" Corinthia replies, "is an adjective referring to sexual matters in an amusing, rude, or irreverent way."

"A wordsmith even under sedation," Marlene jokes.

"Wordsmith, nerdsmith, turdsmith," Corinthia says.

"Who's the triangle from?" Marlene asks, clearly trying to keep things from sliding too far downhill.

"A friend," Corinthia says.

"Cloris?" Marlene asks.

Corinthia doesn't have the desire or energy to broach the subject of Lavert Birdsong.

"Yeah, Cloris the Clitoris," she lies.

"Well, that's sweet of her," Marlene says. "A triangle."

"A three-sided figure, yep."

"But why a triangle?"

"I'm pretty sure it's an inside joke," Corinthia says, and leaves it at that. She giggles and strikes the delicate instrument a few times. "Nurse, oh, nurse," she goofs. She slips the triangle, Lavert's note, and the little wand back into its velvet pouch and places the pouch back in the box and sets it on the table to her right.

"Nurse Regan just told me you're getting your appetite back," Marlene says, standing over her daughter now, arranging a few sweaty strands of Corinthia's hair behind an ear.

Corinthia nods.

"And all the scans came back negative, thank God. Dr. Neboshik says you're right as rain."

"Lucky me," Corinthia says. "Lucky giant."

"He said they'd like to keep you here overnight, but you can come home tomorrow morning."

"You sure you want that?" Corinthia says.

"Want what?" Marlene asks.

"For me to come home."

"Of course I want that, Cori. Where else would you go?"

"I don't know," Corinthia says. "I could probably stay with Cloris."

"You belong at home with your family," Marlene says sternly. "Besides, you wouldn't be *comfortable* at Cloris's house. What in the world would you *sleep* on?"

"I'd sleep in her backyard. In her bounce house."

"Corinthia Lee Bledsoe, Cloris Honniotis does *not* have a bounce house."

"Cool image, though, right, Marlene?"

"Cori," her mother warns.

"Marlene," Corinthia says back, giggling.

"You know I don't like when you call me that."

Marlene's iPhone chirps, and she quickly checks it. Her face suddenly falls.

"What's wrong?" Corinthia says.

And then, just like that, Marlene starts to cry.

"Mom," Corinthia says. "Mom, don't cry."

"I'm not," she says.

"Yes, you are. You're sort of blubbering."

"I can cry if I want to!" Marlene protests, her voice faint and high.

"Don't cry about me, Mom. I'm gonna be okay — you just said so."

"I'm *not* crying about you," Marlene says. Her face suddenly appears to be screwed into itself bitterly, as if she's been forced to suck a lemon.

"Then, why are you crying?"

"Because . . ." Marlene starts to say.

"Because *why?*" Corinthia asks, playing along.

"Because I just found out that FirmaMall is going out of business. They just filed for bankruptcy, and they're not sending out any more catalogs."

"Did they, like, *text* you or something?"

"I get their push notifications," Marlene bleats. Little bits of saliva leap from her lips. She sniffles and holds her breath and tries to stop, but she just can't help herself.

Corinthia is pretty certain that her mother is lying about the source of her sorrow.

What Corinthia doesn't know is that, not twenty minutes earlier, Marlene Bledsoe had contacted Lemon Tidwell to request another rendezvous.

We could meet at that burrito place again, she texted. *Just say the word and I'll be there.*

Sorry, Marlene, he texted back just moments ago. *Can't do today. But I'll see you at Group.*

And when Marlene tries to contend with the twenty-two-caliber-size hole this has left in her heart— yes, it feels as if she's been shot—it's that intense—it makes her want to hurl herself to the pavement behind the hospital, that really foul, venereal-looking pavement out back by the Dumpsters, where the orderlies go to smoke and play grab-ass and check their cell phones. She wants to prostrate herself and bloody her knuckles on this particular slab of extremely septic-looking asphalt and then smear this blood from her knuckles all over her mouth and nose and eyes and neck and keen insufferably like some fallen lunatic queen at the end of a Greek tragedy.

"You got your hair done," Corinthia says.

"I got it lightened," Marlene says, grazing it with salon-fresh nails. "Do you like it?"

"It's nice," Corinthia says, less giggly now, sobered a bit by her mother's tears.

"I just can't stand how many grays I'm getting."

Marlene crosses to the bathroom, fluffing her hair. She enters the room, leaving the door open.

"Where's Dad?" Corinthia asks after a silence.

"He's on his way," Marlene answers, returning from the bathroom, wiping her smeared face. "He was just visiting with Detective Moon."

"Any word on Chan?"

"Nothing," Marlene says.

When Marlene wears too much makeup, Corinthia thinks she looks like an aging porn star. And now that it's smeared, she looks like an aging porn star who's slept with a rodeo clown.

"By the way," Marlene says, her voice lower now, assuming its reliable, post-cry register, "a boy stopped by the house with your desk. Walked it all the way over from the high school."

"What boy?" Corinthia asks.

"His name was Billy. Real nice boy. He said he was a freshman. I was surprised he was in high school. He was pretty small for his age."

"I don't know him."

"Well, anyway, he brought your desk home. Billy Something-or-other. I think his last name was Wall or Paul. He was pretty worn out. He was sweating so bad, I thought he'd just run a 10K! Poor little thing!"

Brill Bledsoe enters the room. He is out of breath and pushing his dark hair to the side with his hands.

"She's up!" he says.

"All the scans are negative," Marlene toots.

"I heard," Brill says. "Just ran into Dr. Nebraska in the hallway."

"Neboshik," Marlene corrects him.

"Nebraska, Neboshik, Nabisco . . . Hey, kiddo," he says, greeting his daughter.

"Hey," Corinthia says.

He takes the side of the bed opposite Marlene and leans over and kisses Corinthia on the forehead.

"Sorry if I stink," Corinthia says.

"You smell fine," he replies.

"Cloris brought her a gift," Marlene announces in a voice that might be more effectively used in an arts-and-crafts class for third-graders.

"What'd she bring you?" Brill asks his daughter.

"A triangle," Marlene says.

Brill says, "I didn't know geometry had healing powers."

"It's the kind of triangle you *play*," Marlene says. "With the little thingy."

"Oh!" Brill says, feigning ignorance. "The *instrument!*"

Marlene says, "Don't be a dang ding-dong. . . . It's

apparently some kind of special inside joke between she and Cloris."

"Between *her* and Cloris," Corinthia corrects her mother.

"I mean *her* and Cloris," Marlene says. "All hail the grammar queen."

"Sounds like they're gonna let you come home tomorrow," Brill says to his daughter.

"But she's gotta take it easy," Marlene interjects. "You gotta take it easy, you hear me, Cori?"

Corinthia says, "Aye, aye, Cap'n."

"And we think it would be wise for you to pay a visit to Dr. Flung. Right, Brill?"

"A session or two couldn't hurt," he says.

"I've already spoken with her," Marlene adds, "and she's real keen on seeing you."

"You good with that?" Brill asks his daughter.

Corinthia nods again.

Marlene touches Corinthia's cheek with the back of her hand and allows it to remain there for a moment. With this forced tenderness, the little ICU room seems to acquire a strange density. When she can't stand it any longer, Marlene pulls her hand away.

"Any news about Channing?" Corinthia eventually asks her father.

"No," Brill replies soberly. "The police looked

in the woods over by the frontage road, their thinking being that maybe those gray wolves had gotten to him, but all they found were a half dozen deer carcasses."

The grisly image renders the room silent. There is only the sound of Corinthia's IV unit pushing fluid through the tubing, as well as some indecipherable hospital ambience beyond the room: murmuring nurses, beeping machines, the squealing wheels of mystery carts . . .

"In other news, FirmaMall went out of business," Corinthia says in a goofy news anchor's voice. "No more stone Sasquatches or Gears of Time Sculptural Clocks to brighten our homes and gardens. What's a consumer to do?"

Marlene crosses her arms and squints at her daughter as if to say, *Okay, you got me this time, missy, but it's open season now.*

Corinthia simply smiles back at Marlene. She's sure to force her lips together, sparing her mother the monstrous vision of her teeth.

"Well, it's good we got Chet when we did," Brill says, half joking. "What on earth would we do without Chet?"

The three of them share a halfhearted familial chuckle that, more than anything else, serves to relieve the tension.

And then, after another silence, Corinthia finally asks what she's been dying to know for the past few days. She's resisted posing the question to Dr. Neboshik or to the various nurses and technicians of St. Anthony's out of fear that they might think she's crazy. As far as they know, she's in the ICU because she had some sort of stress-related breakdown and bumped her head on her living-room floor; that she's being evaluated for concussion-like symptoms; and, because of her past relationship with an exceptional life-altering tumor, they have to rule out certain things. But the fact of the matter is, her actual sanity isn't the thing being evaluated.

She's been looking forward to her father's arrival because she knows he will tell her the truth. She reaches toward Brill Bledsoe and gently grabs his wrist.

"They came, didn't they?" Corinthia finally says.

Marlene looks at Brill, reminding her husband of twenty years about honoring their agreement regarding a particular off-limits subject.

To her daughter she says, "Who came, sweetheart?"

"The geese," Corinthia replies.

Marlene shoots Brill an unblinking dead-eyed stare so intense it almost has a sound. He looks down at his free hand. It appears as if he's somehow seeking its counsel.

"That's why Mom won't let them put a TV in my room," Corinthia continues, "because it's been on the news, right?"

No response.

"Just tell me," Corinthia pleads.

Brill finally looks up.

"Yes," he says to his daughter, "the geese came."

After a breathless silence, Marlene says, "That's some coincidence, huh?"

Corinthia looks to her father, who can only manage to offer a sad, knowing half smile.

The following morning, at home, Corinthia places her prescription bottle of Valium (one pill, twice daily, or as needed; take with food) on her dresser, beside all her other meds. A small clump of mail has been left on her desk: a few more brochures from prospective colleges (St. Olaf College, Grinnell College, Clarke University) and a postcard from her favorite thrift store, announcing a sale.

Corinthia treads downstairs as quietly as she can and goes into the garage, where her custom-made school desk is leaning against the wall. It appears to be relatively unscathed, until Corinthia turns it around and notices two crude rectangular blocks of black paint. Someone has obviously painted over something. From her father's jumbled collection of supplies scattered about a convoluted metal shelving system, Corinthia grabs a small vat of turpentine and an old rag. She douses the rag and gets to work on the first black rectangle.

The chemical smell of the turpentine sharpens her Valium-softened senses. Her entire being seems to expand. Her breath quickens. She suddenly smells the various odors of the garage: spilled motor oil, the nitrogen in the Miracle-Gro that Marlene uses for her little garden in the backyard, the gasoline in the spare tank in the corner.

After a moment, the letters FUM, also in black, emerge. She immediately starts to work on the lower rectangular block, with even greater fervor now. Neither Marlene nor Brill Bledsoe knows what their daughter is up to. Marlene is out running errands and Brill, who stayed home from work today, is on the phone in the kitchen.

Who blocked out these words? Corinthia wonders.

Was it Denton Smock?

Or the freshman boy who returned my desk?

Was it my mother?

After she works the turpentine into the lower, larger block, in what seems like a matter of seconds, the following four words, applied with tar, seem to radiate out of the wood grain as if the desk itself had willed the thought:

DOWN WITH THE GIANT

Just beyond the desk, underneath a pair of old rawhide, multistained work gloves, Corinthia spots a quart of paint and a small edging brush covered in black semigloss, still somewhat damp to the touch.

12

October 1, 2015

Dave,

It's been a few weeks — I know. Have you
missed me?

I'm sorry I haven't talked to you in a
while, but a lot's been happening. Scholastic,
social, and personal events. For instance, at
school, the main building has been repaired
and all the Airstream trailers are gone.

This girl in my social studies class, Britney
Purina, who is famous for her Instagram skills,
left her iPhone in Airstream number two, and
she will likely never partake of this device's
services again. Britney Purina is always text-
ing and Instagramming and Snapchatting
during social studies, practically right in Mrs.
Gluber's face, so I think she is deserving of
her fate.

What was weird and quite unfair was that Britney Purina accused me of stealing her iPhone.

"He's the one who took it," she told Mrs. Gluber, pointing directly at me. "The Ball Boy did it!"

Yes, that's what people are starting to call me now, Dave: the Ball Boy. Not cool, or in any way legendary, I know. I will have to devise a plan to somehow reverse this unfortunate nickname.

But when Mrs. Gluber asked me if what Britney Purina was saying was true, I told her that it wasn't and that I would never do a thing like that because of my various codes of goodness, citizenship, and honor.

"Check the Ball Boy's book bag," Britney ordered Mrs. Gluber. "Check his creepy book bag!"

But Mrs. Gluber refused to, because she said this action would have violated my student rights.

"Ball Boys don't have any rights!" Britney Purina said.

"That's enough, Britney," Mrs. Gluber said to her, and then it was over.

Dave, I'd like to point out that my book bag is in no way, shape, or form creepy. I think it's quite original, actually, because despite the fact that it's a polyester JanSport book bag, it features the face of Sitting Bull, a 19th-century Sioux warrior chief who ruled the Lakota tribe. I ordered this great patch from the Internet and sewed it on myself with skills that I learned in freshman home economics. During the first week of classes, I was named Sewer of the Day, which made me proud, but other students used this information against me and started asking me if I would fix the busted crotch in their pants or sew my own vagina shut, which caused many to laugh and sneer at my expense.

Chief Bull is especially famous for massacring General Custer and his 700 soldiers at the Battle of Little Bighorn. He had visions and was a great leader.

Nothing else came of Britney Purina's accusation, but she was already throwing high-level shade my way. You could almost see it throbbing out of her eyes. If her shade had had a color, it would have been electric pink.

During lunch she came over to the Frog

table, where Keiko Cho, Durdin Royko, and I were minding our own business, and she told me that if I had her fucking iPhone 6, I'd better fucking give it to her or Todd fucking Chicklis and Bronson fucking Kaminski were going to fucking butt-fuck me with my own fucking Fisher-Price baby Ball Boy boner, which doesn't even seem anatomically possible, Dave, but all I could do was sit there and listen to her call me Billy Ball Boy and list the many different kinds of rapes I will receive with my own Fisher-Price baby Ball Boy boner, while everybody in the cafeteria stopped eating and watched.

Dave, my body got so tense that it felt like I was turning into tin. I know you don't actually have a body, because you're mostly paper and cardboard, but if you did possess a human body and you experienced an attack of this proportion from a popular girl of the caliber and prettiness of Britney Purina, I think you would know what I'm talking about. By the way, I just realized that your metal spiral spine thing that keeps these pages together might be tin, but I'm pretty certain it's actually aluminum, which isn't tin but it's close. Or maybe it's copper. And copper is also close to tin. Maybe you know a little bit about this feeling after all.

So anyway, Britney Purina was announcing to me and the rest of the cafeteria how she was going to basically use her pretty-girl power to make Todd Chicklis and Bronson Kaminski force me to rape myself with my own Fisher-Price baby Ball Boy boner, and every time I thought she was getting close to the moment when she might stop verbally assaulting me, it would just get worse and worse, and my stomach started making terrible gurgling sounds, and I thought I would expel gas, and I kept getting more and more frozen. I could even see into the food service area, where Camila, my beautiful Mexican princess, was watching from behind a bin of pizza pockets. When I saw her deep-brown eyes staring back at me, I felt like I was shrinking, like I was turning into a penny, but instead of the penny having Abraham Lincoln's face on it, it was my face. I would no longer be a human, Dave. I would be a penny for the rest of my life.

But then something amazing happened, Dave, something that made me feel like there are good forces in the world, and it was this:

While Britney Purina was unleashing her wrath of words upon me, that extremely tall girl, Corinthia Bledsoe — the one who predicted the tornadoes — stormed into the cafeteria. She stormed into the cafeteria with great force and passion, and she stood between Britney Purina and the Frog table. Corinthia Bledsoe isn't even supposed to be in school, Dave! She's supposed to be serving a suspension for exhibiting extreme behavior. What happened was she accidentally destroyed school property, even though she knew the tornadoes were coming and was just trying to be a good citizen and warn everyone. I'm pretty sure that Principal Ticonderoga, Vice Principal Mejerus, and Guidance Counselor Smock think Corinthia Bledsoe is somehow responsible for general scholastic pandemonium. Or that maybe she's some kind of evil high-school witch. She did break a door, Dave, I will admit that, but it was only because she was trying so hard to communicate her vision. I highly doubt that Sitting Bull got in trouble for communicating his visions. If anything, he was more respected for communicating them.

So anyway, Corinthia Bledsoe stormed through the cafeteria's double doors, and it only took her, like, four steps to reach the Frog table. When she got there, she stood between us and Britney Purina, and she told Britney Purina to go sit down.

She said, "Sit the fuck down, Britney."

And she said it calm, like she was filled with a powerful force; like God was inside her with a secret microphone, telling her to do it, so she could act with tranquility because she knew she was carrying out a master plan of the highest level.

Her calmness was one of the most amazing things I've ever seen, Dave.

All Britney Purina could do was stare up at Corinthia Bledsoe, and like I already said, she's really, really, really tall, like seven feet something, and then Corinthia Bledsoe stopped being calm and shouted "GO!" and then "NOW!"

And then Britney Purina turned and scurried away to the other side of the cafeteria, where she was sitting with her pretty, popular friends, and they had a hard time looking at her when she sat down, because they were so clearly embarrassed for her.

Then Corinthia Bledsoe took a can of spray paint out of her pocket, because her pockets are huge, Dave, and with hissing black spray paint, she wrote the word FUM across the front of her plain white shirt, and then she shouted in a heraldic manner. And this is what she shouted, Dave. She shouted, "THE GIANT WILL NOT FALL!"

It was like she was turning herself into a statue of justice.

What was so cool about it, besides the fact that she defended me, is that since she predicted the tornadoes, all these FUMs have been appearing throughout the school. Someone even painted one on the shed where they keep the track-and-field hurdles. This kid in my homeroom, Willy Binobo, said that there was even a FUM spray-painted on the Lugo water tower. But it was like she took all those FUMs and put them into the one that she spray-painted on her shirt. And it somehow made her more powerful, Dave. I think it made her invincible.

And, yes, this is also the same extremely tall girl who said that those birds would come when everyone was gathered in the field house for the all-school assembly. And they did come, Dave, like three thousand Canada geese arrived and ate all the grass on the football field, and it's now in a permanent state of depression. It took this entire group of animal social workers from the ASPCA in Carbondale to come and help get rid of the geese. It was on the news and everything. You should see the football field, Dave. I've never seen a bigger field of solid mud, and it smells terrible because the Canada geese defecated thousands of gruesome feces droppings all over it.

Anyway, after she shouted, Corinthia Bledsoe just continued to stand there. It was almost like she was in church or something, like God was telling her what to do.

And then she turned and thanked me for returning her desk, because I returned her desk to her because the school was just going to throw it out. I know this because I found it by the Dumpsters, and I knew it was hers because I'd seen her carrying it around the halls. It was one of the most physically demanding things I've ever done, even more demanding than the time I hiked multiple miles of the Indiana Dunes with my dad when I was eleven. The desk was really heavy, but I took several breaks and tapped into the man that I will be after I go through puberty and all my hormones start working properly.

After dropping the desk off at Corinthia Bledsoe's house on Stained Glass Drive, when I finally arrived home, I even went into the bathroom and checked to see if I had grown any pubic hair during my journey, but I was still bald.

Anyway, in the cafeteria, Corinthia Bledsoe said, "Thank you for returning my desk."

"You're welcome," I said.

And then she walked out of the cafeteria and disappeared.

My stomach was gurgling. Keiko Cho and Durdin Royko continued to finish their lunches. No one harassed us for the rest of the lunch period, and I stopped feeling like I was turning into a penny.

The List continues to grow, Dave.

I have officially added the following six people:

       4. Troy Aurora

       5. Nate Bluff

       6. Britney Purina

       7. Todd Chicklis

       8. Bronson Kaminski

       9. Ward Newbury

So, some more stuff happened after the cafeteria incident. I am going to tell you about that now, Dave, but first I have to use the bathroom. Excuse me. . . .

Okay, I'm back. Sorry about that.

Anyway, later, in English, we were talking about the lotus-eaters from Homer's epic poem The Odyssey, which is about King Odysseus and the survivors of his army's journey home after the fall of Troy. The lotus-eaters were these people who lived on an undiscovered island that Odysseus's ship happened upon. Odysseus was headed west to Ithaca, but the mighty north winds blew his vessel off course. So, Dave, the lotus-eaters were the inhabitants of this island and they derived all their nourishment from nutrients found in this special flower called the lotus flower. All these people ate were lotus flowers, which apparently make you really, really, really happy and content and you'll want nothing more than to stay on the island forever and you won't ever get sad.

After eating the lotus flowers, the men in King Odysseus's army had to be physically forced back to their ship because they were suddenly so happy and satisfied and nothing else mattered.

I must say I was really enjoying this discussion, Dave. Those lotus flowers are quite fascinating to me. It made me think of how the Native Americans eat peyote and turn themselves into hawks and buffaloes. I wonder what nutrients and chemicals exist in these flowers to give them so many powers. I wonder how one might obtain a lotus flower. I wonder if they sell them at the nursery at Walmart, or if you have to special-order them. I also wonder what one tastes like. Is it like parsley? Or like something in a salad? I plan on investigating this subject more in-depthly on the Internet. I'd like to maybe give one to Mom, who is still very unhappy about my dad being dead.

Mrs. Kenosha even projected an ancient picture of Odysseus pulling two of his men away from the lotus-eaters by their hair because they had eaten too many flowers and they'd lost their battle helmets and forgotten all their sorrow and pain and the fact that they were trying to get home, where they had wives and children and pets who were waiting for them.

I was raising my hand, about to contribute to the discussion, when Vice Principal Mejerus interrupted the class and walked over and whispered into Mrs. Kenosha's ear. And then she nodded and turned to me and said that my presence was being requested at the principal's office.

"Why?" I said. "What did I do?"

"Please come with me, Billy," Vice Principal Mejerus said.

I wanted to tell Mrs. Kenosha and the class how great it would be to be able to take everyone's pain away by giving them a lotus flower to eat, how forgetting sad stuff can be a good thing.

As I was walking out of class, I tried to ask Mrs. Kenosha where they sold lotus flowers in Lugo, but she looked away.

"Can you get them at Target?" I asked as Vice Principal Mejerus took my arm like we were maybe going to square-dance. But Mrs. Kenosha kept looking away and wouldn't say anything.

As we were walking down the hall, Vice

Principal Mejerus hardly said a word to me. And he wouldn't let go of my arm, which made me feel like I was going to get beaten to death.

"Are you going to beat me to death?" I asked him.

"Am I going to do *what*?" he asked.

"Beat me to death," I repeated.

"Why would I do that?" he replied.

When we got to the principal's office, Guidance Counselor Smock was sitting in one of the two chairs across from Principal Ticonderoga, who was behind her desk, tapping a pencil.

Vice Principal Mejerus released my arm, and Principal Ticonderoga gestured toward the empty chair.

She said, "Take a seat, William."

I asked Guidance Counselor Smock what he was doing there, but he wouldn't answer me.

"Please sit," Vice Principal Mejerus said. He was standing behind me now, sort of blocking the door.

"Are you going to beat me to death?" I asked Principal Ticonderoga.

She said, "William, now why on earth would you think that?"

"Because everyone's throwing so much shade," I told her.

"Shade?" she said. "What's shade?"

Guidance Counselor Smock explained to her that it was a modern expression that means "a threatening attitude."

"Well, we certainly don't mean to throw any shade at you," Principal Ticonderoga said. "That's not our intention. But I think we'd all appreciate it if you'd sit."

So then I sat, and nobody said anything, and I started to feel like tin again, and Principal Ticonderoga was tapping her pencil.

There's this picture of President Obama on the wall behind Principal Ticonderoga's desk, and he's smiling and his teeth are very white and his gums are very chocolaty-looking and he appears to be so kind and helpful, and I wished I could somehow make him come to life and be there with me.

Come on, Obama, I said with my mind. Help me, Mr. President. Don't let them beat me to death.

Then Principal Ticonderoga stopped tapping her pencil, and she leaned forward and said how sorry she was about my dad passing and how she can't even imagine how hard that must be to deal with and that she'd spoken to my mother after he died and how my mother had expressed her concern over my well-being and how everyone in her office at that very moment was also concerned for my well-being, and I think she might have used the word "well-being" three or four more times, and then she got to the real reason why I was called down to her office, which was that she wanted to see you, Dave! She wanted to see you!

"I understand you've been writing in a diary," she said. "And that according to Mr. Smock, you may be in the process of creating some kind of a list."

Dave, I was so angry, I couldn't help throwing Mr. Smock some shade. I looked at him and tried to throw him some of the shadiest shade possible, but he wouldn't look back at me.

Then Principal Ticonderoga said, "It's Mr. Smock's duty as a member of this faculty to alert my office if he feels that the safety of your fellow students is in any way at risk."

From behind me, Vice Principal Mejerus said, "He's just doing his job."

I really tried to get Mr. Smock to look at me, Dave, but he wouldn't.

Then Principal Ticonderoga said, "We'd like to see this list, William."

And before I knew it, I was ribbitting like a frog! I really was, Dave, I was going, "Ribbit! Ribbit-ribbit-ribbit! Ribbit-ribbit-ribbit! Ribbit-ribbit!" And then I stopped, and there was a long silence, and I expelled some gas, and it made a noise like a senior citizen sighing in a basement.

I told them I was sorry for expelling gas and that I had forgotten to take my simethicone after lunch.

"It's okay, Billy," Vice Principal Mejerus said. "We all have to toot sometimes."

I thought it was strange how Vice Principal Mejerus was calling me Billy and Principal Ticonderoga was calling me William. It was like they were playing a game.

Then I said that if I wasn't allowed to go to my locker and take my medication, I might wind up expelling so much terrible-smelling gas that they would have no choice but to suspend me the way they suspended Corinthia Bledsoe, and my stomach made some gurgling sounds like ocean monsters from dinosaur times, and then Principal Ticonderoga looked at Guidance Counselor Smock, and I think he communicated with her telepathically that I was indeed telling the truth, so she let me go. She said I could go take my medication but that I had to come right back to her office so we could get to the bottom of this so-called list. And then I thanked her and turned around and took a step toward the door, and Vice Principal Mejerus moved out of the way, and I left.

But what I did after I left, Dave, what I did was, I went straight to my locker and grabbed my book bag, which has you in it, as well as my simethicone, and I quietly closed my locker and walked very calmly down the hall in a very Native American fashion, meaning I used very quiet feet, so quiet they were like whispers, and I walked through the front doors and across the parking lot and past the new flagpole, and as soon as I was off the school grounds, I ran home as fast as I could.

Luckily for me Mom was gone, but I had to act fast and not get fatigued and concentrate on my next task, which was to tear all these pages out of you, Dave, meaning the

ones I have written so far, which totals fourteen pages. And then in the same notebook,
the same one with the green graph paper
that Guidance Counselor Smock gave me, I
recopied each page as best as I could, with
excellent speed and accuracy, but whenever I
mentioned anything about The List, I added a
bunch of <u>new</u> material that suggested that the
people on The List were all the people who I
<u>admired</u>, not <u>disliked</u> in any way. And I added
a bunch of other people, too, like Corinthia
Bledsoe and my English literature teacher,
Mrs. Kenosha, and the two other Frogs, Keiko
Cho and Durdin Royko. And I even wrote
things I liked about them. For instance, beside
Keiko Cho's name I wrote "polite eater," and
beside Mrs. Kenosha's name I wrote "likes to
teach," and beside Corinthia Bledsoe's name I
wrote "Warrior Prophet."

It took me almost two hours to complete
this other version of you, Dave, and while I
was doing it, the phone rang several times,
and I'm quite confident that it was Principal
Ticonderoga or Vice Principal Mejerus or
Guidance Counselor Smock, or maybe it was
all three of them gathered around the phone
like some witches around a cauldron.

So I have no doubt that I will be in serious trouble when I go back to school tomorrow, Dave. I'm sure Vice Principal Mejerus will be waiting for me at my locker and he'll grab me by the arm in a square-dancing fashion and escort me right to Principal Ticonderoga's office and Guidance Counselor Smock will be there, and maybe they'll beat me with belts or make me do push-ups or certain impossible exercises from the Presidential Physical Fitness Test, like they'll make me do a hundred sit-ups or run in place until I collapse and crack my head open on the floor, but I don't care, Dave. I don't care, because now there's The Real Dave but there's also The Fake Dave. And The Real List and The Fake List. And after they beat me or torture me with physical fitness tests, I will take The Fake Dave out of my Sitting Bull book bag and I'll hand it over to them. It won't be the Dave that I'm writing in now, which is in this completely different notebook, one I used for my eighth-grade American history class. I've even crossed off "American History" and below it I've written "The Real Dave."

And I will continue to add people to The Real List, and no one will ever know what it really is, especially Guidance Counselor Smock and Vice Principal Mejerus and Principal Ticonderoga, who, by the way, are now officially on The Real List.

> 10. Guidance Counselor Denton Smock
> 11. Vice Principal Mejerus
> 12. Principal Ticonderoga

Later, when Mom came home, things got pretty weird. She entered the house, calling my name, and when I came down to the kitchen, she said that someone from the principal's office had called her cell phone, wondering if she'd heard from me, and that she told them she hadn't and was worried sick about me disappearing just like that star football player, and she wanted to know what happened, and I started to tell her, I really did, but I kept getting distracted, and I couldn't keep my focus because, when I really looked at her, Dave, when I stopped trying to tell her what exactly had happened and looked hard at her face, I could see that there was something very different about her. I didn't say anything, Dave, I just stored it, but there was something very strange going on with her face, and when she asked me where on earth I had been, I told her that I came straight home and that this is where I've been since I left school, and when she asked me why I didn't go back to Principal Ticonderoga's office like I'd promised, I told her that I was too embarrassed, that I was expelling terrible gas all the way down the hall, and it was so much gas that my anus and testicles were burning with fire, and that I was worried that the simethicone wouldn't make any difference because my stomach was already gurgling so much, which made me so humiliated and afraid that when I got to my locker and took out my book bag to get my medication, I just left because then I could expel gas in the Lugo community and the terrible sounds and smells wouldn't offend anyone except maybe an old man picking weeds out of his lawn or the Chinese FedEx woman with the knee brace, and then Mom took her phone out of her purse and called Principal Ticonderoga, and when she came on the phone, Mom explained the situation with a sincere heartfelt voice and told her how I was right there with her now and how embarrassed and ashamed I was, and it must have worked, because when she got off the phone, she said everything was okay and that I wasn't in any trouble but that I was supposed to report directly to the principal's office tomorrow morning with my notebook, and that made me feel pretty relieved, Dave — it really did.

And then, as Mom was looking at me and I was looking at her, it suddenly dawned on me. I could see what was so different about her.

Mom said, "What? What's wrong?"

And then I asked her if she was wearing a wig.

I said, "Is that a wig?"

She said, "You can tell?"

I nodded, and then she pulled it off, and she made a face like it hurt when she did it. Underneath the wig was this little flesh-colored cap made of panty hose material, and Mom took that off too and balled it up and threw it to the floor, and her hair underneath the little flesh-colored panty hose thing was all thin and matted and looked like a cat's hair after you throw the cat in the shower and blast the water.

"It keeps falling out," Mom said, touching her hair. "I went to the doctor, but they say nothing's wrong."

One little part above her ear was curling up on its own. It was like an old man's hair.

"It's Dad," I told her.

Mom asked me what I meant by that.

"He's pulling it out," I said.

Then she slapped me hard across the face, Dave. She really hit me hard, and it was loud, too. Some of the slap also hit my ear and made it ring.

"Because you're sad," I said. "His spirit is pulling it out little by little until there's nothing left."

My ear was really ringing, but I just kept talking.

I told her that when it finally grew back she wouldn't be sad anymore.

She asked me how I could possibly know something like this and I told her that I just did.

She said, "Do you read this stuff?"

"I just know it," I said.

She said, "Well, then why isn't he pulling your hair out?"

I told her it was because I'm not sad.

"Why not?" she said. "Why aren't you sad?"

"I'm just not," I said.

"Then, what in God's name <u>are</u> you?" she asked.

She was crying now, Dave, like really, really crying with a lot of dramatic feeling.

I said, "I'm Billy."

"Not <u>who</u> are you," she said. "<u>What</u> are you? Are you a <u>boy</u>? Are you a <u>robot</u>? Do you even have <u>feelings</u>?"

I know I'm underlining a lot of words in this entry, but that's because things were quite expressive, and excessive volume was being used. But I couldn't answer Mom's questions, Dave. I had no idea what to say. The only thing that came to mind was that I wasn't a robot, so that's what I said.

"I'm not a robot," I told her.

She was on the floor now. She was on her hands and knees, facing down like a dog that had broken the rules. She was acting like <u>I</u> was the one who'd slapped <u>her</u>.

"I'm a boy," I said.

But she just cried and cried.

And then I told her I wished he could take my place, "he" meaning my dad, and that

I would trade my life for his if I could, and I meant it when I said it, Dave — I swear I did.

I told her I just needed to find the log.

"What log?" she said.

"The log on the mythical river," I said.

I tried to explain the whole thing to her, about how my dad can't find the log and how he's wandering around in the garden looking for his watch and how the wolves from the newspaper are in the forest by the frontage road protecting the log and how if I did this one thing, this one very important thing, I could help my dad get to it so he could cross the mythical river and pass into the spirit world, but nothing was coming out right, the words were all confused and in the wrong order, and Mom was crying now and her body looked really exhausted and her dark-brown wig was over in the corner and it sort of looked like a shot bird, so I went over and picked it up and started petting it so it wouldn't be so messy and dead-looking, but when I tried to put it back on her head, she said, "Don't you dare, you little shit!" and she sort of hissed that phrase like a feral cat, Dave, so I didn't do it. I didn't dare do that, no way. Then Mom opened the silverware drawer and grabbed something and slammed the drawer shut and forced whatever it was into my hand, and when I looked down, I could see that I was holding my dad's watch.

"There's his goddamn watch," Mom said. "Happy?"

I didn't know what else to do, so I left the kitchen and went upstairs.

Up in my room, I could still hear Mom crying, which went on for a long time. It sounded like she'd been knifed in a forest and left there to die.

The thing about Mom is she's not a mean person at all. She's never slapped me and she's never cursed in front of me, either. These events made me very sad for her.

Later I went back down to check on her, and she was curled up on the floor, at the foot of the refrigerator. It was like she was waiting for a secret knock.

The secret knock would come, and then she'd wake up and stand and open the refrigerator door, and there he'd be, my dad, exactly as he was before he fell face-first into his plate at the dinner table, like he'd just returned from a long trip and had thousands of stories to tell, like maybe he rode an asteroid or communed with some aliens and taught them the state capitals or met God, who sort of looked like that actor Jeff Bridges and was maybe wearing a corduroy coat with a falcon on it.

Then I would hand him his watch, and he'd smile and thank me and maybe pat me on the head.

And after that, they would step to the side, and I would walk into the refrigerator.

"Good-bye, Billy," Mom would say, closing the door behind me.

"Be brave, son," my dad would say. "Don't forget to take your medication."

13

In the basement of the Church of Our Merciful Savior, on Eleventh Street, just north of Muhammad Ali Boulevard in downtown Louisville, with the help of Sturm Fullilove and Clinette Sloper, Marlene Bledsoe is in the process of securing a white sheet to one of the paneled walls. She is first up at PGDC's Tuesday-night meeting—it's going to be her first share—and her hand is shaking so much, she can't quite drive the thumbtack into a channeled groove of the weathered wood. Tonight a faint electricity charges the normally slightly fungal air of the small meeting space.

Knowing about Marlene's important evening through an e-mail from the PGDC leader, Shepard Montrose, everyone is in a festive mood. For instance, Chauncey Shore, normally a quiet man who rarely shakes hands or hugs anyone, gently squeezed Marlene's shoulder when she arrived. And Sturm Fullilove brought twice as many Krispy Kreme dough-nuts. This is the general treatment one receives on the night of their first share.

"Lemme help you, Maylene," Clinette Sloper says. Marlene hands her the thumbtack and steps back.

Others who are present for this week's meeting are Clinette Sloper's husband, Spinner, who just finished arranging a dozen whole-grain apple-spiced muffins on a few sections of paper towels, Shepard Montrose, whose thick white hair seems a little yellow this evening, Chauncey Shore, who, in a matter of minutes has already eaten two of Sturm Fullilove's Krispy Kremes, Amy Rubbentugh, a first-timer with cystic acne who drove all the way over from Lexington, and last but not least, Lemon Tidwell, who walked in only moments ago carrying a big cardboard dispenser of Veranda Blend Coffee from Starbucks.

"Sorry I'm late, everybody," Lemon apologized. The smell of his aftershave sent a jolt of longing through Marlene's kidneys so potent that she almost wet herself. A little might even have squirted out, in fact, and she had to go to the ladies' room to make sure it wasn't showing through the crotch of her Talbots stretch khakis that she's worn especially for him.

Although it's the second week of October, Marlene is sweating so much that she regrets not having worn a darker blouse, which would better hide any pit or neckline stains. But she absolutely *had* to wear the baby-blue Eileen Fisher top with the banded hemline that she picked up from the mall in Kaskaskia.

"That's great on you," the young salesgirl told her after she came out of the fitting room. "It's very Connie Britton. Your husband's gonna love it."

After Eileen Fisher, Marlene spent another hour at the Best Buy back in Lugo, where she purchased a state-of-the-art projection device that plugs into an iPhone's mini-USB port and displays hi-res images in a slide-show format.

Once the sheet is secured to the wall, everyone gathers around the buffet table, except Spinner Sloper, who is stationed by the door, ready to kill the lights when cued.

Marlene stands in front of the projection sheet while the others look on.

Shepard Montrose, who is the last one to settle in, places one of Sturm Fullilove's Krispy Kremes on a napkin, sits, and says, "Whenever you're ready, Marlene. Take your time."

Marlene takes a deep breath and closes her eyes.

"Hello," she says, opening her eyes.

"Hello," the group echoes.

Marlene bobs back and forth in her white, sporty Dexflex Comfort stretch flats.

"As most of you know," she begins, "I'm Marlene Bledsoe and I have a disfigured child and this is my first share."

"You get it, girl," Clinette Sloper says encouragingly.

Marlene nods to Spinner Sloper, who kills the lights. She then touches her phone and the first image is projected onto the sheet. It's a picture of a baby with chubby cheeks, a faint strip of hair, and large, wondrous eyes.

"Channing Taylor Bledsoe was born on May eighteenth, nineteen ninety-seven," she begins, facing the white sheet, standing to the left of it. "A quiet baby who loved to nurse, Channing often slept through the night."

Marlene touches her phone again, and the second image is projected: Channing as a young boy. He is wearing shorts and a baseball shirt with green sleeves and is holding the first fish he caught.

"This is Channing at seven," Marlene says. "Here he is just after he caught his first fish on Rend Lake. A smallmouth bass that weighed over four pounds. Pretty impressive for a kid his age."

She touches her phone again and the next picture is of Channing as a freshman in high school. He stares directly at the camera, and there is a pimple on his chin, the slightest fuzz on his cheeks. He is wearing a blue button-down oxford-cloth shirt and boasts only the faintest smile.

"This is his freshman picture at Lugo Memorial High School," she continues. "I asked him to wear my favorite shirt that day, and he did. Such a sweetheart. Look how thick that hair is. I don't think anyone could possibly anticipate how handsome and strong he'd turn out to be."

She touches her iPhone again, this time producing an impressive action photo of Channing in full cream-and-crimson Lugo Memorial football regalia. He's airborne, flying into the end zone, his body almost parallel with the turf, his muscular arms outstretched, about to catch a football. There is a defender on his heels, also airborne.

"Channing caught this thirty-two-yard pass in the closing seconds of the fourth quarter," Marlene explains proudly, "which sealed the conference championship for Lugo Memorial. As a junior, he was named First-Team All-Conference and First-Team All-State for Class One-A in Illinois. A photographer from the *Chicago Tribune* took that picture. They wound up running a story on Channing, who is believed to be a rare small-school find with Division One —"

Suddenly the lights snap on. Spinner Sloper is standing beside the entrance, his hand on the light switch.

He says, "Where you goin' with this, Maylene?"

Everyone at the table is squinting and shielding their eyes from the harsh light.

"Where am I going?" Marlene replies, somehow unfazed by the blast of fluorescence, but clearly confused.

Chauncey Shore runs his hand through his white-yellow hair and says, "Did somethin' happen to your boy, Mylene?"

"I don't understand," she replies.

"Unless this is goin' somewhere," Clinette Sloper adds, "I don't see how these photos are pertinent."

Everyone stares at Marlene, indignant. Even the new woman, Amy Rubbentugh, seems agitated, her heavy arms crossed in front of her.

Marlene can suddenly hear a faint buzzing in her head.

"Am I doing something wrong?" she asks, bringing her fingertips to her temples. "Can you not see the images?"

"We can see the images fine, Marlene," Shepard Montrose replies calmly. "I'm sorry to say this, but I think Spinner has a point."

"Point?" Marlene says, feeling the room start to tilt a bit. "What point?"

"Well," Shepard Montrose starts in gently, "I'm

not sure anyone here understands what you're *sharing*. We've all shown one another very difficult images. We've shared the most intimate details about our children. This group exists to foster a safe environment in which to have a dialogue about the challenges that come with having a grotesquely disfigured child."

"We showed you our son!" Spinner Sloper says, upset. "All those pictures of DeMarcus! He ain't no superstar quarterback!"

"Is this s'posed to be some typa ignorant joke?" Clinette Sloper adds.

"Mylene," Chauncey Shore interjects, muffin crumbs all down the front of his red-plaid sixties madras shirt, "there just doesn't appear to be anything wrong with your son."

"Do he got like *burn marks* on him or somethin'?" Sturm Fullilove asks.

"Burn marks?" Marlene cries, suddenly beside herself with rage. She is starting to lose her balance and has to push against the paneled wall. "Of course Channing doesn't have burn marks!"

"Did he get bit up by a *dog*?" Spinner Sloper asks from his post near the entrance.

"I thought you were comin' to these meetings because of your *daughter*," Clinette says.

Marlene can feel the walls closing in on her.

She can practically see the grooves in the paneling expanding into fault lines. It suddenly feels as if a cold, invisible hand is squeezing her heart.

Lemon Tidwell finally speaks. His deep, steady voice is like a prayer being answered.

"I think Marlene's just confused," he offers. "I have no doubt that she's here for the right reasons. She's just confused."

"Marlene?" Shepard Montrose says to her. "Can you explain yourself?"

Marlene takes in the group. Her face flushes, and her nostrils flare. Her pupils contract down to pinpoints.

"You know nothing about my son!" she seethes through her teeth. "Nothing! He's a scholastic hero! He's a Lugo legend!"

Marlene quickly turns and claws at the sheet, which tears in one corner. The thumbtack in the opposite corner shoots off the wall and strikes newcomer Amy Rubbentugh, the slope-shouldered shy woman with the heavy arms and cystic acne, square between the eyes, and although it's the flat side that connects with her, a sound flies out of her mouth that's not unlike the shriek of a spooked jungle bird. The thumbtack skitters across the table and into Chauncey Shore's party-size bag of sea-salt-and-vinegar potato chips.

"Careful with those chips," Chauncey warns the group.

And now Marlene Bledsoe is down on one knee, and her body is convulsing soundlessly with some strange combination of grief, confusion, and exhaustion. Her arms swim out in slow motion. It's as if she's performing the animal expression of some unfathomable emotion that manifests equally as flying and drowning.

Amy Rubbentugh, whose own arms are now oddly suspended above her head, is looking at the bag of sea-salt-and-vinegar potato chips with such unblinking intensity, it seems as if she is willing it to transform into a portal through which she can escape.

Lemon Tidwell reaches down and gathers Marlene Bledsoe under her hot, moist armpits and helps her to her feet.

She stares at his bristly mustache and opens and closes her mouth, but no sound comes out.

"Let's go get some air," he says.

The smell of Lemon Tidwell's aftershave—that manly funk of musk and smoky spices—seems to momentarily calm Marlene. She stares up at him and finds the clear cerulean blue of his eyes and smiles the sweetest smile because she knows he understands her. He might understand her more than anyone she's ever known.

"What do you use?" Marlene asks him, drunk with his aroma now, almost swooning. "What *is* that?"

"Come on, Marlene," Lemon Tidwell says, an arm around her waist, grabbing her phone with his free hand, then her purse, while easing her across the little basement room and out the door.

14

At the Lugo district library—at the long, smooth, cherrywood young adult reading table, to be exact—Corinthia Bledsoe is studying her life sciences assignment, which covers the male procreative habits of the forty- to fifty-foot humpbacked baleen whale, whose complex ritualistic mating song is as mysterious as it is incessant. In a matter of a few paragraphs, Corinthia has learned that these stud whales will repeat each ten- to twenty-minute song for hours at a time. *This whale music must sound maddening,* she thinks. *Absolutely maddening.*

Since her suspension from school, this is her first attempt to actually complete one of the many homework assignments she's received via e-mail from Vice Principal Doogan Mejerus's office. Despite her recent lackluster performance, she has not received a single admonishment from Vice Principal Mejerus, Principal Ticonderoga, Guidance Counselor Smock, or any of her teachers, for that matter. She does find it strange that nothing has been said of her total disregard for her schoolwork. Has anyone alerted her parents? Is the faculty simply being super-understanding, considering the community concern surrounding the disappearance of her brother? Or do the adults at Lugo Memorial even care?

According to today's e-mail, Mr. Sluba will be conducting a ten-question pop quiz based on the reading assignment.

Corinthia is doing her absolute best to focus her attention on the male mating rituals of the humpbacked baleen whale, but she keeps getting lured away by the September and October issues of *The Wonderful World of Wolves*. The cover of the September issue features a large white Alaskan wolf perched at the top of a cluster of river rocks that are frothy with rapids. The wolf's mouth is wide open, its enormous jaws angled to catch a flat, airborne salmon, whose expressionless face is so detailed Corinthia can practically see the indifference in its eye. The picture is remarkable. The turbulent river is silver and black, almost gold in places . . . the incandescent flash of the salmon's skin . . . the wolf's frighteningly long, prehistoric-looking teeth.

She opens the magazine, thumbs through its glossy pages, most of which are dominated by ads for outdoor living products and services: RV dealerships, big-game tours, hiking and fishing gear companies.

The cover of the October issue features a thickly

coated black Mongolian she-wolf with eerie blue eyes, huddling with two of her cubs on a snowy embankment somewhere in Siberia.

Corinthia flips through this issue as well, looking carefully at the outdoor-living ads and Alaskan vistas and various articles about mating habits, migration patterns, and hunting strategies.

In her pocket she's been carrying the small wooden wolf that she found in Channing's bedroom. She puts it on the table and stares at it, wondering if there's some other clue as to her brother's whereabouts.

She is continuing to leaf through the October issue when Channing's girlfriend, the beautiful, honey-haired, doe-eyed Winter Hornacek, appears before her.

Did I just somehow summon her? Corinthia wonders.

Is there some sort of homing device hidden in the little wooden wolf?

"Winter," Corinthia says, closing the magazine.

"Hello, Corinthia," Winter says. She is holding a pink subject binder in front of her, her fists clutching either side of it as if she is manning a shield. Her makeup is so immaculately applied, it looks like the work of an entire team of expert cosmetics artists. Her tan cashmere turtleneck is a perfect choice to combat the early autumn chill, and also highlights the smooth slopes of her lovely breasts.

Corinthia starts to ask her how she's doing, but before she can execute the musical lift at the end of the question, Winter Hornacek lets her have it.

"You know something about Channing, don't you," she states rather evenly.

Corinthia just sits there, holding the PDF printout of her reading material.

"I *know* you know where he is," Winter adds. Her pupils and irises seem to be one entity now, both eyes almost entirely dark with the kind of righteous rage befitting a queen, or at least Lugo Memorial's Homecoming Queen.

Corinthia begins calmly, "I'm sorry, Winter, but—"

"But *what*?" Winter shouts. Her pretty face is red now, or sort of orange. She's obviously been holding her breath. Corinthia suddenly thinks her brother's girlfriend resembles the local female TV news anchor Tracy Jeopardy, who can purportedly execute over three hundred floors on the StairMaster in under an hour at Fare Thee Well Fitness, Lugo's new, state-of-the-art health club.

"You saw the tornadoes," Winter Hornacek continues. "You saw those stupid *geese*. And now you're telling me you have no idea where your *brother* is? That you can't see *him, too*? Corinthia, in case you haven't noticed, Homecoming is quickly upon us. *Homecoming!*"

Winter Hornacek breathes again—she inhales and exhales exactly three times—and continues:

"Just three months ago while Channing and I were at Six Flags Great America up in Gurnee, just after we got strapped into the Giant Drop, he gave me this charm bracelet, which he purchased at Zales! *Zales!*" Winter cries, now going into a one-handed hold of the pink binder, thrusting her bejeweled wrist into Corinthia's face. "Just after we got strapped in, he put *this* around my wrist—*THIS!* Can you *see* it?"

"I can," Corinthia says.

"And as we crested to the top of the tower, he attached THIS BRACELET to THIS WRIST with its sterling-silver clasp, and then he told me he LOVED ME and that he couldn't wait for HOMECOMING, where we would again be crowned KING AND QUEEN, and his voice cracked, it practically broke IN HALF, and then we fell twenty stories at a speed of over SIXTY MILES AN HOUR. Can you see this bracelet, Corinthia?"

Winter rotates her wrist so that the fluorescent library lights can dance off its dazzling details.

"It's a PERSONA CHARM bracelet from ZALES, and it has a SUNFLOWER and FOUR MINIATURE HEARTS and CHAMPAGNE GLASSES with CHAMPAGNE IN THEM and my BIRTHSTONE, which is an AMETHYST, and two

CUDDLING KITTENS who are obviously IN LOVE, and a bronze FOOTBALL, and this right here is a tiny MERCEDES-BENZ SL-K conVERTible, which is the car we're going to OWN someday, even though material objects don't mean a THING to EITHER of us, and THIS PERFECT LITTLE THING next to the MERCEDES happens to be a FROSTED CUP-CAKE CHARM, which features PINK and WHITE AUSTRIAN CRYSTALS! DO YOU SEE? Channing even put a little SNOOPY at the end of it because HE KNOWS HOW MUCH I LOVE *PEANUTS*!"

And just like that, Cloris Honniotis—all four feet nine inches of her—has materialized at the young adult reading table.

"Can I help you with something?" Cloris says calmly to Winter Hornacek, who has retracted her wrist and gone back to manning her pink binder like a shield.

"No!" Winter cries—and she's doing exactly that now—she's crying. "You can't help me with ANY-THING, you FERAL MIDGET! You and GOD-ZILLA here obviously can't do a damn thing to help ANYBODY!"

And then, in perhaps the quickest three-part move that's ever been witnessed at Lugo's infrequently fre-quented district library, a move clearly informed by one who seriously practices Brazilian jujitsu, Cloris Honniotis confiscates Winter Hornacek's extremely pink binder, extends her short arms to their vertical limit, and bops her smartly on the crown of her head with it, so smartly that the detonation emits an audible *thwunk* that one might normally associate with, say, a sledgehammer being brought down onto an old sidewalk that needs to be recemented.

Winter Hornacek goes down on one knee, attempts to get up, and then falls onto both knees.

It's amazing how beautiful her brother's girlfriend can look during such a terrible moment, Corinthia thinks, especially one containing such embarrassing, asinine shame that should, by all accounts, belie even the most competent and deserving incumbent Homecoming Queen.

"Stand up!" Cloris Honniotis barks at Winter Hornacek, who makes a swallowing sound and then abides, slowly standing, tears now slicking her lovely pronounced cheekbones, yet miraculously not disturbing her makeup in any noticeable way. At close to five feet nine inches tall, Winter Hornacek, who normally exhibits exemplary posture, is nearly a foot taller than Cloris Honniotis, but at the moment, her physical stature has been rendered meaningless.

"Now, get out of my library!" Cloris Honniotis

seethes through her teeth. She thrusts the pink binder into Winter Hornacek's breasts. Winter then quietly turns toward the checkout desk, a bit dazed, passes through the turnstile, and exits, her right hand grazing the top of her head where she's been thumped with her own binder.

Three hours later, after Cloris Honniotis's superior, Norma Klondike, fields an e-mail from Dr. Gunter Hornacek, Winter's ophthalmologist father and esteemed member of the Lugo Memorial School Board, Cloris Honniotis is relieved of her duties at Lugo's district library, whose carefully curated young adult section will never be the same.

Two days later, in a cream-colored office with handsome midcentury furniture, Dr. Nene Flung and Corinthia Bledsoe sit across from each other on cream-colored leather beanbag chairs. Corinthia sort of lies back on hers, her knees tented, her shoulders, neck, and head kissing the warm, smooth hide of the beanbag. Dr. Flung, on the other hand, is perched weightlessly on hers, sitting with her legs crossed, a steaming earth-colored mug cradled in her hands. The office smells like eucalyptus and green tea.

"So, tornadoes and geese," Dr. Flung says, following Corinthia's explanation of her two visions, their settings and contexts, her physical experience, the migraine-like headache following the three tornadoes, the epileptic-like seizure roughly coinciding with the arrival of the geese.

It's cold today, more brisk than normal for the middle of October—it's actually in the low forties—and Dr. Flung's plum turtleneck gives the effect that her pretty head is floating slightly higher than her body, as if it contains an intelligence that functions better in the room's higher altitude.

Dr. Flung says how curious it is that none of the medical scans produced evidence of unusual matter in the brain.

After a long silence, she adds, "There is considerable evidence that the vast majority of us access only a small fraction of what our brains are actually capable of."

She goes on to cite a recent finding in which a man in Germany was able to predict unusual behavior in a herd of cows. Without any knowledge of farming, the weather, or matters bovine, he was able to predict what fields they would migrate to when left to their own devices.

"He was twelve for twelve," Dr. Flung says. "They came to him in visions."

"I saw a cow, too," Corinthia says. "At center court

of the field house. And when we arrived at school the morning of the tornadoes, this farmer had come to collect her."

"It sounds like you have a gift," Dr. Flung offers.

"A lot of good it's done me," Corinthia replies.

She's been suspended from school for almost six weeks now and is barely interested in her schoolwork. She's stuck at home, where she pretty much completely avoids her mother, who seems to be shuffling around in her own world of confusion, no doubt aggravated by the disappearance of Channing and in no way relieved by the FirmaMall collapse.

"It's your choice to think of it this way," Dr. Flung offers.

"In what way?"

"Cynically," Dr. Flung says.

"I want to stop taking my medication."

Dr. Flung knows not to ask why, but rather to wait for Corinthia to actively offer an explanation.

"I have too many chemicals in me," Corinthia eventually continues. "All these meds are obviously screwing with my brain."

Dr. Flung rotates her mug in her hands and offers the possibility of considering these visions a good thing.

"So few of us have access to what's beyond the realm of normal perception."

"Everyone thinks I'm a freak."

"You've been different from the others since your growth spurt," Dr. Flung says. "And the fact is that for the rest of your life, you're *not* going to be like anybody else. And you know this, Corinthia."

Corinthia has no response. She's suddenly reminded of why she stopped seeing Dr. Flung: it's because this slight woman with the simple, clear vision of her circumstances has been the only person in her life who actually makes her face the truth, and this grew to be too uncomfortable. But now, during this difficult time, at this very moment at least, Corinthia appreciates it.

"You didn't get suspended because you saw those tornadoes," Dr. Flung says. "You got suspended because the administrative leaders at your high school felt you were upsetting your fellow students."

"I didn't mean to."

"I know you didn't. But the fact of the matter is that you're seven feet four and a quarter inches tall, and when a person this large gets excited and damages school property, it can be quite upsetting."

"I only broke one door."

"Still," Dr. Flung says. She sips from her mug of hot water.

"Sometimes I feel like I'm coming out of my body. Like there's an animal inside me."

"That is your rage," Dr. Flung says. "It's perfectly okay to be in touch with it. When you wrote 'FUM' on your shirt in the cafeteria, you were expressing your rage. How did you feel after that?"

"Great."

"Good," Dr. Flung says. "That was a healthy expression of your rage. And you felt relief, no? You forced others to contend with your feelings. This is a healthy step."

Corinthia nods. Since she wrote that FUM on the front of her shirt with black spray paint, she's also written it on the inside of her leg, on the back of Lorcan Nutt's novel *The Smallest Hands,* and on her bathroom mirror in the basement.

"Perhaps the next step in dealing with this is to figure out how to share your visions with poise," Dr. Flung says. "To train your system to respond to the imagery in a calmer, more controlled way, to relax for a moment or two and be *with* the prophecy, to process it internally before rushing toward some irreversible action."

Corinthia nods.

Next Dr. Flung suggests that they do the wall exercise. She uses a remote control to lower the lights and spritzes the air with a small, cylindrical atomizer, releasing more eucalyptus.

Corinthia rolls off her beanbag, removes her old-school size 22 low-top Pony basketball shoes, and lies on her back, extending her corduroy-clad legs flat on the floor, her arms elongated behind her, her wrists extending beyond her plaid flannel sleeves, her palms conjoined, so that she's nearly eleven feet long now, like some supersize human kayak.

In order to make space, Dr. Flung has to dismount from her beanbag and move it to the corner. She conducts the exercise from the other side of the room, where her sleek teak desk and handsome installation of jade plants are arranged.

During the exercise, Dr. Flung paces slowly, padding a slow parabola in socked feet, her hands clasped behind her back, her voice calm and clear.

After the familiar breathing and relaxation primer, which takes a few minutes, Dr. Flung instructs Corinthia that once the slate wall is summoned, she should try to conjure the image of the geese, to *welcome* them as she might a friend, and that once the wall and the geese are alive and present, the goal is to breathe, to relax, to invite a sense of ease, to use the cool surface of the slate wall to calm herself if necessary.

And this is exactly what Corinthia does. She can see her familiar wall, just as it was the last time she conjured it: its gray, monolithic vastness, the air around it cool and molecular. She approaches it, stands very close so she can behold the tiny fissures and imperfections on its surface, infinitesimal as the fibers of silk. She can see the moisture gathering on its exterior. . . . A ladybug passes. She resists the urge to take the insect in her hand. She simply stands before her wall and breathes. She can no longer hear Dr. Flung's voice. She is on her own now.

Moments later, she can hear the faintest honking, the distant beating of wings, almost a figment of sound. It grows more definite as it draws closer and closer. She knows they are coming. It feels as inevitable as the moment she fell to her living-room floor, when she saw the onslaught of their wavering black form, that enormous liquid-like force that seized her mind and body and drove her to the carpeting. She stares up at the top of her wall — miles up, it seems — and there they are, their honking louder now, discordant and violent. But Corinthia continues to breathe, to draw upon the wall's strength to remain poised.

And now there are hundreds of geese, flying over the wall and tacking back in a long arc behind her, their dark bodies powered by the deep, steady, thunderous strokes of their wings. There are thousands of them. She can see the white collar stripe marking their necks. They continue passing over the wall. The scattered orchestra of their honks is almost deafening.

Corinthia turns and faces what appears to be a cyclone of geese. She steps away from the wall and walks toward it. She is in a meadow of long grass now, thousands of geese circling maddeningly above her. But she remembers Dr. Flung's instructions and simply breathes through it, summoning the strength and solitude of her wall.

She closes her eyes.

When she opens them, the geese are gone. They've disappeared into thin air . . . except for one goose, which is sitting in the meadow, a good distance away from her. Separated from its flock, it seems smaller than the rest, somehow reduced by its aloneness, gosling-like. It honks a few times. It rears up, trying to flap itself into the air, but it appears to be lame. It skitters about for a moment and then comes to rest.

Just as Corinthia is about to take a step toward the wounded goose, a wolf appears from behind a stand of trees. It is hackle-backed, gray with yellow eyes. Its sharp, sickle-shaped irises exude a knowing madness. The wolf approaches the goose, circles it. The goose honks and attempts to flap its lame wing, but it can't lift itself off the meadow. The wolf wears what appears to be a smile across its long snout. Its tail hangs low. Another wolf appears from the stand of trees. And then another, and another. They yelp to one another. Their yelps are high-pitched, almost jubilant. They start to circle the goose as a unit, three going in one direction, two trotting the opposite path, their tails low, their smiles wide, yellow-toothed and lunatic. Three more wolves join the pack. The goose cries out, its honks almost human-sounding. And then the wolves start going in, one by one, nipping at the goose, their yelps like children shrieking with joy. A blur of feathers starts to boil above the circle. . . .

Corinthia opens her eyes. She is panting. Dr. Flung is kneeling at her side, holding out a bottle of water.

"I think I lost you for a minute there," she tells Corinthia, offering the bottle.

Corinthia sits up, brings the tips of her fingers to her temples.

"What happened?" Dr. Flung asks. "What did you see?"

"Wolves," she says, taking the bottle of water. "I saw wolves."

Not even an hour later, Corinthia finds herself in the center of town, at Lugo's main municipal building, an impressive, four-story block of brick with a portico and marble hallways, which contains the courthouse,

Lugo's lone Starbucks, a community meeting hall, a small visitors' bureau kiosk, the police precinct, and the office of Dole Ossining, who's been the mayor of Lugo, Illinois, for two consecutive terms. In front of the building, erected on a short lawn and surrounded by park benches, is a brass statue of Captain Clyde Lugo, the legendary Union Army hero and agricultural leader and the town's namesake when it was incorporated in 1865, only months after the end of the Civil War. According to the brass plaque below the large figure, in addition to being a heavily awarded Union Army hero and close friend of fellow Illinoisan Abraham Lincoln, Clyde Lugo was really into corn and soybeans and lived to be 102.

Corinthia has been waiting to speak with Mayor Ossining for over twenty minutes. She's walked all the way here from Dr. Flung's office, some three miles away, and the arches of her feet are inflamed and aching, as are her knees and lower back. While passing through Lugo's business sector, Corinthia came face-to-face with another FUM that had been spray-painted on the glass of an empty storefront formerly occupied by Lugo's lone independent bookstore, Black Bear Books. The three running red letters slashed across Corinthia's reflection in the window, and in that moment she felt like she was fading; fading from her hometown, from her high school, from her family, even from herself. She reached up to touch one of the letters and realized that the word had been painted on the inside of the glass. Did this mean that the proprietor of the storefront was somehow in cahoots with the vandals? Were they planning some sort of Corinthia Bledsoe exhibit? Outside of her parents and Dr. Flung, is there a single adult in Lugo who might actually *sympathize* with what she's been going through?

Mayor Ossining's secretary, a woman in a violet cardigan sweater named Eula who has a face like a stunned rabbit, hangs up the phone and says, "Mayor Ossining will be with you in a moment." She's echoed this phrase four times now, and before Corinthia can nod and thank her, the mayor's office door opens, and Dole Ossining — the mayor of Lugo himself — stands at the threshold. He is tall and old and bowlegged. He possesses thick white hair and smiling eyes.

"Corinthia Bledsoe," he says. "Come on in."

After he closes the door, Mayor Ossining offers Corinthia a handsome leather club chair in the "meeting area" of his wooden office. The mayor chooses to arrange himself on the forest-green tufted leather sofa with many buttons. When he sits, the cuffs of his trousers ride up, exposing hairless pale shins that look like undercooked pork.

"Can I get you anything?" he asks. "Water? A coffee?"

"No, thank you," Corinthia replies.

"You sure? I'm happy to send Eula downstairs for a Starbucks."

"I'm afraid coffee would just upset my stomach," Corinthia says.

"So, what brings you to my office?" he asks.

"I'm worried about the wolves," she says.

"What wolves are you speaking of?"

"The ones that have been living in the woods by the frontage road. The ones killing all the deer."

"Well, that's very thoughtful of you, Corinthia, but why worry?"

"Because I think something bad is going to happen."

Mayor Ossining smiles, revealing bright-yellow teeth, and says, "If this is an animal-rights concern, I applaud your initiative, Corinthia. But you have to realize that we've had a deer problem. A very serious one. Over the summer they were meddling in our gardens and defecating on our front lawns." He reaches down and scratches one of his bald shins. "And as I see it," he continues, "the wolves gettin' to 'em, well, that's just Mother Nature doing her thing."

"But this goes beyond deer," Corinthia says.

"It does? In what way?"

"It's going to become a people problem."

"Meaning what, exactly?"

That yellow smile again. Mayor Ossining suddenly seems to possess more teeth than your average human. Corinthia imagines him eating the carcass of a dead deer, his naked body hunched over it, pawing out its innards like some primitive half-human.

"Meaning the wolves will start attacking the people of Lugo," she says.

"Well, forgive me for saying this, Corinthia, but that just seems awfully far-fetched."

"But it's not," she says. "It's not far-fetched at all."

As Dr. Flung suggested, Corinthia is doing her best to remain poised, continue breathing, and keep her pulse at a reasonable level. She can feel her hands starting to clutch the hide on the arm supports of the leather club chair. She exhales through her nostrils and eases her grip.

"I saw the tornadoes," she continues, "before they came. I saw all three of them. And I told people, but no one would listen. And then I saw the geese — the geese that destroyed the Lugo Memorial football field. You know that happened, too, right?"

"Of course I do," Dole Ossining says. "I'm the mayor."

"Well, I saw those geese coming, and then they

did. And now I'm telling you that something's going to happen with these wolves. Someone's going to get seriously hurt."

Mayor Ossining sucks on his teeth a moment, steeples his hands, and sets their point on the bridge of his nose. He studies Corinthia Bledsoe for a bit.

"Do you realize how you sound, Ms. Bledsoe?" he finally says.

Corinthia doesn't respond. She simply sits there.

"What do you expect me to do?"

"Call County Animal Control."

"And tell them what, exactly? A young woman came into my office with some sort of *vision*?"

"Yes," Corinthia hears herself say.

"And based on this *vision*, this *fantasy*, I'd like your organization to kill a bunch of wolves? The same wolves that are finally starting to rectify Lugo's deer problem? Do you hear how silly that sounds?"

"The tornadoes weren't fantasies. The geese weren't fantasies."

"Then what would you call them?" Mayor Ossining says. "Coincidences?"

Corinthia can feel anger starting to simmer in her hands.

"Can I ask you a question, Ms. Bledsoe?" And before Corinthia can even offer a nod, Mayor Ossining says, "Why aren't you in school?"

"Because I've been temporarily suspended."

"May I ask for what reason?"

Corinthia decides that she's through appealing to this man, Lugo's so-called civic leader.

"Because I destroyed school property," she says.

"I see," he says. "Do your parents know you've made a visit to my office?"

"No."

"What are their names?"

"Brill and Marlene Bledsoe."

"Brill and Marlene Bledsoe," he repeats. "And where are they right now?"

"My dad's at work, and my mom's probably at home."

"And what about you?"

"I'm sitting in your office, talking to you."

"But where are you *supposed* to be, is what I'm asking. Because that's the key to good citizenship, Corinthia: knowing where you're *supposed* to be."

"I'm not exactly sure," she says. She can feel hot tears welling in the corners of her eyes. "The library?"

"Then I suggest you get there."

Corinthia slowly stands. It's miraculous to her that Dole Ossining hasn't made a remark about her size, her height. She stands before him, tears streaming down her face now. She wants to shout, *"Don't you see how enormous I am?"* but she is overwhelmed with the terrible feeling that he does not; that she's disappearing.

So she exits his office, her knees throbbing, her ankles weak with inflammation, and shuffles down the marble hallway, past the Starbucks, where several Lugonites are lining up for their afternoon mochas and toasted graham lattes and shots of espresso.

Corinthia slowly descends the dozen or so steps of the municipal building, crosses the street, and moves out onto the small, well-mown park lawn, where she approaches the statue of Captain Clyde Lugo. She rises up on her tiptoes and stares into the legendary Civil War and agricultural hero's face. She notices the slightest hint of a smile, suggesting pride and humility. His nose is perfect, almost absurd in its symmetry. His blank brass eyes are no more expressive than those of the bloated fish living in her mother's koi pond.

In a flash, Corinthia can feel rage pulsing up her calves and thighs, surging through her hips and torso and chest. Before she can even think about it, with the same explosive force that sent her careening through Bob Sluba's life sciences door almost two months ago, Corinthia throws her shoulder into the effigy of the town's namesake and proceeds to rock it off its rectangular foundation.

The sound that the quarter-ton polished brass statue makes upon crashing down on the little redbrick circular pathway is not unlike a compact car colliding with a U.S. mailbox. Within what seems like seconds, several Lugonites are surrounding Corinthia, who also finds herself on the ground now, on her back, to be exact, beside the statue of Clyde Lugo, arranged almost like his lover.

Corinthia peers up at the cluster of fleshy, jowly adult faces. It's as if she and Clyde Lugo have been caught having sex while picnicking and someone has pulled a blanket off their naked, conjoined bodies. Corinthia is dazed, to say the least.

Although Corinthia recognizes Mayor Dole Ossining's head of thick white hair and his long yellow teeth, the most assertive person emerging through the crowd is Sheriff Burges Beckett, who is uniformed in his crisp police khakis and polished black shoes. The late-afternoon sun glints off the gold badge pinned to his chest. It just so happens that Sheriff Beckett, an old friend of Corinthia's father, was ordering a venti caramel macchiato from Starbucks when, through the street-facing window, he witnessed with his own two eyes the great figure of Clyde Lugo teetering and falling to the earth.

Approximately two hours later, Marlene Bledsoe arrives at the police precinct to pick up her daughter. Through a series of conversations with Mayor Ossining, Lugo

Memorial Principal Margo Ticonderoga, and his old high-school buddy Brill Bledsoe, Sheriff Beckett decides it is best to forgo charging Corinthia with any crime. Destruction of public property would have certainly fit the bill, but knowing of the Bledsoes' recent troubles, benevolent Sheriff Beckett decided it was best to let this incident slip through the system and not mar the permanent record and immediate future of one of Lugo's brightest young women.

"You're better than this," Sherriff Beckett told Corinthia as he tore up the incident report he'd started to fill out. "You Bledsoes are good people."

When Marlene arrives to collect her daughter she tries to write Sheriff Beckett a check for five hundred dollars, but he will have no part of it.

"Just take it," she pleaded with him. "Please."

"I will not take your money," he replied, insistent, and then unlocked the men's jail cell and released Corinthia, who seemed completely drained, her face as bloodless as a cafeteria plate.

It should be noted that Corinthia was being detained in the men's cell because the wooden bench in the women's cell was just too small, and when she tried to sit on it, it snapped in half and caused Corinthia to land smartly on her tailbone, which now throbs along with her knees, ankles, wrists, and elbows. Her entire body is like an orchestra of pain. The men's cell featured a much sturdier bench, one made of brushed steel, in fact, and since the cell was vacant, Sheriff Beckett thought it prudent to keep Corinthia detained in there.

"Please give Brill my best," the sheriff told Marlene when he hugged her good-bye.

Marlene Bledsoe, who shed legitimate tears at the police precinct, has grown cold in the car.

During the ride home, very little is said. Corinthia lies in the backseat of the Hyundai. Her knees are tented, so that, through the rearview mirror, Marlene can see how badly they've been skinned. Corinthia's enormous kneecaps look like hamburger meat, and Marlene is disgusted by the image and has to stop herself from retching.

"Your knees are bleeding," she tells her daughter evenly, swallowing hard. "Please don't get any blood back there."

At home, not quite an hour later, Corinthia is lying on her bed, trying to ignore the pounding in her head, when her mother knocks on the door and enters, holding a bottle of iodine, a blob of cotton balls, and the program for *The Beautiful Apocalypse.*

"For your knees," she says, placing the bottle of iodine and the cotton balls on Corinthia's bedside stand. "And I thought you should have this, too," she adds, proffering the traveling freak-show program she'd brought back from Group some weeks before.

Corinthia accepts it.

"What is it?" she asks.

"Just look through it," Marlene says. "I think what they're doing is very interesting."

And then her mother turns, closes the door, and heads downstairs.

15

October 19, Monday (My Birthday)

Dave,

It was my birthday today. I turned fifteen. But it was not a good day, Dave. No, not at all. It was actually a day of ubiquitous shade. "Ubiquitous" means omnipresent. Manifold kinds of shade, you could say. "Manifold" means multiple and assorted. So that gives you a pretty good idea of what transpired, Dave. Ubiquitous, manifold shade.

I woke with a feeling of hope.

But before I share the details of this inauspicious birthday, I need to tell you that my Fake Dave diary worked, Dave! It worked! I gave it to Principal Ticonderoga, and it's three weeks later now, and I haven't heard a word from her. She hasn't given it back to me, Dave, which I'm pretty certain is some kind of crime against my student rights, but for now

I'm just happy that The Fake List in The Fake Dave was a success!

Generally speaking, since the episode with Britney Purina that unfurled and transpired in the cafeteria (when she threatened me with sexual violence and accused me of absconding with her iPhone 6), things at school have been surprisingly devoid and barren of conflict. For instance, I haven't heard a lot of people calling me the Ball Boy, and for the most part, lunch has gone smoothly, except for the fact that Durdin Royko stopped sitting at the Frog table. Durdin sits elsewhere now, Dave. In fact, he's chosen to sit on the other side of the cafeteria, in the corner, with a junior boy named Keith Kybzanski, who is mildly mentally challenged, meaning he's allowed to attend a regular high school but he takes classes with freshmen.

Once, during a fire drill, Keith Kybzanski defecated in his pants, and this is likely why no one would sit with him in the cafeteria until now. I've seen Mark Maestro and Lars Silence follow him down the hall and call him the Duke of Dooky.

I am disappointed in Durdin Royko, Dave, but Keiko Cho and I are still holding it down at the Frog table, eating quietly, keeping to ourselves.

On the bus, I listened to music on my Android. Currently, my choice musical selection is a band from the '90s called Hootie and the Blowfish. They have this song called "Let Her Cry" that I like to play on continuous repeat. Darius Rucker is the name of the lead singer. He's African American and possesses a very appealing voice. A few weeks ago, I heard Mom listening to their first album, *Cracked Rear View*, in the privacy of her bedroom, and I was quite seduced and bewitched by Mr. Rucker's voice. I think Mom cries when she listens to "Let Her Cry," so for her the song is like an instructional manual and a permission slip to let forth the flow of her emotions. After some Internet investigation, I was able to find this song and purchased it via my Android. After my dad died, I was awarded a sum of money, which is distributed into my checking account on a weekly basis, and this money allows me to make various purchases. I would like to buy a gift for Camila. I'm thinking of maybe buying her a box of high-quality chocolates or perhaps a scarf for the winter.

But back to my day . . .

So the bus ride to school was replete with my favorite song, during which I imagined Camila and me partaking of romantic scenarios, such as playing a round of mini-golf in Shawneetown and sharing a serving of Dippin' Dots in Kaskaskia.

In homeroom, during morning announcements, my birthday was declared, and Mrs. Klubek led the class in singing "Happy Birthday" to me. Everything was going so well until the last verse, when you're supposed to sing "Happy birthday, dear Billy / Happy birthday to you," and Rose Bryant, Breanne Billson, and Rod Benedict sang "Happy Birthday, dear Ball Boy / Happy birthday to you." But, of course, Mrs. Klubek didn't hear them. I was still happy to hear so many of my fellow students in homeroom singing "Happy Birthday" to me, so I tried not to let the three others' mischief bother me too much, but I should've known it was a harbinger of things to come. Dave, a "harbinger," as I learned the other day during the vocab portion of my English class, is an "omen."

So I'll get right to it. In the cafeteria,

Keiko Cho and I enjoyed our lunches, but the normal day ended there. On my way to sixth period, which is algebra, whose classroom is on the second floor, Todd Chicklis sort of kidnapped me by grabbing my belt, and then the door to Corinthia Bledsoe's private bathroom opened, and he forced me inside. Also populating this particular bathroom was Bronson Kaminski, as well as Britney Purina. Britney Purina nodded to Bronson Kaminski, and then, like a magic trick, he made some duct tape appear and tore a few strips off and forced it over my mouth and around my head so that I couldn't make any noise. And then Todd Chicklis locked the door from the inside and Britney Purina started whispering, and her voice was a like a hot wind with wild saws, and she said "Happy birthday" in a rather condescending manner, and then she called me Ball Boy and said she wanted to see my Ball Boy baby balls, and then Bronson Kaminski undid my belt, and even though I kicked and ran in place and tried to turn myself into a human windmill, Bronson Kaminski was successful in overwhelming me and pulled my pants and underwear down to my ankles, and my stomach started gurgling, and I could feel my intestines filling with swampish gas, and then I could see Britney Purina make an expression that I can only accurately modify with the word "ghastly," and I realized she was looking down at my underwear, and then I looked down and I could see that what she was looking at was a feces stain. It was brown and shaped like a rocket flame. Or maybe it was shaped like a canoe. Or maybe it was shaped like a canoe on fire. Anyway, then Britney Purina whispered that I was a fucking idiot Ball Boy and not only was I an idiot but that I was a <u>bald</u> idiot and where's my giant now and why wasn't she protecting me on my Ball Boy birthday, and then I started crying, and she whispered/sang "Happy Birthday," and like Rose Bryant, Breanne Billson, and Rod Benedict in homeroom, she replaced "Billy" with "Ball Boy," and then I was snotting through my nostrils because my mouth was still covered with that duct tape, and I couldn't get enough air, and then everyone was laughing, and Bronson Kaminski was snapping his fingers below my testicles, which was making me flinch and dance, and I wished it was Wednesday, my gym class day, because I would've superglued some of Mom's hair that I'd collected from the bathroom floor to my upper junk area, and I could feel my penis responding to all of this shade, because it was so hard and small like it had turned itself into a light switch maybe so I would reach down and turn the whole scenario off, and then Britney Purina was holding a black Sharpie and she proceeded to remove the cap and write something on my forehead and then she spit in my face, which made me squint hard, and I kept my eyes closed for a moment, and during this moment I thought they were going to beat me to death, that Britney Purina, Todd Chicklis, and Bronson Kaminski were going to take turns slapping me and then break my jaw and then my arm and then my feet and then they'd pull a rib out of my side and stab my eyes with it and then my heart and then they would set me on fire, and part of me <u>wanted</u> them to do this, Dave, part of me <u>wanted</u> this. I wanted to be set on fire and die in Corinthia Bledsoe's private bathroom.

When I opened my eyes, Britney Purina, Todd Chicklis, and Bronson Kaminski were gone. I didn't even hear them unlock the door or gather their materials or leave. They were just gone.

So I locked the door and then I pulled the tape off, which burned my mouth and chin, and then I went to the bathroom because I had been holding in so much gas that it caused me to have to move my bowels, and after I did that, I wiped and threw my stained underwear in the wastebasket under the sink and pulled my pants up and secured my belt, and then I looked in the mirror, and in addition to the irritation around my mouth from the duct tape, I could see what Britney Purina had written on my forehead.

She'd written FUM, Dave.

FUM.

And then in the reflection of the mirror, I could see that someone had spray-painted FUM all over the walls, so now my forehead matched the walls of Corinthia Bledsoe's private bathroom.

I'm just glad they didn't take my dad's watch, which I've been wearing since Mom gave it to me that time in the kitchen.

I never made it to my sixth period and didn't bother going to Principal Ticonderoga's office to report Britney Purina, Todd Chicklis, and Bronson Kaminski, because I just felt so bad and dumb and I didn't have any underwear on.

I decided to skip the bus and walk home, and the air was getting really cold and my teeth were starting to chatter. It took me about half an hour to get home, and when I finally did, Mom was in her bedroom listening to Hootie and the Blowfish's second album, *Fairweather Johnson*.

I just kept sitting at the kitchen table. I felt useless and filled with shade. After a while Mom came downstairs. She was wearing a bathrobe and pajama bottoms and slippers and this Chicago Cubs baseball cap she's been wearing since she threw her wig into the backyard and screamed, "Fuck you, world!" The wig is still back there, Dave. It sort of looks like an animal that got stuck in time. I've been checking on it periodically. Part of me wants to drive a barbecue fork through it and into the cold crust of the ground so it will stay there forever. I'm not sure what this would accomplish, Dave, but I've thought about doing it more than once.

Mom was still humming this one song called "When I'm Lonely," which is the final track on *Fairweather Johnson.* Then she sat at the table and said, "Hi."

And then I said hi back and then we were quiet for a minute.

She seemed too tired to be downstairs, and I worried that she might fall asleep on the kitchen floor again. Then she started to hum the song again.

I said, "Hootie."

"Yep," she said. "They're the best."

Then Mom asked me if I wanted hot dogs for dinner, and I said sure, and then she turned and looked toward the living room.

She said, "Look, it's snowing," and from where we were sitting, you could see through the kitchen and through the living room and into the backyard through the patio doors. And it was snowing, Dave! Snow was falling! They were these huge flakes, and they were falling really fast, as if the mind of the world had something in store for all humans and animals and bugs and crops, and then Mom got up and walked over to the sliding patio doors and just stood there staring out at the snow.

"It's not even November," she said after a minute.

Eventually she went back upstairs and put Hootie and the Blowfish on again and started crying, although she might have been singing, and I just sat there, Dave. I just sat there because I realized that she'd forgotten my birthday and that she wasn't coming back downstairs to make hot dogs or give me a present or a chocolate cake with M&M's on it, and I started to think about so many things, Dave, like, for instance, my dead dad and my gas problems and all the people on The List and about how my heart is shrinking little by little and about how Mom didn't even notice the FUM on my forehead and about this notebook and specifically how you're my only friend but how you're not really a live person, how you're more like a thought, Dave, even though you have a name and I can almost imagine what you look like, like maybe you have light-brown hair and a little mole under your eye and how sad it is that we'll never get to hang out and help each other with vocab words or talk about the Sioux while throwing stones at bottles.

And then I tried to fight this glumness and avoid throwing too much shade at myself by imagining Camila the cafeteria worker, like she and I doing activities together, like picking out apples at the supermarket or going to see a movie or riding in a canoe, and how she would just have to sit there because I would do all the steering and paddling.

And then I saw something in the patio doors, Dave. It was eerie but special at the same time. What I saw was a wolf. I'm almost positive it was one of the gray wolves that the local news has been reporting about for the past few weeks. They've been showing pictures of them in the newspaper. They've been killing huge amounts of deer in the forest by the frontage road and all these carcasses have been appearing in the forest. But now the deer are all dead, or maybe the ones who were left found an effective escape route, so the wolves are looking for other sources of protein.

But anyway, there was this wolf staring into the house from the backyard. You could see its yellow eyes gleaming. Dave, what I did was I walked up to the patio doors. I walked up to them and just looked at the wolf. And it looked back at me, in a sitting position, the way a dog sits when it wants something. And it just stared at me with its yellow eyes. It was like the gray wolf was trying to talk to me. I really felt that, Dave, like it was trying to tell me the greatest secret, or like it was inviting me to go into the forest over by the frontage road and show me where the log is. I know that sounds weird, but that's really what I felt.

I even held my dad's watch up so the wolf could see it.

"I have the watch," I said to the wolf through the patio doors. "Take me to the log."

Then I heard a noise from upstairs, a loud thud, and I turned to this sound. When I turned back to the window, the gray wolf was gone.

I was curious about the thud, so I went upstairs and knocked on Mom's door.

"Mom?" I said. "Mom?"

"I'm okay," she said.

"What happened?" I asked from the other side of her bedroom door.

"I fell out of bed," she said.

"You sure you're okay?" I asked.

"I'm really fine," she said.

"Want me to bring you anything?" I asked.

"No, thank you," she said. "I'm gonna go back to sleep."

"Okay." I said. "Good night."

———————

The List grows.

New additions include those three people from homeroom:

> 13. Rose Bryant
> 14. Breanne Billson
> 15. Rod Benedict

16

By Halloween, almost a foot of snow has fallen on most of southern Illinois. It's a record snowfall for the region, and winter wear is in full effect. Children trick-or-treat throughout the modest neighborhoods of Lugo, the youngest ones being escorted by their parents, the older ones left to their own devices. Their colorful costumes would normally stand out against the pristine white hide of snow, but aside from masks, most costumes are hidden by parkas, ski pants, and even snowmobile suits.

Corinthia Bledsoe and Cloris Honniotis are sitting on Cloris's living-room floor, drinking boxed white wine. They have each taken one of Corinthia's leftover Valiums from her recent hospital visit. Cloris decided to boycott Halloween and has disabled her doorbell and is ignoring all trick-or-treaters. It is her belief that Halloween is just another consumer holiday designed to be a big payday for candy companies that use white sugar and other mass-produced ingredients that actually harm children.

Their backs are set against Cloris's plaid sofa, and they've moved her coffee table off to the side to make room for Cloris's laptop, which rests on the carpet in front of them. Cloris has pushed herself about a foot closer to her laptop by wedging two throw pillows between her back and the sofa, a strategy that will hopefully balance out the extreme size difference between her and Corinthia for the live video-conference they are about to take part in.

The Valium has started to take effect, and Cloris initiates the Skype connection with 103-year-old young adult novelist Lorcan Nutt. Through an impassioned phone call and a half dozen follow-up e-mails, Cloris was able to persuade Mr. Nutt's assistant, an elderly lady named Lorna, to talk the reclusive writer into Skyping with her and her friend, Corinthia Bledsoe. She assured Lorna that it wasn't an interview, that it would in no way be digitally or otherwise disseminated for public consumption, that she was simply a passionate young adult librarian hoping for a conversation with her favorite author. Of course Cloris didn't mention the fact that she'd been recently fired from Lugo's district library. They agreed upon Halloween, which Mr. Nutt doesn't observe either. Lorna was absolutely insistent that Mr. Nutt would be able to give them only twenty minutes of his time, as he was busy finishing a novel.

Cloris and Corinthia primped, Cloris put eye-liner on, Corinthia covered a pimple with Cloris's non-oil-based cover-up, and they're both wearing flattering sweaters; Cloris was sure to put on her charcoal cable-knit turtleneck because Corinthia told her that it brings out the color of her eyes.

After a few rings, the Skype call is answered. An elderly woman's face appears on the screen. She has skin like wet tissue paper, its pallor marked with fleshy folds and little coffee-colored spots. Her unadorned earlobes are almost shockingly long, like dangling tears of putty. Her hair is short and so white it's almost color-less, and she doesn't appear to be wearing makeup.

"Hello," she says.

"Hello," Cloris and Corinthia reply in unison.

"How are you ladies this evening?" the woman says. Her voice is a lively warble, one perhaps more befitting a bird.

"We're fine," Cloris says. "How are you?"

"Oh, I'm fine," the woman answers. "A little tired, but we've had a long day."

"Are you Lorna?" Cloris asks.

"I am," she says. "I'm Lorna."

"I'm Cloris!"

"Hello, Cloris."

"And this is my best friend, Corinthia Bledsoe."

"Hello, Corinthia."

"Hello, Lorna."

"Can you young ladies see me okay?"

"We can see you perfectly," Cloris says. "Can you see us?"

"I can see you pretty good," Lorna says, "but my Internet connection is not the greatest out here in the boondocks. I hope I don't get fuzzy."

"We'll be sure to let you know if you do," Cloris says. "Is Mr. Nutt there with you?"

"He's definitely here with me," she says. "He most certainly is."

"Is he planning on joining you?" Cloris asks.

"Well," Lorna says, "I can't promise anything. He tends to be quite shy."

"It'd be such an honor to chat with him," Corinthia says.

"Could you tell him that?" Cloris offers.

"What exactly is it that you two young ladies want to talk about?" Lorna asks.

"First of all," Cloris says, "we just wanted to tell him how much we admire his work here in Lugo, Illinois."

"He'll be happy to hear that," Lorna says.

"And we'd love to know if he's working on any-thing new," Corinthia says. "I think I've read *The*

Smallest Hands four times now. I'm hungry for a new book!"

"We be hungry!" Cloris adds, definitely loopy from the Valium-and-white-wine cocktail.

"Well, he certainly is working on a new book," Lorna says. "He's been working on it for many years."

"Can you tell us what it's about?" Cloris asks.

"Mr. Nutt normally doesn't disclose this kind of information," Lorna says. "He's quite discreet about the subjects of his books while he's working on them."

"We won't tell anyone," Cloris promises.

"We really won't," Corinthia adds. "You have our guarantee."

"It's about an escaped circus monkey," Lorna begins, "who teaches a small town in the middle of America how to play volleyball and also how to run better."

"How to run better as a town?" Cloris asks.

"How to run better as in *run better*," Lorna says. "As in the verb *to run*. Because the citizens of this particular town only walk and sit in front of their computers. They've forgotten how to run. The monkey teaches them how to jump and play volleyball, too."

"Fun!" Cloris says, giggling.

Lorna goes on to tell them that after the town starts to run and jump and play volleyball through basic edicts of physical fitness and team sports, the citizens come to understand joy and how to sustain a kind of civic well-being that awakens them to the concept of happiness. But they soon forget about the monkey. And one night he is seen hanging from a tree branch, and the authorities capture him and keep him in a cage, and, though he is still trying to speak to them with his learned language skills, they stop hearing his voice. To them he only screeches and makes base monkey sounds. He is now a creature to be kept in a cage. Eventually they even strip him of his circus outfit because they no longer find it to be amusing. And then they starve him. The monkey eventually dies, and local dogs eat his viscera and bones. All that is left is a lump of fur. But the town thrives and becomes one of the most physically fit, highest-jumping, fastest-running towns in America.

"But is it a book for young adults?" Cloris asks.

"I think Mr. Nutt believes his books are for everyone," Lorna replies.

"Is the monkey a young adult?" Corinthia asks.

"No," Lorna says, "but his only true friend in town is a young girl named Hallie Elizabeth, who brings him bananas when no one is watching. They become good friends, and at one point Hallie Elizabeth even tries to free the monkey, but she gets caught and is sent away to a military school in Pennsylvania. The monkey affectionately calls her Hallie Bananas. But once she's sent away, no one else comes to feed him, and he withers and dies."

"Where does the town keep the cage?" Cloris asks.

"In the back of a used-car lot," Lorna replies.

"What's the title?" Corinthia asks Lorna, clearly affected by Lorna's summary.

"Mr. Nutt is temporarily calling it *The Book of Matthew*. Matthew is the name of the monkey."

"It sounds incredible!" Cloris proclaims.

"Really incredible-sounding," Corinthia adds with far less enthusiasm, her voice betraying her a bit.

To Corinthia, Lorna says, "You seem disappointed."

Cloris turns to Corinthia. "Are you disappointed?"

"Why can't Hallie Bananas set him free?" Corinthia asks.

"Because that's not how life really is," Lorna says. "If one is reading purely for pleasure, one can always turn to books about wizards and bespectacled young geniuses who can time-travel and solve all sorts of the world's problems with magic potions and charm."

Cloris says, "Is this what *you* think, or what Mr. Nutt thinks?"

She says, "As far as I see, that doesn't really matter."

"Why not?" Cloris asks.

"Because he is me and I am he."

"You're Lorcan Nutt?" Corinthia practically shouts, exuberant.

"I've been Lorcan Nutt for as long as he's been writing books," she explains, "but Lorna Nuttinger is what it says on his birth certificate."

"Holy shit!" Cloris cries.

Lorna says, "Language, girls, language!"

Cloris apologizes, and she and Corinthia are giddy with excitement.

"You young ladies must keep this a secret," Lorna says. "You must swear this to me."

"We swear," Cloris says. "We swear, we swear!"

"It'll be our little secret," Lorna says. "Now I must get back to work. But before I sign off, you must remember to be good to each other. No matter how bad things get. Don't expect much from people, because humans are generally a very disappointing species. But nevertheless, you must try to give as much love as you can. Endure this life. And help others endure it, too. And fend off bitterness at every turn. Do you hear me?"

"We hear you loud and clear," Cloris says.

"We hear you," Corinthia echoes.

"It was lovely chatting with you," Lorna adds. "Over and out."

And just like that, the Skype session is over and

she's gone. Cloris and Corinthia sit in silence for a long time while snow continues to fall.

Corinthia considers Lorna's advice about fending off bitterness and helping others. Not an easy task of late. Not easy at all when virtually everyone around you thinks you're a witch or a monster or some grotesque combination of the two.

She closes her eyes, and she can see Lavert Birdsong asleep in a hospital bed, his body frail, his face racked with pain. It feels as if a sewing needle is being slowly pulled through her heart.

A few trick-or-treaters pass by Cloris's living-room window. They are bundled in winter clothes, their Halloween masks ghastly and vibrant. One small boy comes through the bushes, presses his face to the glass, and peers in. He is not wearing a mask, but his face is made up like a clown's, painted white with red balloons on his cheeks.

"Trick or treat!" he calls from the other side of the window, his breath steaming the glass.

Cloris rises and crosses to her kitchen. Moments later, she returns with an apple. She motions to the boy to go and meet her at her front door. Then she crosses to it, opens the door, and hands him the apple.

Rather than drive under the influence, Cloris agrees to walk Corinthia halfway home. The soft, slow snowfall passes through the glow of the neighborhood streetlights like flour falling from a baker's mill. They are bundled in winter coats and knit hats. Cloris has wrapped a long plum-colored scarf around her neck. Corinthia walks with her hands wedged in her armpits. Her size 22 old-school Pony sneakers aren't fit for the snow, but they are so long and wide it's as if she is maneuvering on snowshoes.

They talk about Lorna Nuttinger and her pen persona, which has spanned more than half a century, and their amazing Skype call. Though Cloris wishes the great Lorna would publish her new book under her real name, they both swear to each other to protect her alias.

After the boxed wine, which they finished, they are pretty drunk, and they enjoy some sliding. Though Corinthia has a long way to fall, she runs and slides down the middle of the street while the neighborhood trick-or-treaters stop and point.

A few blocks later, they happen upon a boy who is standing beside one of the neighborhood's oldest and largest oak trees. He's maybe seven and wears a khaki uniform with a hazard-orange winter vest, venom-yellow safety glasses, and a red felt Canadian Mountie hat. Slung over his shoulder is a toy rifle.

"Who are you supposed to be?" Cloris asks.

"Yeah, who are you supposed to be?" Corinthia echoes.

"I'm with Animal Rescue," he tells them. "I've been dispatched here to deal with those gray wolves."

"Ahhh," Cloris says, playing along. "You're *protecting* us."

"Yes, ma'am," the boy replies with his deepest, most adult voice. "In the past few weeks, there have been several neighborhood spottings. I think they're getting low on their protein supply."

"What kind of rifle is that?" Corinthia asks him.

"It's not a rifle," he says, adjusting his yellow safety goggles and using his natural, prepubescent voice now. "It's my dad's Red Ryder BB gun. He wouldn't let me load it, but it's still pretty crisp. See?"

The boy pumps the rifle and takes aim at a nearby mailbox. He pulls the trigger, which issues a faint *click*.

"Pretty fancy," Cloris offers.

"Yeah, the last thing anyone wants to see is one of my fellow trick-or-treaters get taken down by one of those wolves." Then, to Corinthia he says, "By the way, how tall are you?"

"Taller than your average gray wolf," Corinthia jokes.

"She's nine feet tall," Cloris says. "And she knows jujitsu."

"Wait a minute," the boy says to Corinthia, lifting his yellow safety goggles. "You're the giant monster witch! You're the one who made the tornadoes and the geese come!"

"She's not a monster witch!" Cloris retorts, poking him in the chest. "She's a *soothsayer*!"

"What's a 'soothsayer'?" the boy asks.

"A prophet!" Cloris replies, and tugs on the brim of his Canadian Mountie hat.

"Prophet*ess*," Corinthia corrects Cloris. "I didn't make anything come. I just saw they were coming."

Corinthia almost slips and falls. Cloris has to grab her arm, and they wind up sliding around a bit, clutching each other until they find their balance.

"Do you see other stuff?" the boy asks Corinthia.

Corinthia stares at him playfully.

"I just saw who's gonna give you your first French kiss."

"I don't wanna know that," the boy says. "That's gross!"

A group of kids shuffle by in boots and puffy coats, their heads hooded, their Halloween masks flecked with snow. They are all carrying plastic pumpkins and pillowcases filled to the brim with candy. The boy stops them, and from a plastic bag he hands them orange hazard whistles with lanyards.

"Wolf whistles," the boy says. "See a wolf and blow it as loud as you can."

The kids accept the whistles, loop them over their masked heads, and continue on.

To the boy, Cloris says, "Wolf whistles?"

"For the gray wolves. Twilight is one of their prime hunting times."

He hands Cloris and Corinthia whistles.

"The sound alone should scare them off."

"What's your name?" Corinthia asks the boy.

"Crispin," the boy says. "Ranger Crispin Kincade Doyle."

Cloris says, "Nice to meet you, Crispin."

Corinthia adds, "Keep up the good work, Ranger Doyle."

They thank him for the whistles, and then Crispin tips his hat to them and they continue on.

Not even a block later, coming around the corner, they happen upon two boys stacked one on top of the other monster-style, with a white T-shirt that has been fitted over a puffy metallic-blue snow parka. There is another, much smaller boy behind them, perhaps eight or nine years old. He is wearing a red cape over a blue parka and wielding a plastic whip. He whips the stacked boys in front of him, shouting "TAME THE BEAST! TAME THE BEAST!"

Cloris stops them. The boy on top is wearing the hood of the metallic-blue parka and carries a Lugo

Junior High School gym bag filled with candy. His cheeks are flushed from the cold.

FUM has been crudely written on the T-shirt worn over the parka of the top boy.

"Hey!" Cloris shouts up at him. "What are you supposed to be?"

The boy looks down at Cloris, then at Corinthia, who stands eye-to-eye with him. She has an urge to push him over, to topple the two stacked idiots and kick the young boy with the whip right in the chest.

"Well?" Cloris shouts again.

"We're supposed to be her," he mutters, pointing halfheartedly at Corinthia.

"Well, you're *not* her!" Cloris almost screams at him. "You're not even close!"

To the boy with the whip, Corinthia says simply, "You really want to whip me? I'm right here."

But the boy is frozen.

"Do it!" Corinthia screams at him.

Some children across the street turn and watch.

"Whip me!" Corinthia shouts. "The genuine article is standing right in front of you! Here's your chance!"

The boy with the whip is crying now. Corinthia knocks the gym bag out of the top boy's hand, reaches inside it, and starts flinging candy in all directions.

"TAME THE BEAST!" she shouts at the entire neighborhood. "TAME THE BEAST!"

When the gym bag is empty, Corinthia just stands there. It feels like all the trick-or-treaters of Lugo are watching her. All three boys are crying now.

"I hope the wolves get you!" Corinthia screams at them bitterly. And then she turns to the rest of the neighborhood. "I hope they get all of you!" she shouts.

Cloris takes Corinthia by the arm and leads her away.

At home, Corinthia is in her basement bathroom, sitting on the toilet with the lid lowered. She has taken another Valium because, after dealing with those cruel boys, her nerves are absolutely shot and she really doesn't feel like doing her homework. There are far more important things to think about, like the fact that on the way home, in an effort to get Corinthia's mind on other things, Cloris handed Corinthia her iPhone and persuaded her to call Lavert Birdsong and invite him to go sledding in Bicentennial Park the next day, which she did. And even though he did say he hadn't been feeling so great, he agreed, and went on to mention that the fresh air might do him some good. So now it's a date.

Since she's been home from the hospital, Corinthia

has tried to call Lavert several times to thank him for the triangle, but he never answers, and she's elected not to leave a voice mail. The two times that his grandmother answered, she promised to leave word for him, but Lavert hasn't called back, so when he answered Cloris's iPhone, it came as quite a surprise.

Bicentennial Park is home to Suicide Hill, a favorite sledding spot, and when Cloris drove past it on her way home from the grocery store, she could see that it was still blanketed with virgin snow.

Despite all of her recent troubles, the very idea of Lavert Birdsong thrills Corinthia to no end, and this is precisely why she's decided to shave her bikini line. She steals one of her father's Gillette Fusion razors because it offers a cleaner, more precise shave than those cheap pink ones she uses for her underarms and legs. She lathers up and carefully sculpts a shape to her liking. She's especially sure to execute a clean flat top.

The second Valium has loosened her mood considerably, and she finds herself giggling and humming Ariel Pink's "Put Your Number in My Phone."

After she rinses and dries herself, she tweezes out a few hairs that are corrupting the perfect line she's been trying to achieve at the top of her pubic area.

When she's satisfied, she brushes away the stray hairs, fine as spider legs, and uses a Sharpie to write across the expanse of flesh between her navel and the newly pristine flat top of her pubic hair.

She stands and beholds herself in the mirror, continuing to hum the Ariel Pink song. She grazes her fingertips across the three letters.

FUM

17

Except on weekends, Bicentennial Park is usually empty, but today it's even more desolate than usual, perhaps because of the unseasonably cold weather. It's only November 1, after all, but it feels like it could be January, with temperatures starting to dip below freezing.

Before they picked up Lavert, Cloris and Corinthia had to excavate Cloris's Beavertail Wild Sled from her jumbled basement and negotiate it into the back of her station wagon. The sled's color is marsh brown, and it's one of the best winter-fun investments Cloris has ever made.

After parking in the empty lot, Cloris, Corinthia, and Lavert cross the picnic area, which features several small barbecue units, all of which are heaped with snow. To get to Suicide Hill, they have to descend a small amphitheater and cross a cement stage, to the other side of a band shell, which leads to the top of the hill.

During the short walk, beyond a comment here and there about the weather, not much is said, and

Corinthia notices that Lavert's movements are slower than they were when she last saw him. He grimaced as they stepped onto the stage of the band shell.

"You okay?" she asked, carrying the sled.

"I'm straight," he said, although it certainly didn't seem that way.

Nevertheless, once they reached the top of the hill and peered down its slope to where it leveled off before a short stand of trees, Lavert perked up.

"Never been sleddin' before," he said.

During the walk over, Corinthia realized that there was no way she would fit in the sled. Although Cloris swore it was big enough for two people, the moment Corinthia hoisted it up on her shoulder, she knew it just wasn't true.

"The hard part is walking back up the hill," Cloris tells Corinthia and Lavert. "My jujitsu keeps me pretty fit, but even *I'm* probably only good for two or three trips."

"Let's do this," Lavert says, eager-eyed, a boyish lift in his voice. "While we're still young."

Corinthia sets the sled down.

"You two go," she says.

"No, you two," Cloris protests.

Though it pains her to say it, Corinthia tells them that she just won't fit in the thing and that she's happy to watch.

So Cloris and Lavert man the sled—Lavert sits in the back and spreads his legs so Cloris can sit between them—and after a count of three, Corinthia pushes them down the hill, and off they go. Cloris shrieks with joy, and Lavert simply cries out, *"You serious?"* over and over.

"You serious? You can't be serious. . . . You serious?"

Their descent lasts not even ten seconds, but it might as well be an eternity. Lavert's arms fly up over his head like he's riding a roller coaster. Cloris is a shrieking loaf of winter wear.

The sled comes to rest at the edge of the colorless, lifeless trees, the tops of which are silver with snow. An enormous blackbird, obviously immune to the unseasonably cold weather, springs from a branch and flies off.

Corinthia feels a barb of jealousy pricking at her heart, but she fights it. She knows that this happy moment shouldn't be about her.

As Cloris and Lavert ascend Suicide Hill, the vapor from their breath plumes above them. Lavert carries the sled as they trudge their way back up toward the band shell. Cloris laughs, and Corinthia can hear her say something about getting snow in the crack of her butt, and Lavert laughs, too, and keeps saying, "That was madness, yo. *Madness.*"

Lavert moves slowly, like he is suddenly very old.

He has to stop twice and set the sled down and put his hands on his knees before he can continue.

When they finally arrive at the back of the band shell, they are both winded. Cloris sits on one of the concrete steps, and Lavert is doubled over the sled with his hands on his knees again. Snowflakes encrust his thick dark eyelashes.

"That was ill," he says, panting. "Ill, yo."

"You guys should go again," Corinthia offers.

Lavert is holding his side now.

"You okay?" Corinthia asks him.

"I'm cool," he says. "I just need a minute."

He removes a glove, unzips his puffy winter coat, and reaches inside it, grimacing.

"Thanks for the triangle," Corinthia finally tells him. She's been waiting for this moment, hoping it would be less fraught with cold and fatigue, perhaps more private.

"I called your house and your moms told me you fell down and hurt yourself. I was worried about you," he says, still doubled over, his breath coming fast.

"It meant a lot," Corinthia says.

Lavert's hand emerges from his side and he puts his glove back on.

"Once more?" Lavert says to Cloris.

"You better believe it," she replies, and they're back in the sled.

Lavert has to stop and clutch his side once more.

"You sure this is okay?" Corinthia says.

"Positive," he replies.

As she did before, Corinthia counts to three and pushes them down the hill.

That evening, the snow continues to fall, slow and steady. Brill Bledsoe is in the kitchen, boiling water for his nightly Sleepytime tea, when, through the living-room patio doors, he sees his wife, Marlene, building what appears to be an enormous snowman. It is much taller than she is, more of a rectangular creature than the classic three-part snowman with a spherical base, midsection, and head. In order to access the top of her creation, Marlene is using a dinette chair that had been retired to the garage. Her breath freezes above her in white gusts. Brill stands at the counter with a tea bag poised over his mug, waiting for the kettle to whistle.

His wife's face looks chapped and glistens with perspiration. She shapes the top of the snow beast with her hands and reaches into the pocket of her puffy coat and produces what appears to be a plastic bag of light-blue candy. She places a piece where each of the snowman's eyes would be, makes a nose, and then adds four or five more pieces to create a mouth. It's more of a straight line than a smile, but it's a mouth nonetheless.

Marlene then steps down from the dinette chair and adds buttons down the center, equidistant, carefully considered.

When she is finished, she stares up at it with what appears to be a wistful expression. Brill Bledsoe has never felt further away from his wife than he does in this moment.

Later, in the middle of the night, Brill sneaks out of bed and comes down to the kitchen to boil another kettle of water. He boils two kettles, in fact. And after putting on his shoes and a hooded sweatshirt, he quietly lets himself out through the sliding patio doors and goes into the backyard with the two kettles of water. He sets the kettles down and simply looks up at the grotesque monstrosity that has taken over his backyard. He removes one of its buttons. It's a piece of salt-water taffy. He removes all the buttons, places them in the front pocket of his sweatshirt, then climbs onto the dinette chair and removes the mouth, the nose, and the eyes. He puts all the taffy in the sweatshirt pocket and then steps down from the dinette chair, grabs the first kettle, steps back onto the chair, and begins pouring the boiling water over the creature's head, which melts away with alarming velocity. He pours slowly. Thin ribbons of steam rise through the cold early-November night.

After he empties the first kettle, he grabs the second one and resumes pouring the boiling water over the now half-melted snow creature.

Is this supposed to be Corinthia? he wonders. *How could Marlene be so insensitive? Has she completely lost her mind?*

As the lower half of the snow creature melts down to nothing, a picture frame emerges. Brill recognizes it. It's from the living room, where all the other family photos are arranged on the old credenza. It's Channing's junior class portrait, the one featured in the yearbook. He is handsome and confident, a slight smile lifting his face. His hair is parted on the side, the same way Brill wears his. Channing looks like the kind of kid who has the rest of his life in front of him.

Brill Bledsoe goes to his knees, clutching the framed photo, and begins to sob as quietly as he can while the even, silent snow continues to fall all around him.

18

In the little ranch house belonging to Florida Birdsong, her grandson, Lavert, has just adjusted his hospice bed to a more upright position when his nurse, a soft-spoken white man named Nick, returns with a clean bedpan, which he places on the lower shelf of the bedside table. This room, which used to be filled with the many sewing machines and yarn-spinning devices that Florida Birdsong has collected over the years, was cleared out some three weeks ago, and the good people from hospice came and transformed it into a room for Lavert. Prior to this, Lavert was sleeping on a small twin bed in the basement, but Mary and Chad and Roberta from the hospice organization really felt it would be best for Lavert to spend his remaining days in a room that not only could be easily accessed by their nurses and various medical professionals but was also filled with a good amount of sunlight during the day.

"Your visitor's here," Nick tells Lavert, who nods and drinks from his water glass. His upper right arm has been outfitted with a pain-relieving unit from which extends a plunger that Lavert has free rein over now. It's the second week of November, and the baseboard heating system in Florida Birdsong's home isn't as good as it might have been some ten or fifteen years ago, so a small space heater has been set up beside Lavert's bed.

"Can I get some mouthwash?" Lavert asks his nurse.

"Of course," Nick replies.

He exits and returns moments later with a small bottle of mint-flavored Listerine. Nick undoes the top for Lavert, who drinks from it, swishes the liquid around his mouth, and then spits into a small kidney-shaped plastic basin that Nick holds just below his chin.

Save for a few patches of hair, Lavert is almost bald now, and his weight loss over the course of the past few weeks is startling.

Lavert adjusts his automatic bed once more so that he's the slightest bit more vertical.

"I'm ready," he says.

Nick exits, then returns moments later with Corinthia Bledsoe, who has to duck under the door's upper casing. Corinthia is wearing her favorite sweater, and she's put on just the slightest hint of makeup. Her winter coat is folded over her arm.

"Hi," she says to Lavert.

As soon as she sees him, tears well up in her eyes. She'd promised herself she wouldn't get upset, at least not this quickly. She swallows the lump in her throat and manages to hold it together.

Lavert says, "Hey, lady."

Nick says that he'll leave them alone and that he's just outside in the living room if they should need anything.

Corinthia thanks him, and then Nick exits, shutting the door.

"Come closer," Lavert says. "I ain't gonna bite you."

It's only been two weeks since she's seen him, but he looks like he's been starved and tortured for months.

"Bring that chair over," he says, pointing to a comfortable overstuffed chair in the corner. "Gramamma can move it, so it can't be too heavy."

Corinthia crosses to the chair and pulls it closer. She sets her coat on the floor and sits.

"So, how you been?" he says.

"Good," she says. "I've been good."

"Stayin' outta trouble?"

"Trying to," she says.

"They let you back in school yet?"

She tells him that she spoke with Principal Ticonderoga just yesterday and that they'd like her to start coming back to classes after Thanksgiving break.

"You lookin' forward to that?" he asks.

"I don't know," she says. "Not really."

Then she asks him how he's doing and quickly apologizes.

"I'm sorry," she says. "Stupid question."

"I'm not dead *yet*," he says, joking. He smiles. Even with the weight loss, his smile has the same undeniable power. He says, "I still got a little fight left in me."

"I brought you something," Corinthia tells him, and from her pocket she takes out her copy of Lorcan Nutt's *The Smallest Hands* and gives it to him. It's the same copy that's been overdue at the library for some time. Out of solidarity for Cloris's termination, she's decided to keep it.

"Not sure if you're reading much right now," she says, "but if you get bored . . ." She has to swallow hard again. "It's one of my favorites."

And then she loses it.

"Hey," Lavert says. "Hey, now . . ."

Corinthia leans forward and lets her head fall onto the side of the bed. Lavert places his hand on her hair. Her sobs rise up out of her like wet wads of cotton.

"Sh-sh-sh," Lavert says. "None of that now."

"I'm sorry, Lavert," she manages to say. "I promised myself I wouldn't do this."

She sobs some more, and he keeps his hand on her head. He even pets it a little. After a few minutes, she lifts her head off the side of the bed. Her face is slick with tears and mucus.

"Some tissues right there," he says, pointing to a box of Kleenex on the bedside table.

Corinthia takes a few tissues and blows her nose. The noise is so loud, it sounds like an enormous brass instrument in a marching band.

Lavert says, "Damn, girl!" and they both laugh a bit.

When they are quiet, Lavert thanks her for the book.

"I thought you might like it," she says.

He says, "I'll definitely check it out."

Then Corinthia tells him how nice his grandmother is.

Lavert says, "I assume she told you everything."

"Pretty much."

"So you know things ain't gonna get no better."

Corinthia nods.

"Which means they're only gonna get worse."

She nods again.

And then she asks him if he's in a lot of pain.

He slowly nods. "Thank God they gimme this," he says, looking at the pain-relief plunger. "I just hit the little red button, and off I go."

"What is it?" she asks.

"Morphine," he says. "Answer to all my problems."

There is a thick sheen on his forehead. It looks as if a substance has been applied to his flesh rather than secreted from it. His collarbone is prominent, his cheeks sunken.

"My body can't make no more nutrition," he explains, "so I'm basically starvin' to death."

Corinthia nods.

"I thought about callin' you a coupla times since we went sleddin'," he says, "but I figured you wouldn't wanna see all this."

"I don't mind," Corinthia says.

In the other room, the TV is turned on.

"There goes Gramamma, watchin' her programs."

"What's her favorite show?" Corinthia asks.

"She likes *Survivor*," he says. "*Survivor* and *Judge Judy*. She can't get enough of *Judge Judy*. Always talkin' back at the TV, carryin' on. Poor Nick's gotta sit through all of it."

"He seems nice," Corinthia says.

"Yeah, he's cool," Lavert says. "Nick's my boy."

Corinthia tells Lavert how she was planning a trip to Northland College in northern Wisconsin; how she walked into the principal's office at Lugo Memorial in the middle of third period, even though she was still technically suspended, and persuaded Principal Ticonderoga and Vice Principal Mejerus to help her set up a special student visit. After conferring with each other for a few minutes, they thought that it was actually a very good idea, a productive use of Corinthia's time, and that it showed strong initiative on her part. And then Principal Ticonderoga called the Northland College admissions office right there and even asked to speak with the academic dean and proceeded to sing the praises of one of Lugo Memorial's "most advanced students," and it all worked out, so she and Cloris, who is still unemployed and more than happy to have something to look forward to, are planning to leave in a week.

"What part of Wisconsin?" Lavert asks.

"Ashland," Corinthia replies. "It's basically as far north as you can go in this part of the Midwest."

Lavert says, "I've never been that far north. It's prolly mad cold."

They are quiet. During the silence, Lavert places a clear mask over his mouth, which is attached to a tube that is connected to an oxygen tank. He releases a valve on the tank and breathes in and out several times. It's hard for Corinthia to watch. His cheeks cave in even more when he inhales. His eyes bulge. The space between his collarbones hollows grotesquely.

When he has had enough oxygen, he shuts the valve and removes the mask.

He stares at Corinthia a long moment and says, "So, can I come with you?"

The question shocks her.

"Of course," she says. "But is that a good idea?"

He says, "At this point, pretty much everything there is is a good idea."

"Will the cold bother you?"

"I'm burnin' up all the time now, anyway," he says. "That kinda cold'll prolly feel good."

"Will your grandmother let you come?"

He says, "I'm a grown-ass man. I can do what I want."

Though it goes against her better judgment, the idea thrills Corinthia. She pictures Lavert, Cloris, and her in the car together. A road trip! A true adventure!

"But you gotta do something for me," Lavert adds.

"Okay," Corinthia hears herself say. "What?"

"When we get up there," Lavert says, "and I want to go to sleep, you'll help me sleep."

Corinthia says, "That sounds easy enough."

"But *really* sleep."

The idea of what he's suggesting is suddenly lodged deep in her like a coin she'd been forced to swallow: indigestible, irreducible.

She recalls the premonition she had some weeks

ago, after she'd taken his hand in hers . . . the certainty of that feeling.

"All you gotta do is make sure I got plenty of pain relief," Lavert explains quietly, "and when the time is right, I'll just take off my oxygen mask and my heart'll slow down so much I'll fall asleep."

"How do you know that'll work?" Corinthia says.

"'Cause Nick told me it would."

"Then why can't you ask him to do it?"

"'Cause he could get in serious trouble for it. Prolly lose his job. Besides, he's my boy and everything, but I don't care for him the way I care for you."

"What about your grandmother?"

"Not in a million years. I bring this kinda thing up with Gramamma, and that woman'll get so amped, she'll have me put in a hospital with guards around me twenty-four seven. Security cameras, shit like that."

"Okay," Corinthia hears herself say. "It's a deal."

He says, "You gotta promise me, Corinthia."

"I do," she says.

"Say it."

She looks at him long and hard, and he won't look away. Finally she says it.

"I promise."

19

November 19, 2015

Dave,

This will be my final letter to you. Everything is set in motion. I'm going to go find the log. It's been great sharing all of my personal thoughts and feelings with you. I think it has helped lead me to a new place. Dave, you are a true friend, and I've valued our time together.

I leave with you The Official Real List, which, as you know, I've been compiling over the course of the past few months.

Be well, Dave.

Billy Eugene Ball

The Official Real List

1. Cinthia Hauk
2. Mark Maestro
3. Lars Silence
4. Troy Aurora

5. Nate Bluff

6. Britney Purina

7. Todd Chicklis

8. Bronson Kaminski

9. Ward Newbury

10. Guidance Counselor Denton Smock

11. Vice Principal Mejerus

12. Principal Ticonderoga

13. Rose Bryant

14. Breanne Billson

15. Rod Benedict

16. Gerald LaPasso

17. Kirk Batis

18. Dennis Hill

19. Bliss Ford-Chadwick

20. Ben Krabbenhoff

21. Bo Fitzgerald

22. Terry Fitzgerald

23. Anton Walkup

24. Jodi Glibbenshautz

25. Gordon Gosser

26. Richard Schotmaker

27. William Hughes

28. Doug Shapiro

29. Anna Fugatz

30. Jake Dowdell

31. Chuckie Ishwerwood

32. Charles Fuchs

33. John Bell

34. Dave Bell

35. Oscar Unitas

36. Susu Plesac

37. Brian Antoon III

38. Paul Respert

39. Sandra Wick

40. Scooter Peeples

41. Frank Batavia

42. Ingrid Snell

43. Robert Yoder

44. Fin O'Neill

45. Brenda Underwood

46. Sean Black

47. Shawn White

48. Mike Stith

49. Rider Waddell

50. Boyd Kingman

51. Lloyd Rhodes

52. Samantha Poose

53. Floyd Taphorn

54. Octavia Blintz

55. Ryan Schroeder

56. Ben Hilliard

57. Austin Lee

On Tuesday, November 24, two days before the onset of Thanksgiving vacation, a white delivery van from lugoblooms.com arrives in the parking lot of Lugo Memorial High School.

A deliveryman wearing a navy-blue outfit with a matching visor proceeds to enter the main school building with three red delivery crates containing sixty-four purple lotus flowers. Each one has been individually set in a protective plastic container.

It took some careful maneuvering, especially when it came to opening the van's double doors, but the deliveryman was able to bring the full complement of flowers into the building in one go.

Following meticulous instructions, after conferring with a woman from the administration office, he specially delivered each lotus flower throughout the school, one at a time. Although over half of the sixty-four students were found in the cafeteria during their lunch period, it took the deliveryman a little over an hour to complete his task.

The recipients were Cinthia Hauk, Mark Maestro, Lars Silence, Troy Aurora, Nate Bluff, Britney Purina, Todd Chicklis, Bronson Kaminski, Ward Newbury, Guidance Counselor Denton Smock, Vice Principal Mejerus, Principal Ticonderoga, Rose Bryant, Breanne Billson, Rod Benedict, Gerald LaPasso, Kirk Batis, Dennis Hill, Bliss Ford-Chadwick, Ben Krabbenhoff, Bo Fitzgerald, Terry Fitzgerald, Anton Walkup, Jodi Glibbenshautz, Gordon Gosser, Richard Schotmaker, William Hughes, Doug Shapiro, Anna Fugatz, Jake Dowdell, Chuckie Ishwerwood, Charles Fuchs, John Bell, Dave Bell, Oscar Unitas, Susu Plesac, Brian Antoon III, Paul Respert, Sandra Wick, Scooter Peeples, Frank Batavia, Ingrid Snell, Robert Yoder, Fin O'Neill, Brenda Underwood, Sean Black, Shawn White, Mike Stith, Rider Waddell, Boyd Kingman, Lloyd Rhodes, Samantha Poose, Floyd Taphorn, Octavia Blintz, Ryan Schroeder, Ben Hilliard, Austin Lee, Walker Cash, Ed Rene, Scott Dale, Walter Riggan, Buddy Mikelson, Kate Doss, Hayden Mangione, Timothy Eubanks, Winona Street, and Peter Elms.

With regard to Principal Margo Ticonderoga, Vice

Principal Doogan Mejerus, and Guidance Counselor Denton Smock, their lotus flowers were delivered directly to their offices and placed in the center of their desks.

A brief, typewritten note accompanied each plastic container, which read:

Dear _____,

Eat this lotus flower. It will make you forget all the things that make you sad and you will feel better.

Sincerely,

Billy Ball

Lugo Memorial High School

Class of 2019

Earlier that same morning, just before dawn, Billy Ball got out of bed, already fully clothed. He was careful not to wake his mother, who was asleep down the hall.

After putting on his shoes, winter coat, and hat, he quietly exited his house on Pinewood Drive and walked approximately two miles through the snowy neighborhoods of Lugo, toward the edge of town.

It was a peaceful morning, with only an occasional crow's caw marring the silence. It felt to Billy like his entire hometown was sleeping, and he was pleased about this.

It felt as if the world was ready.

When he reached the frontage road, he walked north for a little more than a quarter mile. There was very little wind, and the snow made everything seem calm and placid. When Billy came to a stand of trees that looked inviting, he crossed the threshold of dead, frozen grass and barren brambles and proceeded to remove all his clothes and leave them at the edge of the woods.

The air was crisp and cold, and the earliest hint of morning sun was starting to blue the sky, which Billy could see through the canopy of trees.

Snow chilled the bottoms of his naked feet and his body shivered, but he steeled himself and walked into the depths of the forest buoyed by a calm sense of certainty.

The following evening, just before dusk, having been devoured by gray wolves, Billy Eugene Ball, devoid of his heart, lungs, liver, intestines, cheeks, eyeballs, hands, and tongue, was discovered in the woods along the frontage road. On his wrist, undamaged, was a men's Timex Expedition analog/digital watch.

20

The trip up to northern Wisconsin takes approximately eleven hours. Corinthia is determined to arrive on the campus of Northland College no later than 4 p.m., as this is the last hour that the admissions office is willing to conduct a tour. The dramatic setting, featuring Lake Superior and a nearby national forest, happens to be one of the school's major selling points.

With the help of Lavert's nurse, Nick, they are able to load up Cloris's station wagon, whose muffler Corinthia paid to have replaced three days ago. In the back of the station wagon is Lavert's wheelchair, Corinthia's Lugo Memorial gym bag containing a change of clothes, and a few extra blankets.

They depart Lugo at 4:30 a.m. Though an absurd notion, considering his current state of decline, Lavert did offer to drive if necessary, but Cloris insisted that she take the wheel the entire way. It's the only option, really, as Corinthia can't fit in the front seat.

The plan is to head north on Interstate 39 at Bloomington, continue on past Rockford; Madison,

Wisconsin; and then Wausau, where they will switch to Highway 51 and drive past other Wisconsin towns, called Merrill, Tomahawk, Harshaw, Hazelhurst, Woodruff, Manitowish Waters, Mercer, and then Ironwood, Michigan, where they will have to change to Route 2, which will lead them west for some forty miles before they arrive in Ashland, Wisconsin, a small port city near the head of Chequamegon Bay, which is an inlet of Lake Superior.

The first few hours of the ride are relatively uneventful as they ascend through South Central Illinois, with its modest snow-dusted farmlands marked with silos, corncribs, lopsided barns, and an army of windmills so vast, it almost looks like the setting for a science fiction movie.

Lavert sleeps in the passenger's seat, the paperback edition of Lorcan Nutt's *The Smallest Hands* in his lap. His head, which is covered with a silk do-rag and a thick wool cap, rests against the window. His oxygen mask covers his mouth, the fog of his breath clouding its surface.

Nick was kind enough to provide a portable, battery-operated morphine cartridge. "It should be plenty for what you need," he quietly told Corinthia.

The red-buttoned plunger rests in Lavert's left hand, which Corinthia keeps a keen eye on from the backseat, where she reclines on a pillow, extending her legs as comfortably as she can, though the peaks of her knees nearly graze the station wagon's ceiling.

It's still dark in the early predawn, and Cloris drives with the radio quietly playing early eighties classic rock. It's a rock block of REO Speedwagon.

"What does he normally listen to?" she asks, finding Corinthia's eyes in the rearview mirror.

"I think he's into Tupac."

Cloris scans the airwaves, lands on a hip-hop station.

The beginning of their journey is overcome with quiet. There is the sense that they are going much further than the six hundred miles and eleven hours that was predicted by the travel website.

Three hours into the trip, they are passing through Rockford when Cloris speaks after a long silence.

"Do you love him?" she asks Corinthia, finding her eyes again in the rearview mirror.

Corinthia stares back at her.

"He's asleep," Cloris tells her.

Corinthia nods.

"Are you afraid?" Cloris asks.

Corinthia considers her promise to Lavert, then nods again.

When they cross the Wisconsin border, Lavert stirs in the passenger's seat. They've completed almost half the trip, and after Madison they talk about food. They pull into a Wendy's rest stop. Cloris asks Lavert if he'd like to order anything, but he says he isn't hungry. She and Corinthia get cheeseburgers and small Frostys and eat in the parking lot. It's barely 11 a.m. and after Cloris finishes eating, she goes inside to use the bathroom.

Lavert is staring out the window, his oxygen mask still fogged. He seems troubled, far away.

"You still want to do this?" Corinthia asks.

He nods.

"You sure?"

He nods again.

As Cloris is returning to the car, Lavert removes his oxygen mask and, with a voice that is at once hoarse and faint, says, "Just lemme know when we're an hour away, and I'll start hittin' this plunger."

As they travel farther north on Highway 51, the towns are smaller and their populations begin to dwindle. It's as if this region of the country has been besieged by some sort of plague. Snow covers everything. It almost feels as if there are no other seasons here, only winter and variations of winter.

They stop for gas in Mercer, and just before Ironwood, a town so small it seems to exist purely for fast food, a few motels, and diesel fuel, Corinthia alerts Lavert that they're roughly an hour away.

He nods and begins depressing his morphine plunger every ten minutes.

They arrive in Ashland just before 4 p.m. The sky is gray and the air contains a brutal chill that Corinthia has never experienced before. It's the kind of weather you read about in books, like the bone-freezing damp that beleaguered sailors must endure in epic novels about whales and lunatic ship captains.

Stretching into the horizon before them is Lake Superior: first the frozen bay, and then the storied Great Lake, which appears to extend into infinity, like an ocean.

Cloris parks at the threshold of the small beach and helps Corinthia unload Lavert's wheelchair from the back of the station wagon. There are no other cars. Corinthia brings the wheelchair around to the passenger's side, and when she helps Lavert out of the car, she's stunned at his weightlessness. His arms are slack and his legs are puppet-like. He seems even thinner than when they started their trip, some eleven hours ago.

After Cloris closes the station wagon's back door, she says good-bye and heads to the Northland College admissions office, where she will masquerade as Corinthia Bledsoe of southern Illinois's Lugo Memorial High School. The fake ID that she made at the library, along with Corinthia's Social Security card, is tucked into her back pocket.

Corinthia watches the station wagon pull away. Once she gets Lavert seated comfortably in the wheelchair, she arranges a few blankets over his lap, secures his oxygen mask, and checks to see that his morphine unit is still properly inserted into the port in his upper arm.

"You good?" she asks him.

He nods, his eyes sunken and enormous.

She pulls his knit hat a little lower on his head and begins wheeling him across the parking lot, past a stand of tall, ancient, snow-heaped evergreen trees, and then onto a gravel path, which leads to the beach.

The sky looks iron, Superior an expanse of slate. Beyond the bay, far out in the depths of the Great Lake, there is only the slightest hint of moving water. It ripples like the troubled hide of some prehistoric sleeping beast.

When they reach the frozen beach, pushing the wheelchair becomes cumbersome, but Corinthia presses on. Lavert keeps his chin tucked into his chest, his oxygen mask snug over his face.

Improbably, a gull arcs toward the shore and lands on the ice. It trots around, wings tucked, all skinny legs and clumsy, like an old man looking for a lost coin, and then flies off.

Corinthia parks the chair some twenty feet from the water.

"It's cold," she says.

Lavert nods, his oxygen mask still fogging up, his eyes peeking out from under his hat.

"You warm enough?"

He nods again.

They stare out at the Great Lake. It feels like the end of the earth, as if there's nothing beyond where the water meets the cloudless, colorless horizon.

Lavert gestures with his hand, pointing toward the lake.

"You want to get up?" Corinthia asks.

He nods.

Corinthia comes around to his front and removes the two blankets from his lap. Lavert reaches inside his parka and disconnects the morphine cartridge from its port, then hands it to Corinthia, who puts it in her coat pocket.

He then motions to Corinthia in a manner suggesting that he'd like to stand, so she helps him out of the wheelchair. She offers her forearm for support and he uses it to pull himself up. Once on his feet, he teeters a bit but then bends his knees a few times. After a moment, he lets go of Corinthia's forearm. She drops down to her knees, as if looking after a toddler, ready to catch him if he falls, but he shoos her away, determined to prove that he's able to stand on his own.

They take each other in.

The same hungry gull returns, unleashing a screech as it wheels overhead. Its cry is almost human in its desperation.

Corinthia nods to Lavert, and he returns the nod and then removes his oxygen mask and hands it to her. He pivots toward Lake Superior. Corinthia places the disconnected oxygen mask in her other coat pocket and starts to follow him, but Lavert turns back to her and shakes his head.

"Okay," Corinthia says. "Go, then."

Lavert stands on the frozen beach, hunched, holding his side with one hand, his knee with the other, like a much older version of himself considering the shape of the simple moment he's arrived at.

He then pivots again and starts to walk.

When he reaches the edge of the frozen bay, he stops for a moment and takes in the enormous expanse before him, and then he eases himself onto the ice, moving very carefully.

Although she has an impulse to go to him, Corinthia stays where she is, still on her knees.

Lavert shuffles out a few more feet and then starts to lift his arms high in the air. He slides to and fro, a few feet to his left, a few feet to his right. He slips a bit, his arms jerk out. He almost falls backward, but somehow he regains his balance. He has to go to a knee.

Corinthia can hear the wind whistling through the evergreen trees behind her. She arranges one of the blankets on the frozen beach, folds it into a square, then sits on it, with her legs crossed.

Lavert rests for a bit, still looking toward the horizon, and then manages to get to his feet and slowly walk back to the beach.

The light is starting to fade. Corinthia studies his thinned silhouette as he approaches. Each step is careful, intensely considered. His winter boots look huge, too heavy for his legs.

When Lavert finally reaches her, he is winded. His body is racked with fatigue, but his face is joyous. Although it seems to be getting darker by the moment, Corinthia can see that his eyes are bright and filled with a boyish wonder.

Lavert manages to lower himself to his knees and then leans toward Corinthia. She gently pulls his body into hers, his head and neck and shoulders easing into her torso, his legs bent at the knees, his feet tucked under his seat, the whole of him held in the bowl of her legs.

Corinthia closes her arms around him.

Once they are comfortable, they simply sit there,

staring out at everything: at Lake Superior, at the fading endless horizon, at the stand of evergreen trees off to the left, at the snowy gusts skirling across the beach.

"How was that?" Corinthia asks.

"It was good," Lavert says. "Real good."

His voice is faint, dreamy.

"Thank you," he says.

As his breathing slows, it starts to snow. The wind causes the flakes to tumble in many directions. It seems odd that it would snow on a beach, like it's one of the world's cruel secrets.

It is a brief, fitful snow, not even a minute long.

Corinthia lowers her face to Lavert, who is turned into her now. She adjusts his head, turns his face toward hers, hopes to feel his breath on her cheek, her eyes, the skin on her lips . . . but there is nothing.

They stay this way for a few more minutes—Lavert cradled in her lap—warming each other on the cold beach.

Eventually Corinthia rises and hoists Lavert into the wheelchair. She folds the two blankets, places them on his lap, tucks his hands underneath them. Then she gently closes his eyes with a fingertip.

As she wheels him along the gravel path toward the parking lot, she can see that Cloris has returned with the station wagon. She is standing beside it, next to the driver's seat. They wave at each other.

At the station wagon, Corinthia wheels Lavert to the passenger's side, and Cloris slides in and helps her arrange his body in the front seat and secure his seat belt. Cloris then scoots over to the driver's side and starts the car and puts the heat on.

The headlights of the station wagon shoot out over the short beach, new gusts of snow swirling through their beams.

EPILOGUE

Three months later, Brill Bledsoe, traveling alone in his wife's Hyundai, pulls into a parking lot in the town square of Venus, Texas, a small hamlet in Johnson County, thirty miles south of Dallas, just below the state's panhandle. He has traveled some seven hundred miles in the middle of February—it's the only time he could take off from work at the meatpacking plant—so he can witness firsthand a nomadic freak show known as *The Beautiful Apocalypse*, specifically its newest attraction, a soothsaying giantess billed as "Fräulein Feffi Fum: Seer of Dread."

As outlined in the four-color brochure, which also features an alligator-skinned child called Gator Gary; a young woman covered in thick simian-like fur called Weird Wendy, who rides a unicycle while playing the flute; and some creature altogether surreal called Plato the Potato Boy, for a mere five dollars, you can sit with clairvoyant phenom Fräulein Fum, and if you simply allow her to take one of your hands in hers, within sixty seconds, she will tell you a terrible thing that will happen to you. The brochure promises it to be a one-on-one encounter like no other.

Brill parks the Hyundai just below the Venus water tower, which is quite similar to the one in Lugo, with its white block letters inset in a baby-blue band. It's 72 degrees, with bright, clear skies, but Brill expected it to be hotter. Nonetheless, it's a far cry from the frigid temperatures of southern Illinois. Last week, an ice storm felled several branches of the older trees on Stained Glass Drive. Since mid-November, Lugo has been impacted in a crusty hide of snow, so, as he weaves his way through the hundreds of cars in the parking lot, it's nice to be able to walk around wearing only a knit shirt and his Bazoo Meatpacking Windbreaker.

An enormous white big top has been erected on a park green. The tent is so large, it almost dwarfs the lawn, whose discernible fringe of grass is dry and faded. Hundreds of people mill about food trucks, merchandise tables stacked high with T-shirts and trucker hats, and a fleet of portable bathrooms that has been set up around the tent's perimeter. A banner with THE BEAUTIFUL APOCALYPSE has been draped across the entrance. As Brill stands in line to purchase a twenty-dollar admissions ticket, he is surprised to see how many parents have brought their children. The website images alone are the stuff of nightmares:

humans with spired teeth and cloven feet and donkey tails and extra limbs. Although they update their web content regularly, they have done a good job to keep Fräulein Feffi Fum an enigma, as the description of her attraction is limited to a field of mysterious text floating in an hourglass.

CLAIRVOYANT GIANTESS!
SEER OF DREAD!

At the box office, as the very normal-looking young woman with the ponytail protruding from the back of her Houston Astros baseball cap runs Brill's bank card, he asks her where he might find the giantess.

"Triple F is all the way in the back of the tent," the woman says.

"'Triple F'?"

"Fräulein Feffi Fum," she says. "You won't miss it. There's a long line. She's become our main attraction since Tulsa. She has her own wigwam now."

"Wow," Brill says.

"It's an additional five dollars to see her, and they accept only cash in there. Do you have cash?"

"I have cash," Brill assures her.

When she hands his bank card back to him, Brill realizes that her right hand is shaped like a lobster claw. It's a shocking image, but Brill manages to maintain his composure. He thanks her and makes his way through the big top's entrance.

Inside, it smells like popcorn and human breath and mosquito repellent and deodorant spray, and hundreds of fellow ticket buyers walk slowly through the various installations with stunned expressions on their faces.

Not even ten feet inside the tent, he's approached by an armless woman in a red gingham dress who is pulling a Radio Flyer wagon filled with pink blobs of cotton candy. The wagon is attached to a chain that's been belted around her waist.

"Cotton candy?" she says to Brill, who finds her voice almost as beautiful as her face. She wears her dark hair in French braids, and her eyes are stunningly green.

"How are you able to serve it?" he asks, surprising himself with the uncharacteristically potentially insensitive question.

"With my hands," the young woman replies.

In a swift move, she hops onto one leg and grabs a long cone of cotton candy with what at first appears to be her left foot, but it turns out to be a hand, complete with an opposable thumb. Brill Bledsoe is dumbstruck, to say the least. It's not an ugly hand by any means. In fact, it looks to be a hand worthy of her beauty. Her fingers are long—delicate, even—and their nails are painted red to match the color of the woven plaid in her dress.

It's the hand of a pianist, he thinks.

The young woman offers him the cotton candy and says, "I can make change, too. I even do foreign currency."

"No, thank you," Brill says, and she deftly returns the cone of cotton candy to its slot in the wagon.

He can't help noticing the other hand, connected to the bottom of her other leg. It, too, boasts attractive, fluted fingers and red fingernails.

Brill wants to ask this young woman so many questions, such as "Do you like doing this job?" and "Do you have a family somewhere?" and "Doesn't being gawked at all day make you sad?" and "What do they pay you?" and "Do you browse the Internet with your feet—I mean hands?" and "Does your condition force you to contend with all sorts of personal hygiene issues?" But the words are lodged in his throat, so he simply thanks her again and moves on.

It's hot in the tent. Or maybe Brill's just incredibly nervous. He's always prided himself on maintaining his composure. His entire life he's been praised by doctors and nurses for his low distance-runner's pulse. But now he can feel himself sweating through his knit shirt, so he removes his Windbreaker, folds it over his arm, and continues on.

Moments later, he happens upon a small group of five or six people peering down into a large white box. On a post that's been pounded into the earth, a small placard reads THE TEN-INCH MAN. A woman moves away from the gathering of people, and Brill steps into the vacancy.

Inside the box, dressed in a white tuxedo and holding a walking cane, is a miniature man, perhaps no taller than the coffee thermos that Brill takes with him to work every morning. The little man seems to be deeply recessed in the box, several feet down.

It has to be an illusion, Brill thinks. *They must have dug out several feet of earth to achieve the effect. It's a trick of forced perspective.*

But when Brill really looks, the Ten-Inch Man doesn't seem far away at all. In fact, his features are distinct. The man is old, perhaps sixty, with slicked-back gray hair and light-blue baggy eyes.

The Ten-Inch Man simply stares back up at his small audience. At one point, the Ten-Inch Man waves up at them, and a few of them wave back. "Hello," a heavyset woman in a Dallas Mavericks jersey calls to him, waving. It troubles Brill to think that this poor man's life has been relegated to spending untold hours in a white box, staring up at normal-size people's stunned faces. Brill is overwhelmed with the impulse to reach down and grab him and put him in the pocket of his Windbreaker and take him back to Illinois. But then what? Would he drop him off in the center of town? Would he set him free at the edge of a cornfield? Keep him in the basement? Would the Ten-Inch Man insist on living in another box?

When Brill catches himself turning into one of his fellow gawkers, he decides he's seen enough and moves away.

Just get to the wigwam, he tells himself. *Keep moving . . .*

Some fifty feet deeper into the tent, a group of fifty or so students stands before a large terrarium with PLATO THE POTATO BOY advertised on a neon archway. Brill stops and watches from the back of the crowd. Inside the terrarium, it appears, a man without limbs has been planted into rich brown soil. He is shirtless and bald, and possesses a disarmingly deep voice, which is amplified over a public address speaker. Several dandelions have been arranged in the soil around him. He speaks into a lavaliere microphone hanging around his neck, which boasts perhaps two of the thickest veins Brill's ever seen.

Plato the Potato Boy proselytizes passionately about the evils of the digital world. "Throw your smartphone AWAY!" he cries. "Talk to each other FACE-TO-FACE! Write a freaking LETTER to someone, with a freaking PEN, and put it in the freaking MAIL, you FREAKS! Do something VICTORIAN for a change! Or go live in a NATIONAL FOREST and learn how to build a FIRE and use a HATCHET and FISH and CAMP and get inspired to start this awful world OVER!"

The students are rapt. Many are wearing Plato the Potato Boy T-shirts.

If this isn't a cult, then I don't know what is, Brill thinks.

Brill looks around and finally spots the wigwam at the back of the big top.

Plato the Potato Boy's amplified voice fades as Brill moves away.

There is a huge line to see the clairvoyant giantess. Many have brought portable stools and beach chairs, and the procession snakes this way and that. If Brill had to guess, there might be fifty to sixty people waiting to have their dread told to them. Many fan themselves with freak-show programs. Some have actual miniature battery-operated fans, which they hold in front of their tired, sweaty, beleaguered faces.

Brill takes his place at the end of the line.

A bare-chested African-American man wearing a top hat, suspenders, and white pants makes his way through the line, collecting money. After he takes the five dollars from Brill, he says, "Will you be offering your left or right hand?"

"Excuse me?" Brill replies, confused.

"Will Fräulein Fum be taking your left or right hand? For your prophecy."

"Oh," Brill says. "My right hand."

The man then takes Brill's left hand, turns it so the knuckles are facing up, and stamps it with what appears to be a cylinder of ChapStick. Then he removes the top hat and bows to Brill, revealing a six-inch, flesh-colored horn protruding from the crown of his head.

"Thank you, sir," the man says, and then places the top hat back on his head, covering the horn.

After the man moves on to the next person, Brill looks down to see three small purple *F*s marking the flat surface above his wrist.

Fräulein Feffi Fum, Brill thinks.

Did Corinthia rename herself or did some freak-show higher-up assign the name to her?

Is my daughter now speaking with a German accent?

So much has changed in the past year. First Channing disappeared and then his only daughter never returned from a college visit, and then, just six weeks ago, on Christmas Eve, in the middle of the night, he received a call from a neighbor who had discovered Marlene, his wife of twenty years, walking barefoot down the middle of Stained Glass Drive, wearing only her nightgown, trudging through the falling snow, carrying a laundry basket full of Channing's workout gear, babbling indecipherably. Since then, Marlene's been staying at Streamwood Manor, a private psychiatric hospital up in Centralia, about an hour north of Lugo, where Brill goes to visit her on weekends.

Brill learns from a Houston man who gets in line behind him that Venus used to be a kind of layover town for crooks on the lam.

"That motel on the other side of the water tower is where they'd stay," he tells Brill. "Then they'd head to Louisiana and try to disappear in Shreveport or Monroe or someplace like that."

The man is referring to the very motel where Brill is staying tonight.

"Don't worry—it's safe now. I'm Russell," the man says, extending his hand. He is wearing a colorful Hawaiian shirt and possesses a face like a walrus, distinguished by an impressive, platinum-colored handlebar mustache.

Brill shakes his hand. "Brill," he says. "Brill Bledsoe."

Russell goes on to tell Brill that this is his third visit. Feffi Fum has already correctly prophesied two "bad things" that have come true. First, his German shepherd, Julius, died. And then his house got robbed.

"All they took was my sixty-inch flat-screen TV," he explains, "but I did get robbed."

"And you're back again," Brill says.

"Here I am," Russell agrees. "I guess dread is sort of addictive."

He tells Brill how he first saw the Fräulein at Lyon College in Arkansas. And then, after Julius died (kidney failure), he just absolutely *had* to see her again, so he followed *The Beautiful Apocalypse* to Belhaven University in Jackson, Mississippi.

"Waited in line for three days before I finally got to see her again," he says. "And that's when she predicted the robbery."

"After her prophecy about the robbery, did you do anything to *prevent* it?" Brill asks.

"That's the thing," Russell cries. "I just sort of waited around for it to happen! And then it did! Fate is so cool!"

According to Russell, *The Beautiful Apocalypse* was initially visiting only college towns, but when Fum came along, they had to expand beyond the higher-education circuit.

"Popular demand and all that," Russell says.

Brill wonders how this makes his daughter feel. Is she proud of helping to increase the demand for *The Beautiful Apocalypse*? Is she even aware of it?

"So, why are you in line?" Russell asks. "You want to know something specific, or are you just thrill seeking?"

"Well," Brill says, "my son disappeared back toward the beginning of the school year. I was thinking maybe she could tell me something about him."

"That's a damn good reason," Russell says. "Sorry about your son."

"And I'm sorry about Julius," Brill offers.

As they slowly inch their way closer to the white wigwam, Brill starts to worry that he might not get to see his daughter. The line is just moving so slowly.

An hour passes.

And then another.

Brill and Russell talk about many things: Russell's son, Hans, a young marine who is serving his third tour of duty in Afghanistan; Brill's various over-the-counter health supplements (fish oil, glucosamine, and a probiotic called Vital Biotics); Russell's love of dove hunting and bass fishing (Falcon Lake is the very best spot, down in Zapata); and the story of Channing's disappearance the night of the tornadoes as well as his many athletic achievements.

Finally, improbably, it seems — some three hours later — Brill is next up.

A middle-aged female security guard stationed beside a short velvet rope cautions Brill against taking photos or videos and tells him that he will have a five-minute encounter, after which he will be expected to leave the wigwam, and that if he wishes to spend more time with Fräulein Fum, he must go to the end of the line, pay another five dollars, and get restamped. The woman's face is tattooed with hundreds of thin green pinstripes. She wears a black T-shirt with *The Beautiful Apocalypse*'s initials on the front and SECURITY on the back. She speaks in a military manner, and Brill notices what appears to be a remote control holstered to her waist.

"What's that?" he asks, pointing to it.

"My Taser gun," she says.

"Do you ever have to use it?"

"Not very often," she says.

Do these dread seekers try to hurt Corinthia? he wonders. *Is my daughter in danger?*

Moments later, the person who had been in line in front of him — a thin, dark-haired woman holding a photo album — emerges, dabbing at her eyes with a Kleenex. Brill wants to go straight in, but the security guard lady with the pin-striped face closes the rope and holds her hand up.

"She's done for the day?" Brill asks, indignant.

He feels as if his heart has dropped into his stomach.

"We always give her a minute for recovery," she says. "Her seeing takes its toll."

After what feels like an interminable sixty seconds, she unclips the rope.

"Good luck," Russell calls to Brill as he enters the wigwam.

His daughter is seated on an enormous wooden throne. On her head she wears what appears to be a nun's white wimple and neckerchief. She also wears a long blue robe. The costume creates a religious effect. Her face is tastefully made up, and she looks clean and beautiful, perhaps a bit thinner. A smell of frankincense taints the warm, thick air, though its source is unseen. The low, moody lighting brings out his daughter's cheekbones and brows. Before her is a small round table dressed with white linen, on top of which rests a large hourglass containing fine white sand.

Opposite Corinthia, a normal-size chair awaits Brill.

"Hello, Cori," he says, his Bazoo Meatpacking Windbreaker folded over his arm.

Corinthia stares at her father for a long moment. She doesn't blink — she just looks straight at him.

Brill searches her face for love, for excitement, for the smallest recognition, but it remains neutral.

Brill can feel a thread of embarrassment thickening in his kidneys and bowels. He's fully aware that his hair has gone grayer since she last saw him. He knows his eyes look tired and puffy. The recent events have aged him.

"Please sit," she finally says.

Brill does so.

"You've come a long way," Corinthia says.

She uses her normal voice. Brill is hugely relieved that she isn't affecting an accent.

"I drove over seven hundred miles," he says. "I took your mother's car. The Audi's in the shop. . . . You look good. I like your costume."

"It's not a costume," she says.

"Oh. Sorry."

"A costume would suggest that I'm performing something," she explains. "This is far from a performance."

"But you're using a character name," Brill retorts, perhaps a hair too objectionably, because Corinthia flips over the hourglass, and its sands start to empty.

From his pants pocket Brill produces a green-and-yellow lanyard, about six inches long, with a little clip on the end.

"Your mother made this for you," he says. "She's been staying at a, well, a kind of *health center* in Centralia. After you didn't come home, she sort of had a . . . well, let's just say she's had a hard time. But she's doing better. She wanted you to have this. It's for keys, or a whistle."

Corinthia accepts the lanyard.

"Thanks," she says, placing it in her lap. She points to the hourglass. "You have about four minutes and thirty seconds."

Brill nods. He can feel a lump forming in his throat, as if he's been forced to swallow potting soil.

"Don't you want to know your dreadful prophecy?" she says.

"Yes," he says, "of course."

Brill clears his throat a few times, tries to swallow that awful lump.

"I think your mother and I would like to know if there's any information about your brother."

"You have to ask me directly," she tells him. "I take your hand in mine, and then you look into my eyes and ask the question. That's how it works."

"Okay," Brill hears himself say.

Then he reaches across the small table and offers his right, unstamped hand, which disappears in his daughter's soft, warm hands like a playing card. They stare at each other a long moment, and then, with a slight tremor in his voice, Brill asks her the following:

"What is going to happen to Channing?"

Corinthia closes her eyes and takes a slow, deep breath. Her eyes appear to roll back in her head, which starts to twitch back and forth ever so slightly. Brill has the strange sensation that he is turning into a much smaller version of himself — that he's literally losing size and volume. He will emerge from this wigwam as the puppet version of Brill Bledsoe and go climb into that box and spend the rest of his life with the Ten-Inch Man. He could even take over the attraction after the Ten-Inch Man dies; that way, he'd always be near his daughter.

Corinthia unleashes a long, steady exhale and opens her eyes. She releases Brill's hand and tells her father that Channing will be coming home.

"Well, that's good!" Brill says, excited. "That's a *good* thing!"

"But it won't be good," Corinthia says. "It'll be far from good."

"In what way?" Brill asks.

"They're going to find him upside down. Attached to the water tower. As if he's fallen from the sky."

"Oh," Brill says. "I see."

He suddenly feels sick to his stomach. He has to bring his hand to his mouth to keep himself from retching.

"But where on earth was he?" he asks.

"I can't tell you that," she says.

"Why not?"

"Because I don't know the past. I only know the future."

Brill imagines his son hanging upside down from the Lugo water tower. Will he be dead? Will he be somehow maimed or blinded? He has to swallow hard again.

"And what about you?" Brill forces himself to ask.

"What about me?" Corinthia says.

"Will you be coming home anytime soon?"

"No," she says.

Brill nods slowly and then reaches into his back pocket and retrieves a thick envelope, folded in half and cinched with a rubber band.

"Here," he says, setting it on the table.

"What is it?" she asks.

"Money," he says.

"I don't need your money, Daddy."

Hearing her say the word *Daddy* almost takes his breath away. He may have come all this way just to hear that word.

"Please," he says.

"They give me forty percent of the daily take," she explains. "I'm fine for money."

"Use it for your medication, then. It's so expensive."

"I'm no longer taking medication," she says serenely. "Things are so much clearer now."

She passes the envelope back across the little table.

Brill accepts it, and then he starts to cry.

"Will you at least think about coming home?" he pleads, his voice faint. He can't remember the last time he cried in front of his daughter, or in front of anyone, for that matter. His voice sounds strange, far away, like that of a small, lost boy.

Corinthia tells him that she has a new home.

"I finally found my place," she says.

"But don't you want to go to school?" Brill says. "I spoke with Principal Ticonderoga the other day, and she said you could come back to Lugo Memorial and make up your schoolwork, and that if you agreed to take a few summer school courses, you could start your senior year with the rest of your class."

"I'm done with school," she says.

"What about Cloris?"

"What about her?"

"Don't you miss her?"

"Cloris and I will always be friends. She's going to come see me in South Carolina next month."

"I helped her put chains on her tires the other day," Brill says, wiping his eyes. He can hear his normal voice coming back to him. "Lugo's having its biggest snowfall in over fifty years," he adds. "It seems like they're plowing the streets every other night. You wouldn't believe how many people are using cross-country skis."

They are quiet for a moment. Brill spies the hourglass, which has run out of sand.

"When I walked in, this woman with hands for

feet tried to sell me cotton candy," he says, hoping to extend his brief visit.

"That's Wendy," Corinthia says. "She's from Slippery Rock, Pennsylvania. You should see her play Frisbee. We're going to be roommates once the tour hits Florida."

"She seems very nice," Brill says.

"She is."

"I know I can't make you come home," Brill says. "You're of legal age to do what you wish. At seventeen, you're fully emancipated. And I respect your choice, I do. I don't completely understand it, but I respect it."

Corinthia nods.

"But are you *happy* doing this?"

"I've never been happier," Corinthia says.

The female security guard with the pin-striped face enters the wigwam.

"It's okay, Phyllis," Corinthia says to her. "I know him."

"We gotta keep that line moving," Phyllis says. "There's a lotta people out there."

"Another minute," Corinthia says.

"You can have sixty seconds," Phyllis says, looking at her watch, "but if he's not out of here after that, I'm coming back in."

Phyllis turns and exits.

"Can I at least take you to dinner tonight?" Brill says.

"I can't tonight," Corinthia says. "It's Family Friday. We do potluck. Wendy and I made deviled eggs."

"What about tomorrow?"

"I'm not sure," Corinthia says. "It depends on how I'm feeling. Seeing takes its toll."

"Okay, then," Brill says.

He waits for his daughter to say something, but she just sits there. She seems to be filled with a powerful tranquility.

"Should I go get back in line?" he asks.

"If you'd like to," Corinthia says, "but we only go till eight tonight. It's already past seven."

Brill consults his watch and slowly stands. He then leans across the small table, relevés onto his toes, and kisses his daughter on the forehead.

"Good-bye, Corinthia," he says. "I love you."

She squeezes his hand firmly and smiles, but remains silent.

After her father passes back through the door of the wigwam, Corinthia looks down to discover a small, perfectly constructed, yellow origami crane. She takes it in her hand, admiring its meticulous folds and corners. She sets it beside the hourglass and then reaches into the pocket of her robe and produces the small wooden wolf that she found in Channing's room some months earlier. She places it beside her father's crane. And then she arranges her mother's lanyard beside the wolf. She stares at the small keepsakes for a moment.

She can briefly feel the story of her life shifting, turning away from its beginnings. Her hometown, her school, and the house she grew up in on Stained Glass Drive are more and more remote now, like when a distant silo becomes smaller and smaller in a rearview mirror, until it becomes a figment of itself, a pinprick, and then nothing.

Corinthia knows she may never see her father again. Deep within, underneath all of that mysterious tissue and fluid, she feels a dull, revolving ache.

But it, too, will pass, she tells herself, *just like everything else.*

"Need another minute, Fräulein?" Corinthia suddenly hears.

Corinthia didn't even see Phyllis enter.

"No, I'm good," Corinthia replies, clearing the origami crane, the wooden wolf, and the lanyard off the table. "Send the next one in."